The AWAKENING

*A VAMPIRE
HUNTRESS
LEGEND*

L.A. BANKS

St. Martin's Paperbacks

THE AWAKENING

Copyright © 2003 by Leslie Esdaile.
Excerpt from *The Hunted* copyright © 2004 by Leslie Esdaile.

Library of Congress Catalog Card Number: 2003058354

ISBN: 0-312-98702-1
EAN: 80312-98702-2

Printed in the United States of America

St. Martin's Griffin trade paperback edition / January 2004
St. Martin's Paperbacks edition / January 2005

St. Martin's Paperbacks are published by St. Martin's Press, 175 Fifth Avenue, New York, NY 10010.

10 9 8 7 6 5 4 3 2 1

THE AWAKENING

"An intriguing portrait of vampiric society, reminiscent of Anne Rice and Laurell K. Hamilton."

—Library Journal

"With *The Awakening*, Banks solidifies her intriguing, dark series as a project worth watching."

—Booklist

"Again, Banks brilliantly combines spirituality, vampires, and demons (and hip-hop music) into a fast-paced tale that is sure to leave fans of her first novel, *Minion*, panting for more, but nothing seems quite as hot as the steamy, often tense relationship between Damali and Carlos . . . a newcomer to the vampire genre . . . [Banks] lends a fresh and contemporary voice."

—Columbus Dispatch

MINION

"*Minion* is arguably superior to the *Buffy* franchise . . . while Banks relies on an established vampire-slayer mythos for part of her story, she is also wildly creative and invents a totally new and refreshing milieu. Its social hierarchy and politics are fascinating, and the author's reinterpretation of the seven levels of hell is brilliant. Another inspired detail is her explanation for how some otherwise 'normal' humans end up as cannibalistic serial killers. *Minion* is an entirely delicious read, leaving the reader licking one's lips and wanting more, cursing the cliffhanger ending. Luckily, this book is the beginning of the Vampire Huntress series, so there's more to look forward to."

—Fangoria

"Banks's mastery of character creation shines through in the strong-willed Damali . . . a sure-fire hit . . . pretty dramatic fiction."

—Philadelphia Daily News

"*Blade* meets *Buffy the Vampire Slayer* in this first of a trilogy about a no-nonsense guerilla leader of a rock-n-roll vampire-killer band . . . a pulsating blood-booster."

—Kirkus Reviews

MORE . . .

"With L. A. Banks's debut novel, *Minion*, a tough, sexy new vampire huntress challenges the dominance of Anita Blake and Buffy . . . Damali is an appealing heroine, the concept is intriguing, and the series promising."

—Amazon.com

"Readers, run out to your bookstore now or order online *Minion*, the latest and the greatest in the vampire books. It will scare the living daylights out of you at times so keep all the doors and windows locked while reading this enthralling book about Damali Richards, vampire huntress . . . I don't know how Ms. Banks thought of all the material that is in this intelligent, well-thought-out book, but believe me, it is compelling, fascinating and grabs your interest immediately. If you like Buffy, or Anita Blake, Vampire [Hunter], you are going to love this one that stars the first multi-cultural vampire huntress series with a multi-ethnic, multi-religion cast of characters. Ms. Banks is a master storyteller that will stun you with her talent when you read *Minion*."

—Suzanne Coleburn, *The Belles & Beaux of Romance*

"*Minion* is the first book in a . . . series that will appeal to fans of Laurell K. Hamilton's Anita Blake, Vampire Hunter novels. L. A. Banks has written an urban fantasy novel that deals with several social issues in a manner that is both educational and entertaining. The character that is the most intriguing is the man who will be either the [Neteru's] savior or doomslayer which is why readers will want to read *Awakening* as soon as it is published."

—BooksnBytes

"L. A. Banks does an excellent job giving these characters depth . . . and she gives us a cliffhanger ending rarely seen in novels."

Book remarko.oom

"L. A. Banks has woven a fascinating modern-day vampire saga that will keep you reading until the last page. Hooked on the storyline, you find that you can't wait for the sequel and Damali's new adventure."

—Alice Holman, RAWSISTAZ

Awakening to a new reality, perspective, or understanding is a process. For some, it happens in the blink of an eye, a millisecond of time when one's life is irrevocably changed. For others, the awakening within is gradual and complex. But fast or slow, all awakenings require change . . . and as humans, the one thing we most resist and tend to fear is change. Therefore, consciously awakening is perhaps one of the most courageous things an individual can do. This book is dedicated to those who have awakened and were brave enough to open their eyes—even while in the dark.

ACKNOWLEDGMENTS

Special thanks go to my editor, Monique Patterson, and my agent, Manie Barron, who took this entire project to the next level. To my husband, Al, and Constance O'Day-Flannery, who began this mission with me as dear friends. To all my *tights* who stood with me through thick and thin; you know who you are! And, as always, to my family (especially my mother, my daughter, my sister, and aunties), who are always there for me with deep spiritual backup, no matter come what may.

Special thanks also go to the wonderful "master authors," Tananarive Due, Brandon Massey, and Susan Sizemore, who supported this new legend series with generous blurbs; to Robert Flemming and Donna Hill, for their always positive vibes; to Lorene Carey (a community treasure), Jeff Hart, and Bebita Metellus of Art Sanctuary, for their steadfast friendship and encouragement; to Christopher Bonelli, for his *fabulous* Web site development that launched our Neteru into cyberspace with flair; to Vince Natale, who captured the very essence of our vampire huntress with a visually dynamic book cover, as well as to Michael Storrings, for his awesome cover design work; and to Liza Peterson, who gave Damali Richards's voice living energy via her *off da chain* spoken-word rendition of Damali's poem. THANK YOU! This deeply appreciated collaboration of allied artistic support created the complete package and could not have been accomplished without a team effort by serious, visionary individuals.

The Awakening

PART ONE

In order to cause the enemy to come of their own volition, extend some [apparent] profit. In order to prevent the enemy from coming forth, show them [the potential] harm.

—Sun Tzu, *The Art of War*

Se wo were fi na wo sankofa yenki.
(It is not a taboo to go back and retrieve what you forgot.)

—Sankofa proverb

ROLOGUE

Standing in the Middle of Hell . . .

CARLOS ASSESSED his situation fast. Payback for all that he'd done in life was a true bitch. There was no way out. He was dead. Or, more like half dead—undead—a vampire. Topside, he had a woman who he'd give his life for. Perhaps, to some extent, he already had . . . only to find out that the sister he was protecting was a vampire huntress. Not to mention the fact that the woman he wanted more than his next breath was surrounded by a gang of weapons-toting brothers and an off-the-hook momma who could fight. Crazy.

The old vampires had called Damali a Neteru, and then thinking him ignorant and stupid, and being themselves arrogant, had attempted to simplify the concept for him by describing her as a slayer. Carlos smiled. The tension in their faces was a dead giveaway that, for all their power, they couldn't hide. Yeah, they had reason to worry.

But didn't they realize what he'd known all his life? Now dead, there was no loss of that knowledge about what she was—special. Always had been, to him. There was no simplifying Damali. Neteru fit her. To call her anything else would be a clumsy summation of what she was.

His awareness from just a quick hit of Nuit's throne had given him a glimpse of all who had hunted vampires in the past. For centuries humans had cast spells, or those with mild forms of extrasensory awareness had come for what was now, unfortunately, his kind. Shamans had performed rituals and secret societies had made their own legends. But this one, this huntress . . . a Neteru was divinely created and specially anointed. Damali was something that he could not put into words.

Carlos drew a hard breath just thinking about her. This woman could shift the balance of world power, realign the energies in the universe. She had every gift to go along with her force of nature—not all of them realized, but definitely there, waiting—and a team of seasoned hunters at her side to give guidance, then ultimately follow her lead. From her womb great empires could be birthed, on the side of light or dark, and she held the key: her choice in the matter—the ultimate power of free will. The sister had divine authority. Even the old boys were awed, nervous, and craved what she had come by as a birthright.

And she is mine . . .

But he couldn't worry about all that right now.

Above ground, he had the Asian, Russian, Dominican, and Jamaican drug mobs, plus the federal authorities and another master vampire, looking for his head on a silver platter. Beneath the earth's surface, he had the entire Vampire Council on his ass. And now he was about to receive a tour of Hell itself.

This was beyond fucked up.

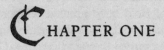

CHAPTER ONE

THE DENSE black smoke that swirled in the abyss-like ceiling high above the Vampire Council table formed a moaning funnel. A long strand of it touched down as though a violent twister, depositing a hooded messenger before sucking back into itself like a giant vacuum to resume its previous whirling mass. Now Carlos understood what was in the screeching cloud—things that went for food, bodies, and anything else the Vampire Council requested.

The messenger used his scythe to motion for Carlos to follow him. "The Vampire Council occupies the sixth realm, with which you have been made familiar. What you have not seen here is for the knowledge of the council members only. As we go, we will stop on each of the five demon realms with brevity. I am told you are valuable cargo, and the upper realms have formed a resistance."

Carlos nodded. The council chairman waved his hand. Just as quickly as he'd consented without words, the funnel reappeared, creating a whining turbine sound. A putrid wind rushed against Carlos's face. This time no terror entered Carlos as the bony messenger's hand clutched him and the tornado-like cloud enveloped them. He was on a mission. He'd been granted temporary immunity. He'd cut *the deal of life.* The powerful strength of master vampire status surged through his veins. Curiosity about this strange new life replaced fear.

Soon the jettison slowed. Carlos landed hard on his feet and heard a crunching noise under them like twigs snapping. Screams of agony met him as they echoed through the distance. The messenger's eyes narrowed as he pointed ahead of them with his scythe. They were standing in a clearing at the edge of dense black woods. Tall, disfigured trees with no leaves rose and twisted amid a climbing bramble of thorns that seemed alive with motion. It was so dim that even with his heightened ability to see in the dark, he had to strain to differentiate the shapes of objects before him. Slowly but surely, he could begin to make out the strange new environment, relying partly on his physical awareness, and partly on his mental sight.

"Look deeply," the entity whispered. "This is the were-realm."

As soon as the messenger had spoken, Carlos heard several mournful howls echo in the distance. The screams that sounded human were everpresent, and the wolf-like mourn pierced those cries to create a chilling call and response in the darkness. Within seconds, golden-yellow eyes opened in the shadows within the thicket. Carlos glanced down at his feet and saw human skulls and bones instead of twigs. He was speechless.

"There are many different mutations within a demon species. The were-creatures are one evolutionary turn from vampiri. Vampires have their wolfen trait from one of their particular lineages, but are more sophisticated. The were-creatures can deliver a vicious bite, turn their prey, or eat them, but they cannot hold their shape permanently. They are beholden to the moon. This is what gives the vampire realm the advantage. Our bite is permanent, hence our superiority. Our human turns do not shapeshift based upon the phases of the moon."

Curious, Carlos glanced around. "How do you keep humans alive down here so the werewolves can feed on live prey?"

The messenger chuckled. "Ah, you refer to the perpetual night sounds here?"

"The human screams," Carlos said impatiently.

"Those are harvested souls, not living humans. The were-creatures, like other demons, are released through their topside portals by a curse or ritual levied by a human with a soul. They eat topside, as do we all. But what remains here are the souls of the damned to also be feasted upon in perpetuity. The damned fuel the transformations and give each demon species strength. The damned feel each topside human attack."

Carlos rubbed his jaw and continued to monitor the distance of the sounds, which were advancing. "The souls take the weight?"

"Correct." The messenger nodded. "Each demon is created by the deepest, darkest, most twisted human thought and desire. You are aware that thoughts and beliefs manifest?"

"I am now."

"Good. You learn fast. The thoughts create the density of the demon. Determine its range of power, or its horror. The lower realms are of the darkest thoughts, most twisted human conception of evil . . . with a little creative license from our Dark Lord. And, so it is with the souls. The greater the sin, the deeper the soul is sent into our realms to contend with the most ravenous of our demons. Sometimes the soul of an unredeemed sinner is ripped apart to experience multiple levels of Hell. Their harvest location all depends on what the primary focus of their human life has been; vengeance, lust, greed, murder, pick one. As we visit the upper levels, you will notice that the density is less, as is the darkness. It is all relative."

A series of howls turned into snarls, and Carlos could detect misshapen, low stalking forms advancing just from the increasing volume of the sounds. Thoroughly intrigued, he decided to wait until they had found a less dangerous location before he'd fire another round of questions. The messenger had said two things that he wanted to learn more about. One was the part about souls being harvested. If he was damned, and if he was dead, then where was his own soul and what was feeding on it? The second issue was the question of unredeemed sinners. The messenger had not just plainly said sinners. By now Carlos had learned that everything meant something here, and an omission of a word spoke volumes.

"We go to level four. The were-creatures—wolfen, panthers, jaguars, bears, all manner of earthly predators made hybrid with human—envy vampiri. It is not safe to linger."

Again Carlos nodded, and felt the touch of the messenger's hand. Growls and snarls continued to draw near him, and oddly it sent adrenaline through his system. He felt his jaw become filled with a sharp hardness as the golden eyes stalked forward. His shoulders now also felt thicker, more powerful, and he was not afraid, just poised for attack. His own fingernails sliced into his fists like razors as he clenched them, prepared to ward off a potential lunge from something in the woods. But a sudden wind encircled him as the beasts before him hesitated. He heard the messenger chuckle. It was so dark in this realm he couldn't even make out the blackened smoke that was lifting them to safety.

"You are coming into your master's strength," the messenger noted, as soon as they'd landed again. "The were-creatures would have rushed a weaker vampire. They are excellent trackers . . . you gave them pause."

Interesting. If he was a master, then the messenger couldn't enter his mind. His thoughts had been sealed, even against Nuit. This was good. There was much to think about. There were many strategies to grapple with. He needed a plan.

"Where are we now?"

Carlos glanced around a damp, mucus-coated area that was the color of dark-gray charcoal on all surfaces. Everything dripped from the slick, smooth surfaces and smelled dank. Clingy vines, Spanish moss, and wet spiderwebs made advancing treacherous, as he brushed them aside to see farther into the infested terrain. Maggots rained intermittently from overhead, making little plopping sounds as they splashed into the unmoving waters.

Tiny flying gnats and other insect pests added a bothersome distraction as Carlos swatted them away. Glowing-eyed vermin scurried and disappeared into the endless network of standing water ponds, wider black lakes, and puddles within the caverns. Moans of despair vibrated through him as he stared off in the distance toward a tar gully that had a low blue flame burning on its thick, slow bubbling surface. Carlos took a step forward and was suddenly knee-deep in vile standing water. "Shit!"

Things wriggled in the sewer-like swamp at his calves and he immediately jumped back from the cesspool that sent the rotting smell of human flesh, feces, and garbage into his nose, the smell covering his tongue. Ugh! It wasn't as dark as the previous black forest, but it was much wetter.

"Shake it off," the messenger chuckled, "and stay close. Use thought to clean and dry yourself. In fact, change your clothes, if you so desire. Always remember that you are from the lowest realm, which gives you authority over the weaker realms. Sheer thought. Use your ability to materialize your comfort—or safety."

Point well taken. Carlos released his disgust and focused his thoughts on having the crap off of him. Instantly he felt dry, and even the smells around him abated enough for him to think. "What's on level four? It doesn't feel as dense." He had a sudden, inexplicable need to know what souls were trapped here.

"We are in the realm of nightmare entities . . . things that swim and slither and creep. These are dark dreams, creatures made of dark desires and black thoughts. There are so many varieties of this demon, and they remain hidden, stay within the haunted spaces of the human mind." His guide waved its arm as it spoke. "Pure hatred lives here, incest lives here, as well as many other dark emotions that become manifest. Vampires have lost the wet, slithering, snakelike forms of these amorphous creatures, but have retained the sophistication of their ability to permeate dreams and thought. Their whispers are mesmerizing. We go now. You are not strong enough to fight the mental pull of these alluring creatures yet. Soon, however. This is a realm of dark desires where even seasoned vampires can go mad. Nuit remained here too long."

Carlos didn't even nod as the messenger beckoned him. Sinister thoughts were attempting to attack his brain, and invisible tendrils slithered up his legs, stroked his groin, and dazed him. The pull of his transport broke the spell, but he looked down as he ascended to the next realm, awed by the power he'd just been wrenched from. Oddly, his eyes adjusted to the speed this time. This was some twisted shit, indeed. Somebody should have shown him this much earlier in his life. Had he only known. . . . But where was his soul? Where was Alejandro's?

"We are on level two," the messenger announced as they landed in a barren, desert-like place that was merely dark gray all around.

Rocks and jagged gray cliffs surrounded him, and Carlos looked up from a deep canyon to a lighter realm above. He was glad it was dry at least. "We skipped level three," he murmured, listening to his voice echo. Sobs surrounded his voice, sending it back to him with piteous wails.

"Level three is where the Amanthras reside. That is not a part of our tour. Too dangerous."

"Why?"

"The Amanthra are poised to detect any vampire encroachment in their territories. The many species of vengeance demons are formidable."

Carlos nodded, continuing to stare at the barren crags above.

"This is the realm of lost hopes, lost dreams, lost faith. Angry ghosts live here." Rocks began to fall and pummel them, and the messenger held out his cloak to protect Carlos. "Poltergeists. A pain in the ass," it sneered. "Nothing here to see. They have no form, just move matter, but we have retained their ability to transform into nothingness, and to move about as mist. We go. Very boring here, but useful."

"Let me ask you something, though, *hombre*," Carlos said fast, holding the arm of the messenger. "Where do vampires' souls go? Assuming we're all damned . . . our essence must go somewhere, right? Who feeds on us?"

The messenger gave him a suspicious, appraising look. "They go to the Vampire Council's vault where they are registered; hence nothing feeds on us . . . unless that soul gets tossed into the sea of perpetual agony—which you crossed to enter the council chambers. Why do you ask?"

More rocks skipped down the cliffs, but Carlos held up his hand, stopping the assault as a huge boulder came toward them, but was deflected. He looked at his hand, assessing the awesome power it had. The messenger smiled with approval.

"Just curious," Carlos said slowly, still awed at what he'd just done. He continued to look at his hand as he pressed his question. "So, my soul is in the vault . . . and so is my brother's, right? Safe?" He had openly displayed concern that his spirit would be kept by the council to throw off the messenger's concerns. It apparently worked when the messenger seemed to relax.

"Yes. Your brother's has been registered, as have your friends." But then its voice took on a strange tone of worry. "Yours, we are still trying to locate, however. There was a dispute, and it was wrested away during the border battle at the edges of Purgatory. No matter at this juncture. We have rightful ownership . . . after all our years of work on you. We will find it, or reclaim it."

"No matter?" Carlos was incredulous. "After seeing this shit, you tell me no matter?"

"No matter. We are predators. The density of your unredeemed soul will have to bottom out, unmolested, on level six—the realm of predators. This was your lifestyle. You preyed on the weak-minded for material gain. Power, blind ambition . . . yours will come to where all like you come."

The dissection of his life gave Carlos serious pause. While he was aware that his business transactions required the weaknesses of others to keep the cash flowing, it never really dawned upon him. "Tell me two things, and then we can go," Carlos hedged, "since you guys have been sloppy—seems only right."

The messenger cocked his head to the side and waited.

"Which souls get cast in the lava around the council's chamber? You feel me? I'm just trying to know: What could get a man thrown in the joint?"

"Wise information to have," the messenger replied. "Those without a prayer who get staked by us for transgressions . . . should they violate the council's policies, or those who fall victim to the humans. If a made vampire was an innocent victim, was turned without agreement, when that vampire is extinguished he goes to the realms above—assuming he didn't have other issues to damn him. But, alas, if he was of the redeemed, he is escorted to the province of the angels by the warrior legions."

"Now that's some deep shit."

"Yes," the messenger stated flatly. "This is why we try to kill all innocents, first, then feed. They are a waste of energy in our realms. This is also why the cleric being turned was such a flagrant violation—it brought warrior angels deep into our realms to collect his soul . . . and they also tried to take additional borderline souls up with them in the battle . . . and were successful in a few cases.

We speak of that no more. It is a history that nags the council. But those under our aegis that are cast by the council into the pit around the sacred council chamber feel us feed on every victim, as well as feel the blood hunger that cannot be quenched while in the pit."

Dozens more questions entered his brain, but Carlos focused on the one priority he had: Nuit. "Then if Nuit was cast into the pit, where's his soul now? Can't the Vampire Council just—"

"No," the messenger spat, cutting him off. "His was in the pit, and in our registry. His lair was sealed and he writhed in pain for only a short time—until his lair was disturbed. After his term of incarceration, his soul was to be sent through the demon realms for them to have their rightful torture split, since his damnation levels were manifold . . . but when Nuit escaped, he was able to convey it to a hiding place on level three where the Amanthras control. His deal put his spirit in their safety zone. They have it, but do not attack it. This is what makes him so dangerous—he is rogue, with no way for us to sanction him like the others."

"And if I drive a stake in his heart for you guys? Where will it go?"

The messenger chuckled. Carlos wished it had a face so he could read more into the thing's voice or expression than just the scant narrowing or widening of its glowing red eyes.

"Straight to level seven, beneath even the Vampire Council's realm. If Nuit fails his betrayal of us, he will have a permanent appointment with the Dark Lord . . . and ask me no more, for I do not want to even fathom what that consequence could bring."

"Sho' you right." That's all he needed to know. For now.

This time, Carlos anxiously awaited the last level, curiosity pulling him upward as much as his guide's hand. They landed in a light gray, barren sandy area, and there were illusive human figures milling about seeming disoriented, arguing, bickering, and screaming invectives at each other—some laughing with insane, vacant stares.

"Pathetic," the messenger spat. "The realm of confusion . . . addictions, excesses, wantonness. Some of these transparent specters don't even realize that they're dead. We don't use much from this realm, save the ability to create turmoil and their capacity to throw voices, which rise to the surface. When humans hear ghostly sounds that frighten them, or hear voices that propel them to evil deeds, more often than not, they come from this region. Sometimes we bring one of them up as a zombie, but it is a tiresome, noisy realm that I cannot tolerate."

"I hear you," Carlos muttered. "Let's roll. This is getting on my nerves."

"Yes. A vampire's sensibilities are utterly invaded by this clamor. We go now."

Again the black smoke pulled at Carlos's body, and his guide didn't bother to touch him. Somehow Carlos could sense that he was in no imminent danger in the upper levels. The only thing he'd been there was aggravated.

"The council felt it wise to deliver you to the gray zone here, in Fallon Nuit's territory. It is necessary that he continue to believe that he has control over you. Kill well on the topside, and feed heartily. You will need your strength," the messenger said with a nod, and was gone.

Carlos stood in front of his grandmother's house and stared at the front door. A pang of mourning inside him became a dull ache. His family . . . things would never be the same. The tiny, impoverished house seemed so frail

against the night. Carlos shook his head. Why hadn't his
mother and grandmother simply agreed to his offer to
move them to a lush home in a much better place? Just
look at it, he told himself, as he stared at the aged clap-
board frame, peeling, ugly gray paint, and flimsy metal
bars that covered the screen door and windows. The front
yard was a postage stamp of withered grass. They should
have let him do what he could, when he could, to move
them all to somewhere safe. But they were so stubborn,
the women in his family.

The porch seemed like it could barely support the white
plastic chairs on it. Cheap flowerpots sat on the steps filled
with half-dead plants. The windows were covered inside
with cheap, sheer fabric curtains. Traffic and night noise
blared around the huddles of young-bloods standing down
the street on the corner. This was no way to live.

However, a wave of concern came over him as the
hunger for blood regained its topside strength. Perhaps it
was the scent of humanity in the air that had ignited it, he
wasn't sure. While on his zoo-exhibit-like tour through
the dark realms, looking at all the grotesque abomina-
tions of demons, he hadn't felt it. Not this strong and not
like this. Not here, he admonished himself, but the familiar ground had such a pull.

He wanted to wrap his arms around his mother, beg
her forgiveness, see that she was all right. He closed his
eyes, breathed in, and saw within the home. Yes, she was
on the telephone in tears—just as he'd witnessed as he
was dying. His grandmother was in her room, her lips
moving in what he knew to be a fervent prayer, but he was
now deaf to it. Juanita was inside trying to comfort his
mama. She was always a good girl.

Tears of earnest remorse welled in Carlos's eyes. What

had he done . . . what had he become? The paradox claimed him; when he had been alive he could not submit to live like them, and now dead, he still could not.

Yet the need to eat created a ravenous draw to the front steps of what had once been his home. These were the people who had given him life, and this was where he'd grown up. The alpha and the omega; his beginning in life through them; their end of life through him. Full circle. He could smell the living behind the door. Their blood was so ripe, so thick . . . Carlos licked his lips. Guilt and shame battled with the hunger and loss.

Like a junkie, he was drawn up the front steps. Like a junkie he knew he would pillage his own home for one hit. Like a junkie he knew that he would prey on his own family—just as every junkie he'd created had. As a dealer, he'd made humans that were like vampires, too. They were also the living dead. They would feed on their families, with remorse. They would make excuses and apologies, but would quench their hunger. Fair exchange is no robbery, he told himself, as he prepared to enter through the mail slot as smoke. His family would hesitate to fire a weapon, fight off an attack, or drive a stake through his heart—just like living families always hesitated when a junkie of theirs came home.

It was the way of predators, junkies, addicts. Bring down the weakest in the herd. Pick off family first. Open a sitting pocketbook, steal money from a drawer, but feed your hunger. Family, for a while, will not bar the door or change the locks. They'll weep. Family, unlike an outsider, would try to beg and plead and hope. Family would try to negotiate and get their predator help. Family would hesitate in the crucial moment of truth. Family had love, and that made them vulnerable.

He almost cried out as the images flashed through his mind. Hot tears rolled down his face and spilled with knowing. He couldn't even call out to God to help him. The thought made him bring his hands to the sides of his head as a stabbing pain shot through it. But it was enough to sober him slightly. Carlos knocked on the door, and immediately his hand was scorched.

Yelling with pain, he drew away his wounded knuckles. Immediately, he heard the locks turn, and his mother stood inside, just beyond the threshold with Juanita and his grandmother behind her. Tears were cascading down his mother's puffed face, and she covered her mouth with her hand for a moment as she stared at him.

"Oh . . . my son . . ." she whispered. "*Madre de Dios,* you have taken all of my children." Her voice faltered and broke into a sob.

Carlos glanced at his appearance. He was normal, projecting pure human. What was she talking about? Even her mind was shut to him.

"Mama," he crooned. "Come outside. We should talk. I know Alejandro's death is killing you, but you still have one—"

"No!" His grandmother wrapped her aged, gnarled fingers around his mother's upper arms. "You may not enter! You are demon now!"

What? His own grandmother . . . and how did she know?

His mother turned from him and sought her mother's shoulder. Juanita's stricken expression drew him and he entered her mind. His grandmother had anointed the house. She had put down a barrier and had been screaming about demons and vampires all day. It was her house, too, shared with his mother now. He could not cross the line without permission of the owner. Juanita thought it was all superstition and was torn. She still loved him. Her heart was breaking as she watched his mother give in to the old ways. He called her with the most seductive voice he could muster within his mind.

Juanita opened the door as the eldest of the women shrieked and grabbed at her. His grandmother and mother were screaming in Spanish, shouting prayers, trying to get her to come back into the sanctuary of the protected home. But his focus was singular. Juanita walked toward him, down the steps as the older women yelled behind the now locked screen. They called him vile things. They said his grandmother had had a vision . . . a dream. Yes, the humans did indeed have gifts. Blood.

"Come to me, baby," he whispered, drawing Juanita farther away from the house. "Just a few more steps, and I will make it better. The pain will go away . . . you won't ever have to be afraid. The old women are foolish, look at how they've hurt me, have turned on their own son. They break my heart."

The smell of her as she entered his arms was intoxicating. The smell of her sweat, her blood, fused with the smell of her cheap perfume. He could feel her pain flowing under her skin. She'd yielded so easily, was so trusting as she clung to him. Desire kindled within him. He'd make it easy for her, would make sure she enjoyed it. She trembled against him. He smelled the moisture of her vulva. This was power. *Yes, come to me.*

Foolish child had leaned her head against his chest and hugged him. Carlos closed his eyes and nuzzled the damp hair away from her neck with his face. Street traffic noise disappeared. The sobs beyond the door were so distant. Boom box music had gone mute. All he could hear now was the sound of Juanita's heartbeat and the blood that gushed through her veins. He felt his jaw tense, his incisors painfully release from their captivity behind his gums.

"Yo, man, sorry to hear about your brother and your boys!"

Carlos's incisors instantly retracted, his head jerked up and he turned, training his glare on his neighbor who was crossing the street.

"It was fucked up, man," his childhood homeboy continued, a large silver cross hanging to the center of his chest. "Your mama and gran'ma are all freaked out. Me and my posse will help you find the motherfuckers, *hombre*. Nobody should roll on one'a ours like dat." The twenty-year-old extended his fist for Carlos to pound. "We need revenge."

Carlos studied the hand, eyed the huge crucifix, released Juanita with a shove, and then returned the fist pound, collecting himself. He warily avoided the thing that would burn him. Juanita seemed dazed, but he sensed that she'd attributed his abruptness to his righteous anger over his brother's death. His boy came near to hug him in respect. Carlos jerked back.

"You see that?" his grandmother shrieked. "You see!"

"Yo, what up, man?" His neighbor glanced at him, confused.

"I'm just freaked myself. Gotta go," Carlos murmured. He turned and looked back at Juanita. His mother's sobs were now fusing with his grandmother's piteous wails. "Mama!" Words became trapped in his throat. Total despair claimed him. He'd almost taken from his beloved family, his inner circle. He was a predator and truly damned.

Oh, the realm of confusion was indeed at work, and he had not been the master of it tonight. "Mama!" Carlos called again, regaining his composure. He studied her weeping form as Juanita slipped back into the house to join the huddle of women. "I am so sorry . . . forgive me. I will never hurt you—but keep the seal on your house. Stay in at night, and keep Nita protected, too. Do that for me . . . it's the last thing I'll ever ask you." He burned their images into his mind for the last time. "I love you."

His friend put a hand on his shoulder. "Damn, man. This is all fucked up."

"Word." Then Carlos was gone.

Carlos glanced around the desolate underground parking garage, moving with silent footsteps. Guilt stabbed into his gut as much as the hunger for blood consumed him. He'd almost jacked his own family. He had to summon the mental control of his rank—a master. Never again, he repeated like a mantra. *Never again.* He would have discipline, patience, strategy, finesse. He would *not* be a beast.

But, he needed to feed. That was real. There were certain practicalities that had to be addressed. Half stooping from the pain, he sucked in a huge inhale and kept walking. The thought of going back to Raven to feed from disgusted him. He'd dropped so low that he'd actually fucked and fed from something that could transform into a panther, something that had eaten the entrails of men. Yet, he needed a body, and what better place than to lie in wait for another of Nuit's minions in the lot beneath his enemy's office building? At least he could feed from something he hadn't screwed.

Yeah. Made sense. He'd drop one of those vampire fuckers, for sure. He'd gut them, fill his hunger on whatever they'd already eaten, just like Raven had demonstrated could be done. He'd never submit to having an innocent's blood on his hands . . . at least not right away. He refused to be made into a junkie, be it drugs or blood. Then, he'd find Nuit.

Profound hunger tore at him as he quickened his pace and he gasped, breathing hard, fighting against the urge. Perhaps after he killed the bastard Nuit, *tonight,* he'd go find a crack-head, a homeless person, or some other society castaway, something—but *never* his family again. Shame christened his eyes with new tears, making his vision blur as he skulked through the parking lot, picking up the trail of where one of Nuit's weaker vampires had just been.

There was so much he didn't know yet about the power he now possessed, but one thing was for sure: he was clear about the existence of Hell.

Carlos passed the security attendant's booth and stopped, the lingering scent of blood drawing his attention. When he peered through the shattered glass pane, he sniffed the dead victim. Raven. Oh, yeah, he was definitely near Nuit's operations.

He bent to siphon what little blood remained in the limp, fat body. The man was a slob and stank. But he kept pulling the salty, thick fluid from the body with abandon. He despised himself as he did so. Now he was a garbage picker, accepting sloppy seconds from a female vamp. His ego was revolted. Had he no dignity left? Then he pulled back and studied his bite signature. Something was different. Two small puncture wounds, instead of the brutal mess Raven had left. A twisted satisfaction filled him. The Vampire Council's action had worked.

At least the small amount he'd consumed staved off the hunger a bit. Yet, at the same time, it made him thirst for another hit. He lowered his head, hoping to find one more drop. Just like a fucking addict. Carlos lifted his head from the dead body and wiped his mouth on his sleeve, then spat with disgust. This was definitely no way to live.

Quickening footsteps forced him to glance at the security monitors. He also noticed that he had no reflection in the mirrors within the tiny space. Deep. The sight of a young blond male entering the parking lot with a terror-stricken expression made Carlos become very still. He stared at the image on the small screens, trying to remember where he'd seen the face, heard those same steps. His own club came into focus. This was the young wannabe who had relentlessly pestered his people to allow Damali to perform there, initially without her consent.

Then it dawned on him—this human could be a tool to get him closer to Damali. He had to warn her. Just thinking about where he wanted to go, Carlos felt a swift wind lift him as though he were air. To his surprise, he immediately found himself standing behind the trotting man in a silent, drifting manifestation. Very deep. Then Carlos breathed in a hint of sulfur and went on guard.

From between two parked cars Raven appeared, hissing and spitting and bearing fangs. Tacky. No style, he thought, as he watched her hunt. The blond intended victim yelled in horror and crouched down as she was on him in two paces. Carlos quickly took on solid form. Knocking the man aside, Carlos came between the would-be victim and Raven. She jumped ten feet back, obviously prepared to duel for her potential kill until recognition spread across her face.

"He's mine," Carlos snarled at her. "You just ate."

"That's because you drained me, lover. I was going to

bring this one to you—so you could also finish where you left off with me. You left me hanging." She moved closer to him with a lazy, sexy lope in his direction and tilted her neck for him to consider. "You know you want it. It's fresh. The guard was okay, save the forty of beer—and the spaghetti he had for dinner," she murmured in a seductive tone. "Want some . . . or something else?"

Carlos shut his eyes briefly, staving off the hunger that she and the scent of the recent kill on her lips created. "Go back to your lair. Not this one."

"What is with you? Is he marked or something?"

"Don't argue with me, bitch. I said to leave this one alone!" He hated the fact that he'd even considered her offer for a moment. Rage filled him as he fought against both urges she produced.

Snarling, Raven backed away, glared at the cowering man on the ground, and vanished into the shadows.

"Oh shit, oh shit, man!" the innocent yelled as he scrambled up from where he'd dropped to cover his head with his arms. "What the fuck was that—man, if you hadn't come along, I would have been dog meat. Did you see that shit? I'm not high, I swear to God! I saw it—you saw it, and it wasn't human. I knew something was following me—I could sense it, but damn! *A fucking vampire?* This cannot be happening—shit like this only happens in the movies. God in Heaven! I must be losing my mind!"

Each time the innocent had said the word that named the Most High, it had sent a stabbing pain through Carlos's head, intestines, and the center of his chest. The words hurt so badly that Carlos staggered away for a moment and held on to the side of a car for support. Powerful. Just the name alone . . . but it had also loosened the mental hold of the Vampire Council's trackers, he noted. As he recovered, he sensed another presence. He'd felt it earlier, but had been too hungry before to address it. Hmmm . . .

Carlos turned around slowly with renewed calm. The hysterical man was walking in circles, babbling to himself and shaking his head. Carlos could feel his fangs retract. When he faced the human, evidence that he was a vampire had vanished.

"What's your name?" Carlos asked coolly.

"Dan, man! Daniel Weinstein. Oh shit." The human named Daniel continued to walk around in a circle, hyped, clutching his head in his hands.

"My advice is that you chill," Carlos said, low in his throat. "There could be others, and you just missed being dinner."

Dan stared at him, sweat pouring down the sides of his blanched face. His lips had gone light blue, and he seemed to be in mild shock. "More of them?" He leaned over and began to retch.

"Get yourself together, and go somewhere safe." The smell of the human's adrenaline, terror, and blood were making Carlos's hands tremble with need.

"Somewhere safe! Where in God's name is that?!" Dan wiped his mouth with the back of his hand and breathed in huge gulps of air. "I'm not going home alone. The only things that saved my ass were probably you and my Star of David," he said quickly, bringing the small gold piece of jewelry to his lips to kiss it three times. "Damali told me not to come here at night, she said there were barracudas and shit, not fucking vampires!"

"You're with Damali's crew, right? Go seek sanctuary with them."

"I *used* to be with them," Dan corrected. "I . . . I . . . was just here in Beverly Hills to seal a deal with Blood Music and Warriors of Light, though."

Dan's frightened eyes darted around the parking lot, but each time they landed on Carlos, he edged closer as though Carlos was a protective shield. It took Carlos everything within him to keep from reaching out for the fool. All he had to do was snatch the quivering body to him, snap his neck, and fill himself with the elixir of life. So very, very close with the scent of life wafting over him. A heart beating so hard it slammed against the innocent's breastbone and nearly vibrated within Carlos's own chest. The human's pores oozed with sweat and fear. Carlos licked his lips. "Talk to me," he murmured, forcing himself to remain smooth. "I need an address."

"I got Light a hookup on *Extra, Access Hollywood, Evening Mag,* for the big concert, dude. But, truth be told, we always work by phones—I never knew exactly where they actually camped, ya know? Last gig, I showed up at the club, but they wouldn't let me go to their spot. I wouldn't know how to get to them if my life depended on it—*and it does.*"

"Yes, *it does,*" Carlos said with a wry half smile.

Daniel spun around, tears rising in his eyes as he glanced at his car with fear. "I'm no punk, usually—and I know, running Club Vengeance and all, you see a lot of shit, maybe even had to do a lot of shit—but seriously, I can't get in my car. I'm about to drop a brick in my pants behind this shit. Oh, fuck me . . . you got a gun, man? In your line of business, I know you have a gun."

"Bullets don't work on them," Carlos muttered, walking over to the man's car and opening the door without a key. He glanced in to check that it was clear, hesitating as he again saw that his image made no reflection in the side or rearview mirrors. But he kept his motions fluid to keep from tipping off the innocent. Deeply disturbed by what he'd just seen, or not seen, Carlos's focus splintered for a split second. What had he done?

Once he was sure that the coast was clear, Carlos then nodded to Daniel who still appeared so traumatized that he couldn't seem to move.

"Get in, say a prayer, and roll up your windows, for all the good that will do. Call Damali on your cell phone and get her to bring you in to a sanctuary. And, you need to move fast."

"You need a ride, man—I mean, we can share. It might be better if we found her, or a place to go together, right?"

Carlos shook his head. "I left my car a ways from here and—"

"You're going to *walk around* out here in a *deserted lot* at *night* with *vampires* stalking people? What, are you crazy? Either that, or you are one bad motherfucker. Me, I'm out."

Carlos held the car door open for Daniel; the sweet smell of his blood that close became so tempting that Carlos had to quickly shut the door and step away. Dan was a walking blood drug, a beacon for vamps as his terror carried every flash hormone of fight or flight—much of it being flight.

"Don't stop at the barrier," Carlos instructed. "Take it out. Run right through it if you have to. Don't put your arm out the window to try to drop a token. Make the call while you drive. Get D to bring you in." He moved away from Dan's car, watching him.

Dan nodded, his hands fumbling with the keys, dropping them once before he got the right piece of metal into the ignition. In an instant, Dan gunned the motor, slapped the gears in reverse, hitting both parked cars on either side of his silver Honda when he backed out of his space. Carlos didn't relax until he heard the sound of wheels screeching level by level, rubber burning as Dan rounded each curve, metal scraping the divider walls. A heavy snap echoed, followed by more rubber burning as Dan tore away from the building.

"Carlos Rivera poses an unfathomable risk for the Vampire Council," the attorney murmured once the messenger reported that Carlos was topside.

"A dangerous variable," another council member agreed.

"He died with a prayer in him," another insisted.

The chairman's gaze swept the group. "We must find his soul for our vault. What happened?"

"We don't know, exactly. But if he doesn't deliver the vampire huntress in three days when she ovulates, or during the fragile period . . . and we miss this lunar cycle of fertility, her womb will be immune to our seed. An opportunity will not present itself again for years—till her next Vulnerability. Even if he brings her to us, after her twenty-first birthday, later in the month during this first ripening, for every successive day that passes her antibodies will build, and the heir will be at risk of spontaneous abortion. Or, Mr. Chairman . . . even if our seed takes, it could be deformed—it could be *human,* or worse. Part Neteru human."

"I know, Parliamentarian Vlak. I am aware of the situation. But please try to calm yourself," the council chairman sighed. "So sad. Rivera has such potential, too bad that we must drive a stake through his heart when he brings her in. Rivera should have signed. I do not like dangling threads. He could have ruled Latin America, and picked up Nuit's territories, too."

"Too much of a risk, Mr. Chairman," the member at the far point of the table argued. "I don't like being leveraged. In our own haste and desperation, we've protected him from Nuit's call, and given the humans Rivera has designated amnesty. Once we set that in motion, it is irrevocable—so, if he reneges, we have an imbalance of negotiations. That makes us vulnerable, and I don't like it. I was against this from the onset, but was overruled."

All heads nodded and loudly murmured the concern amongst themselves until the chairman spoke again.

"We had no choice. We had to take risky measures. But, we must deal with the severely problematic issue that none of us wants to discuss."

"Yes," the attorney agreed. "The prayer. He hasn't technically died, just transformed. We had to intercept Rivera before he was completely expired in order to get around the loophole in the supernatural law governing Nuit's aegis over him—and while he hovered in between states. If the light should suddenly attempt to begin litigation to place a claim on Rivera as their asset, particularly given the preponderance of evidence, the religious relic and a prayer . . . gentlemen, this could be a long-waged, resource-intensive dispute for this soul—which by right, should be ours. Almost his entire adult life, if not all of it, has been under our purview. But, the redemption clause—"

"Don't utter it. Words have power. You have left topside roadblocks?"

"Absolutely. We need him to hunger and feed on an innocent to drive away the forces of light. He has only taken his first feeding from the veins of the already damned, and now from a dead man. You just never know—Rivera seemed more aggressive and didn't strike me as a second-tier carrion feeder. Another variable. He needs to feed the traditional way."

"He's a master now," the chairman said with forced confidence. "The disorientation from our cloak to Nuit just confused him, perhaps. No master will accept carrion, or blood from another vampire's veins, indefinitely, gentlemen. Let us not panic. That is not our way. He will also want to experience the erotic rush of the kill."

The council members returned skeptical glances. The attorney nodded, and that seemed to mollify the group.

"We can only hope that our esteemed chairman is correct. However, Rivera's car and the money are still near two dead Minion members that we'd compromised, but Nuit discovered among his ranks. Another innocent will find Rivera's artifacts and link him to the crime, should he not sign the eternal contract—and make the wrong choice to side with the light. That contract is the only way we can ensure his soul gets correctly deposited into our realm . . . as we have a bit of an inventory problem now— we can't find it. Like the others sent here, no contract would have been necessary, his lifestyle would have given it enough weight to sink . . . but something happened. We are still investigating."

A hush fell over the group. The chairman stood slowly, leaning in the counselor's direction as he issued him a warning glare. "I suggest you rectify this before yours accidentally gets placed in the pit beyond our doors."

"Rivera will have no life in the gray zone, if the realms

of the place that shall remain nameless above earth try to give him a second chance," the attorney assured the council nervously, glancing around the group. "He will not renege, if he is a thinking man."

"Very good, then," the chairman sighed, sitting with effort and pushing back in his throne. "And, we also need to continue to monitor him . . . as we have more than an illusion-projected master topside now. Rivera is indeed a real master who has direct connection to our Neteru. I don't like the windows of invisibility with a master on the trail of a huntress in near ripening."

"Extremely dangerous."

"Our concern all along, Mr. Chairman."

"Mine, too. Which is why we must have him under complete surveillance at all times. Although his thoughts are impenetrable to us at this juncture—given his master status—have our people keep abreast of his activities. His lair, unlike Nuit's, will be accessible. We only need him to lead us to her, beyond the blind spot of the Neteru's protective prayers. Her trust in Rivera gets him through that barrier . . . even Nuit cannot fully see her, can only track her remotely, and cannot get through her barriers without three layers of light forces battling him. Nuit knows that, which is the only reason he walked away from that meeting in the woods without Rivera's head in his talons. Once Rivera is in, we must move in unison— he will be eliminated; she will have the barrier around her breached. She already desires him, so we use Rivera as an instrument to gain her compliance, then we eliminate him."

The attorney nodded. "This needs to happen before Nuit turns two hundred and fifty thousand concertgoers on each of the five continental shelves with his armies in the audiences. This concert is an abomination to the order. Our spies have told us his plans . . . before the two of them were so brutally fed upon in the woods. The North Hollywood incident . . . it was very disgusting, and I will spare the council the details."

"I could care less about two FBI-agent humans who were vampire hopefuls! What is of greater concern is why would Nuit care about our policies when he and his army will be able to walk by day, feast at will on more than blood, and retain all the powers of darkness? He will not have to worry about empire exposure—within short order, he would be able to sweep the gray zone, and food supply won't be an issue for him—only for those of us left to perish with the blood thirst." The council member at the table's far point closed his eyes.

"Have a messenger bring more blood to the council from above. This will be a long siege—three tense eves when all of our concentration must be focused. We cannot go under the heel of demons turned high-ranking vampires prepared to flood the sixth realm, and Nuit's Minion to take over the gray zone as daywalkers. He will be unstoppable. It will be an end of a civilized era. Plus, the Dark Lord is becoming supportive of these efforts . . . he has grown anxious for the Armageddon ever since the millennium turned. We are losing support from below."

"Council members, gentlemen, I understand your concern," the chairman hissed. "There is much at risk. Stay near Rivera at all times.

"There could be brief times when Rivera eludes our monitors, who must be weaker family members to avoid the possibility of our monitors attempting a double cross."

The members at the table nodded, their expressions grave.

"We may experience our own intermittent blackouts when we cannot track him or sense his motion, Mr. Chairman," the attorney warned. "Our power over him could also occasionally waver because it is not solidly aligned with supernatural law. This can occur when his strong maker, Nuit, a past council member, struggles to locate him . . . or, if the forces of light make contact and render us blind."

"Will we know which of our enemies is blocking our location-monitoring thoughts, should this happen?"

The group waited, seeming to hold its breath as the attorney stood, leaned across the table, and lifted the crest before him with a claw. Not even a murmur transpired between them as he produced a huge leather-bound black book with the seal of darkness on it, and began flipping through the code.

"Parliamentarian Vlak. Our patience escapes us. Your verdict indicates . . . ?"

The attorney shook his head. "We have a serious problem."

"Damali, get dressed, a nine-one-one in the weapons room!"

Marlene had said the words so fast and had dashed away from her so quickly that, without hesitation, Damali pulled on her jeans and a T-shirt, and then shoved her feet into her boots. So much for chilling. She picked up Madame Isis and shoved her little sister dagger into her waistband.

Damali got down the hall within minutes, and she could hear Shabazz and Marlene trying to talk Daniel down from a hysterical state, to no avail.

"Dan, where are you?" Marlene walked in a circle of frustration as Dan's voice boomed. Traffic could be heard in the background.

"I don't know! I was in Beverly Hills at Blood finishing the deal and this female vampire jumped out of the damned night on me! I can't go home, and Carlos told me to keep my windows up. Shit!"

"Carlos?" Shabazz bellowed.

"God bless him! He saved my life."

"Where is he?" Damali asked, trying to keep her voice level and authoritative.

"He said he didn't believe in that shit and stayed behind to walk to his car!"

Daniel's voice had broken off into sobs. "I shoulda made him come with me, but I was too scared to wait for him—and he was arguing and shit, D. I practically begged him!"

She walked over to the steel-protected window, closed her eyes, and pressed her palm to it, watching the heat of her hand fan out and make a ring of mist.

"Okay, okay, Dan, it's not your fault," Damali said as calmly as she could over her shoulder, ignoring the glare Shabazz and Marlene gave her. "What streets did you pass?"

"I was on Rodeo, then shot up to Sunset, then—then, I guess I'm on Coldwater Canyon Drive! I'm lost; my tank is on a quarter—whaduIdo? What the fuck do I do?"

"He's headed north, if he passed those streets in that sequence," J.L. confirmed from the map showing on the wall from the computer projector.

"Dan, head east, that's going to be toward your right, onto Mulholland, toward Hollywood Hills," Damali said, her heart slamming inside her chest as she tried to speak calmly for Dan's sake. "Okay? Dan?"

"Yeah, yeah, okay," he stammered. "I can't go home, Damali. I'm scared."

"We're not going to leave you out there. We got'chure back. Stay calm."

"Stay calm! Stay calm? You should have seen that thing! I could feel something creepy walking up on me and I started running. I had on my star like you said, D. Swear to God!"

"She's bringing him in—oh, we're fucked with a breach," Rider said, beginning to pace in an agitated state.

"No, not a good idea," Big Mike agreed.

Marlene pushed the mute button as Dan hysterically railed on.

"Look, guys, we can't in good conscience leave an innocent man out there like that. Jesus, y'all!"

"Damali—what if this is a setup?" Shabazz walked around the table, studying the weapons array.

"Listen to him," Damali urged. "The man is about to piss himself. The guy is traumatized. He's no vamp—and Carlos is out there, too. We need to bring them both in."

"No!" J.L. said, making a swift cutting motion with his hand. "What if Carlos is already compromised from being in that parking lot too long? Bad move."

Damali paused for a moment. "If we coach him in, we can hit Dan's ride with UV when he pulls into the garage, and wait until the sensors tell us there's nothing left to materialize, then open the door and let the poor guy in. Or, we can go get him and keep his eyes covered—if that would make you feel better. Same with Carlos. What is with y'all? We've got an innocent being pursued, plus another in serious danger."

"Guys, guys, talk to me! There's something hovering near my back windows!"

Damali slapped the mute button. "Step on it, Dan!" she yelled. "That's it—I've heard enough. We're coming to get you. When you see our Hum-V, pull over on the shoulder, but do not jump out of the car until one of us comes and gets you.

"Rider, Big Mike—grab a coupla heat seekers and a cannon, crossbows . . . let's rock and roll!"

"You are not going out there tonight!" Marlene said fast. Her expression was frenzied and her words had come out in a quick rush of horror.

"Marlene, I love you, but save it. Keep talking to him, guys. J.L., keep us on a Lo Jack radar blip, and keep com going, and I want a three-way to the vehicle with you guys and Dan so I can hear him and talk to him— Shabazz, you got the compound. Bring Jose into the weapons room and let him rest in here. We all stay in eyesight of somebody. *Nobody* goes it alone."

Damali was in instant motion and the team begrudgingly nodded as she harnessed herself with shells, a handheld cannon, holy water grenades, and her Isis blade. As long as she could hear Dan's voice she was okay—but she wasn't sure of what she'd do if she heard him scream, or heard the sounds of him being ripped apart and eaten alive. It was as though everyone shared the same thought all at once as they each paused and looked at one another. Big Mike and Rider grabbed an armload of artillery and followed Damali, who was already halfway down the hall.

CHAPTER TWO

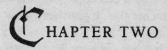

CARLOS WAS in the process of dematerializing into unseen vapors when Damali's worry for him stabbed into his skull. How ironic. His plan had been to follow Dan's scent to her, when she literally called out into the night with her mind and was pulling *him*! How could that be? She'd broken into a master vampire's mind, a human? No one had told him that she would be able to invade his thoughts, draw him to her. Fascinating, and thoroughly electrifying. A shudder of anticipation ran through him.

Carlos became solid form as he closed his eyes and opened his mind to Damali's panic. He could see her driving, could see the perspiration cast a slight sheen to her lovely brow. He licked his lips, tasting the salt of her skin. Her deep brown eyes had opened wide, her pupils expanding until they eclipsed her irises. Night vision . . . like his kind?

Damali's pull was so erotic that he swayed and held on to the hood of a nearby car. *Damn* . . . As she clutched the steering wheel of the Hum-V she drove, he could actually feel her power. No longer shielded behind the walls of her compound, he could detect a light blue aura of energy emanating from her skin. It gave her a glow. He could feel himself needing to touch her, drawn like a moth to a flame. Carlos reached out trembling fingers into the night air and let out a deep moan, and immediately censored himself. He quickly withdrew his hand. They should have told him that she would be like a drug to him. He would have to learn to control his reactions around her, if he was going to protect her from Nuit.

But her hair, her skin . . . *her voice*. The timbre of it issuing battle commands . . . her lack of fear fueled by fury-induced adrenaline shot through him. Shards of pleasure created bands of colors in his head. She was a magnet. He wrestled with the effect she produced and focused on what was around her. Her guardians were formidable, but in this state of aggression he could take them. Then he saw her weapons—a blade, a dagger . . . she had no fear of hand-to-hand combat . . . she had bloodlust in her heart, driving her like a bullet. Carlos shuddered again as the scent of her now filled his nose, creating a hunger that matched his craving for blood.

Delirious, he stumbled forward, away from the parked car. He inhaled her again, and it produced a rush like no other he'd ever experienced. Immediately his fangs came down, the muscles in his body tensed and built. He could feel his density shift, become stronger. He glanced at his hand, awed that it was larger, his nails a deadly eighth of an inch longer, but he was amazed that he did not have claws. Why?

He rubbed his palm over his face, wondering what he looked like now. He used his fingertips to make the assessment. His awareness of her had only strengthened him, but had not disfigured him. Why? He stared at the side of a minivan. Two red gleaming points reflected off the shiny black vehicle. His eyes ... daaayum ... Damali could make him feel like this, miles away? What would an encounter with her be like face-to-face? Maybe the Vampire Council would have to drive a stake through his heart after all—unless she had to plant the blade she carried for her own protection first.

"Unbelievable," Carlos murmured into the nothingness, now identifying the fragrance that he'd always detected from her when he was human. A creature so special had been in his midst all along. He raked every detail about her through his awareness, to understand what this whole thing called a Neteru truly was.

Most importantly, she was safe. He had to go to her. His form began to lose density and shape as he composed himself and summoned control.

Then the shadows moved, and he smelled a sickening musty-sweet scent—incense-like ... frankincense and myrrh.

Ready for an attack, Carlos braced himself, his eyes keened to the movement. There were twelve forms. He could feel his jaw unhinge by reflex and every body muscle twitch as it regained bulk in preparation for mortal conflict. The incisors inside his mouth were different, wider, more lethal than what Damali's image had caused. Erotic desire was instantly differentiated from battle mode. He glanced at his hands. Long, hooked talons came from the tips of his fingers like a lion's retractable claws. Now he understood. He narrowed his gaze as differently clad assassins came from the darkness. But he stood still, assessing which one to bring down first.

The eldest slowly advanced. He wore a huge silver cross with a bleeding heart in the center of it topped by a crown of thorns, and was dressed in royal blue. The aggressor unsheathed a three-foot-long blade that glinted in the dim, yellow parking garage fluorescent lights. Two more came out of the nothingness and were in black Ninja gear. Each had clearly visible weapons in their hands, a morning star and a dagger. Another who seemed to be a sheik wore all-white cotton, his gold star and crescent in the center of his chest dangled like a dare, and his grip tightened on a machete. More and more of them stepped from the darkness behind cars until they circled him—each bearing a different religious emblem and a weapon. Humans. Innocents. But how and why had they found him?

Carlos looked up, considering his options to make an overhead retreat along the ceiling ductwork.

"Demon," the first one who'd approached said, "why did you save the innocent? Is he marked?" The man's tone was wary, but his voice held a hint of confusion.

"Who are you?" Carlos shouted back, his gaze holding on to the cross, remembering his own that he'd dropped when the insanity began. The fleeting thought entered his mind only for a second and then was gone, as he spun to protect his own back.

"I am a knight of Templar," the royal-blue-clad assassin announced. "The others are my brethren from the twelve scattered churches. We make up the Covenant. You are surrounded."

Momentarily confused, Carlos let his gaze rove over the multi-ethnic hit squad, smelling their blood. These were men—but somehow protected men. "So, state your business. Whassup? What do you want with me? I have places to go."

"You let an innocent escape, and that drew us. And you left the gray zone with your mother and grandmother's prayers upon you—and with one in your heart. You had an emblem of God on your person. Do you seek redemption, demon? Are you seeking sanctuary?"

Carlos's shoulders relaxed, although he wasn't sure why, and he could feel his fangs and claws retract. The Vampire Council's monitoring had again retreated as soon as these *hombres* had shown up. Redemption? He thought of the tour the messenger had taken him on through the realms. Sensing an opportunity in the offing, Carlos hedged a bet. "I need to be able to talk to you without my conversation being monitored. I'm tapped. Anything you can do to ensure our conversation stays private?"

The team nodded and lowered their weapons, and soon their voices began in a low chant, each speaking in a different language, saying what Carlos could only determine as different prayers—simply because the one man in blue before him said the Twenty-third Psalm in Latin. Carlos smiled. He couldn't hear the words, but he knew the cadence of the prayer. Knew the beat of it, how it was uttered. His mother's insistence that he attend Catholic Mass as a child had finally come to some good use. But it didn't stab into his brain. Interesting. They had somehow not attacked him with it.

"You are shielded," the blue knight announced as the group fell quiet.

Carlos nodded. "Thank you."

"We are the keepers of the sacred texts, and the

guardians of the transition corridors. We keep the passages to the realms above clear of demonic manifestations and blockages so that ascending souls may pass unharmed. Yours was hijacked during sure descent, from the keepers of the sixth realm of darkness. Supernatural law was broken by the old vampires. You have to make a choice quickly. We don't have much time."

"If my soul got jacked, where is it?" A tingling sensation entered Carlos's fingertips as he waited for their answer.

"In Purgatory, until a final determination can be made about which realm has right to it," the blue knight said. "There has been a dispute over it."

The group nodded, but Carlos could see their grips flex on their arsenal. "Your business with me, then, is . . . ?"

"You have not eaten of the innocent yet, but soon you will have to—the blood thirst will be too strong . . . then you will be lost to us. You must make a choice. There is only one, and you have three days in which to make it. Choose wrong and the vampires own you."

"What choice?"

He studied the assembled warriors carefully as nervous glances passed between them.

"Bring us Damali Richards," the spokesman said in an even tone. "Then who knows? Perhaps mercy may befall you."

Carlos smiled. Damali was in high demand. He almost wanted to laugh it was so mad-crazy. "I already have an offer on the table for her, at present—by another council. Two pending deals, in fact. Want to raise the stakes? No pun intended."

The knight of Templar narrowed his gaze. "Yes. How about if we raise the stakes?" he threatened. "Literally."

A red-swathed Indian monk spoke through his teeth. "We do not negotiate with the underworld!"

"In Tibet, we have one resolution for evil," another in a yellow robe sneered, brandishing a long, thin blade. "We behead it."

"Bullshit," Carlos said. "DEA negotiates with the underworld here on earth, and the human underworld mob bosses negotiate with the feds from time to time. As above, so below. That much I've learned in the last few hours. So, if you don't have anything substantial to put on the table, here ends our conversation—and I'll go about my business in a puff of smoke. Pullease, gimme a break. You *hombres* have to do better than that!"

"Infidel!" the Muslim said.

"Finish this," a rabbi insisted.

"No, think about it, man," Carlos said calmly as the knight circled him. "I'm in a pretty fucked-up position— you are on one side, offering no guarantee of amnesty, and on the other side I've got eternal life, money, fame, and a fifth of the world's territory . . . all for one chick. Talk to me."

Carlos kept his gaze steady, although anticipation coursed through him. Every side was after his precious Damali. Sooner or later one side would win, he just needed to assess which side he'd aid—if any at all. But there had been some policy breach within the spirit world. It might protect her . . . might save his ass, too. "I don't want her to fall into the wrong hands. How do I know I should trust you?"

"Lower your weapons," the knight murmured. "He still has human compassion."

Carlos stared at the man; his dark brown eyes were boring into him and making it hard for him to breathe.

"Demon, you are right to seek her protection and to try to assess the most suitable arrangement for her. Honorable." The knight bowed slightly and leaned on his sword.

For a moment there was silence. Very light traffic could be heard in the distance along with the hum of the fluorescent lights. Moths fluttered overhead, not heeding the remains of their fried, dead comrades that had gone toward the light as a warning. It made Carlos assess his own circumstances very carefully.

"He may still have some of the three weapons available to man," one of the Ninjas murmured. "He obviously cares for her."

When Carlos cocked his head to the side, the other Ninja spoke.

"Faith, hope, and charity—charity defined as love. If a man has faith, he can have hope; with hope, he can love. It is a trinity and without one, all others are weakened. If a man loses faith, hope dies. Without hope, one cannot love. And love is the greatest of all gifts from On High."

"And how is any of this a weapon against anything?" Carlos walked in the confining circle they had made around him.

"These three gifts of the spirit make humans a risky variable to both sides," the blue-clad knight said slowly. "We have lost many people from the houses of worship because they lost one or all of these gifts, hence the variable to our side. Thus we put a young woman in the new arena that draws the focus of millions—the entertainment industry. Her words inspire, inspiration gives birth to hope, hope fuels faith and love. She touches the young, while their impressions of the world are still forming, and instills hope. She composes lyrics from her heart that others her age can identify with. She galvanizes masses with her universal message. Crowds of young people follow her, want to imitate her. Therefore, she's valuable beyond measure for many reasons beyond your comprehension— you must choose wisely."

The rabbi cast his nervous glance around the group. "He doesn't understand the importance of a chosen voice, or art upon a culture." He then addressed Carlos, his eyes possessing an urgent expression. "Art, it's a universal language. It comes from On High, and every culture that evolves to the higher levels brings forth masterful work— to show the beauty and goodness in the world, in all the senses down here on earth. Sound, sight, touch, smell, taste—the various arts invoke emotion, through emotion the human heart can find compassion, which opens it to the three gifts."

The one identified as a Templar nodded, his eyes never leaving Carlos's face. "Why do you think that when cultures are conquered, art and books are the first things burned? Why are artists jailed and persecuted . . . yet they keep on pursuing their craft like they're on a mission? Because they are, even when they don't know why they have this desire inside them that must get out and into the world. But the dark realms destroy such beauty and replace it with their perversion of it."

The Muslim let his breath out with impatience. "This is what they want to do to our Damali. But the art always seeps back into the world and gets a foothold—and is always the advance cry of a revolution of the mind. We are in the throes of an era that requires humanity to glean to higher priorities. We need positive young voices to fill the void, to reestablish hope and faith and love for all races.

We need them to draw peace, not war, as the adults have poorly modeled when they lost their way."

"The darkness has come to know this secret, too," the blue knight said in a sad, quiet tone. "And the dark also uses the airwaves to influence negativity—the Fallen Angel was given principality over the airwaves, as you recall. His realms have begun to use this to their advantage in our digital age where everything is airborne. Why not the vampires? They are, after all, the most evolved of the dark species."

"This is bullshit! I know you didn't come here to give me an art philosophy lesson. So, let's stop jerking each other off." Raking his fingers through his hair, Carlos stared at them for a moment. No anger reflected in their eyes. Pity did, and it disturbed him. Yet their conviction was palpable, and he could not deny that Nuit had built a recording empire in short order. But he needed to get on with his business, get to Damali. These men were wasting his time.

"Why me?" Carlos finally said. "Why didn't you all just surround her with a bunch of your church assassins—what makes you have to come to a vampire?" The pure irony of it made him laugh. "This makes no sense!"

A low murmur swept through the group and the one in all white spoke.

"I am of the Moorish Order, and we must inform you of your value, by right." The Moor waited for the others to nod before he proceeded. "One sinner, damned almost beyond redemption, is worth in soul-weight that of one hundred holy men. We have lost many holy men, and you represent a valuable asset to the forces of light to help tip the scales. You had the destiny to be a tracker guardian . . . Damali was sent to you first, but you chose the wrong path and she was taken from you for her safety."

He'd heard the part about the worth of a soul, but needed to consider what he'd been told about Damali. Parts of his life quickly careened through his mind . . . the way they met, his ridiculous urge to always protect her—never wanting her to be a part of his drug life . . . but never being able to get her out of his system, though she made him so angry at times he could wring her defiant, stubborn neck. The Vampire Council, or one of those insane groups of vamps he'd met had said he was a tracker, had a nose for her. Deep. Now some church guys had the same story. He stared at them hard, assessing them, trying to read the prayer-blocked minds to no avail. But they were indeed humans. Very strange.

"Hmmm . . ." Carlos nodded slowly again, his hands behind his back now as he walked and thought, taking his time to speak. "If I choose your side, what happens? I have seen the dark realm—shortly, I'll have regional maps to the five demon layers as well as the old route to a rogue master vampire's lair."

He could sense a restrained excitement sweep through the group, and their eyes shifted nervously between each other.

"That is valuable information," the knight said quietly, but still on guard. "If you lie, we slaughter you, and send you to the place from which there is no return."

"See, now you're threatening me, and that doesn't put me in a willing frame of mind. It makes me feel no love and want to go where I'm getting more positive vibes. You dig?"

The guardians grudgingly relaxed their stance.

"What do you want, for the maps and Damali?"

"Oh, now, hold up," Carlos said, chuckling. "Maps *and* Damali? You just raised the ante."

"Speak, demon. We lose patience."

"Everybody's in a hurry. Hmmm." Carlos chuckled and let out his breath, remaining cool and in control. "I do not want to have to fight this blood thirst while I'm also fighting other vampires and demons. I want to be able to blind them to my whereabouts at will—if I decide to join your cause. Let's begin there."

Again the assembled men conferred.

"We'll have to take this On High. We have no jurisdiction over these matters."

"How in the world can you come to a negotiating table without the authority to act and cut a deal?" Carlos shook his head as he walked in a tight space. "See, that's the problem with layers of bureaucracy—the other side can make swift, decisive decisions based on a power formula. Just like the difference between the DEA and the mob. Unbelievable!"

The group said nothing but nodded to each other in a way that made Carlos nervous.

"And," Carlos pressed. "This daylight thing—"

"That you will never have, unless you make the right decision after three days has passed, and even then you may die . . . your wounds might have been too severe. The most we can offer is that you may be allowed to live in eternal peace."

"Oh, man . . . what is that shit anyway?" Shaking his head, Carlos passed through their circle and began walking away, so totally despondent and weary of the fruitless discussion that he didn't even care if they came after him.

"Show him," a voice behind Carlos called out.

It made Carlos stop and turn around and stare at the no longer fearsome-appearing group. Their eyes still held a level of pity that disturbed him.

"Witness," the blue knight whispered, pointing his sword toward the black-tinted windows of a nearby parked van.

From a distance Carlos saw what could only be likened to a slow-frame video. He saw himself laughing as a kid, running in the street, playing ball with his brother and his friends. His mother leaned out of the window and yelled for them to come in and eat, and he saw his father sit down at the table and kiss his mother's cheek with love for her in his eyes. The pain of the beautiful memories of his life made him turn away. Then he heard his sister's laughter . . . she was gorgeous, healthy, young, and was running down the street to catch the ice cream truck for him and Alejandro. Carlos swallowed hard.

The pain that filled Carlos was so profound that he had to look away for a moment, but was drawn back to the vision despite his efforts. A part of him wanted to see the pureness of his existence, something lost. Another part of him bled inside from the memory. "That was a long time ago, and all of it's gone."

"Not all of it," the knight murmured, pointing his sword to the van again. "What I have shown you is free joy, peace, grace—none of it costs a cent, and lasts so much longer than what you grasped for in your delusion of power. There is only one true power. This is life in the light."

The vision moving along the van blurred as Carlos blinked back hot moisture from his eyes. Damali was sitting with him at the beach and he was tracing her cheek with a finger. The sound of her laughter was innocent and gentle and it washed through him, making him close his eyes. Her voice stabbed at him as she read him her poems in a whisper.

"Even in your iniquity, you have had a good soul, Carlos," the knight said quietly. "Look further and see what we have seen."

Carlos breathed in deeply, watching parts of his life unfold. It came in fast flashes of altered reality. He saw the schoolyard brawl on behalf of a friend that saved Juan's life. He watched himself push Juanita away from him when his drug business became too hot . . . she was an innocent, and he begged her to fall in love with someone else. He saw himself breaking off stacks of illegal monies, and sending runners to neighborhood homes that he knew needed help. He saw his hatred retreat in the middle of the woods, when he asked that one of the Minion be spared a horrible death—regardless of how his own brother had been killed. Then he saw Dan drive away, frightened but unscathed. And then the van window went black again, leaving him with no reflection.

"An angel of mercy heard your prayer and bound it to those that had already been sent up for you. That was transmitted to warrior angels at the border of the gray zone. It's the only reason you have three days . . . and because the dark side broke supernatural law."

Through a deep breath, Carlos steadied himself and swallowed away emotion. The dark side had a vulnerability. What law had they broken, and what did that mean for him? he wondered. "Can these warrior angels offer a guarantee?"

The group shook their heads no, but then conferred.

"We can try to call them, but we don't know if they

will appear in the presence of sure evil. The only reason we had been allowed to step in and make contact with you is because of the breach . . . and because we have a desperate need to ensure Damali Richards's safety."

A brief wave of panic crested within Carlos for an unknown reason, and he found himself walking toward the assembled, wanting to strike a bargain. He understood weight, product, amassing followers, and building armies to defend one's territory. There was always room to open an alliance.

"Wait," Carlos argued. "Ask them. I mean, if a sinner is worth his weight—then . . . ?" Carlos remained very still while they stared at him. "You guys haven't been honest," he pressed, panic lacing his tone. He couldn't let them leave. Not yet. Not before he knew more, and not after what seeing his old life had done to him. "This ain't about art," he pressed. "It's the fact that she's a vampire huntress—a Neteru. Talk to me."

Again the group mumbled quietly amongst themselves, and a low murmur began.

"So, the breach is correct," the Templar said, glancing at his team. "Only a master vampire would have known of the existence of a Neteru or her importance to the equation . . ." The men around him nodded. "The old vampires are in clear violation. Rivera died tonight, bitten by a master—Nuit, the warrior angels reported—but here he stands before us as a master, not a second-generation creature . . . that explains why even I, a seer, cannot get past his block to read his thoughts."

The Ninjas nodded in unison. "We have a rightful claim in the soul dispute. This must be taken up to higher realms for a decision . . . as long as he does not take an innocent, or pollute the Neteru."

"We'll get back to you," the Templar stated flatly.

One by one the religious men slipped into the shadows without a word. Carlos stood quietly, thinking about it all. No promises or commitments had been made. He was screwed. But he was still surviving the worst-case scenarios.

He needed motion, but preferred to walk for the moment. He took comfort in hearing his footfalls echo through the empty garage. It made him feel real, grounded, and somewhat normal. He'd find Damali in a little while, but he needed to first clear his head. A lot had transpired in such a short period of time. He'd literally been to Hell and back, been killed, raised from the dead, eaten from the dead, and seen his whole life flash before his eyes. His old life had been stripped away, his brother and friends had been murdered—his mother and grandmother had cast him out as the monster he now was. And he was only twenty-three. He'd also learned of Damali's true value, a vampire huntress, slayer, the Neteru. A diamond hidden in plain sight. But she'd been so much more to him than that, if they only knew.

Carlos exited the lot and crossed the street, avoiding the glass windows of the stores on Rodeo Drive by staying close to the curb. If he played his cards right, he could keep Nuit blinded by the Vampire Council—but get on the inside of his operation and close enough to hit him. He could also keep the Vampire Council blinded by the upper realms, who might be still hoping in vain that he'd go for their no-win deal. He could also keep the rest of his family from being turned, marked as off-limits, as well as manipulate the Vampire Council's extra boost of power to ensure that he stayed alive for a few nights, long enough to avenge his brother's death—and then slay his boys to hopefully release their souls. May Alejandro's soul rest in peace.

A long sigh found its way up from Carlos's lungs. He'd find all his family, and release them. Then what? At the end of the equation it still came back to the fact that he had to get to Damali, and in the end he'd be the walking dead, or worse. The Covenant hadn't even told him where to bring her, should he be so foolish as to bring her to them . . .

Carlos slipped into an alley, the streetlights and the normalcy of pedestrian traffic too much for him to bear. The lights flickered and he willed them to blow out. Only moonlight shone down the narrow asphalt corridor. An alley cat fled the Dumpster when he stared at it. Wise choice, kitty. Carlos stooped down and touched a glass-block basement window. Leaning his cheek against the coolness of a tiny cube of darkened pane, he spread out his hand, which now gave off no heat, and looked at the glass, trying to get it to shine back a reflection of his hand. What had he done? He wanted to weep, but his heart had no tears left in it—all it would produce was a mournful moan that made him close his eyes once more, and breathe in the only living thing that gave him comfort. Damali.

Static on the compound radio crackled as the guardians listened to Dan's voice lead Damali to him. Marlene glanced at Shabazz, who was sitting beside Jose's prone body. J.L. peered at her, and then fixed his line of vision on Jose.

"Put it on mute for a minute," Marlene ordered, going to Jose and Shabazz, and placing her hand on Jose's forehead. "He's burning up."

"I know," Shabazz said quietly. "We've gotta get him to a hospital."

Jose's complexion had turned ashen, and he was shivering so hard that he had to keep his eyes closed and breathe in quick, labored pants.

"They're inside my head, but the transmission goes both ways. They're splitting up the herd," Jose whispered through bursts of exhales. "Breaking her off from the group, and drawing her out. I'll be fine—stay with Damali."

Marlene and Shabazz exchanged a glance as J.L. stood.

"He's right," J.L. said, trepidation clear in his tone. "But we have to move the man."

Jose leaned over the side of the sofa and clutched his abdomen, retching. Marlene grabbed a nearby wastebasket that Shabazz had brought into the room—just in case—and thrust it under Jose's face.

"They're crawling inside of me." Jose choked, heaving and trembling, holding on to the side of the wastebasket.

"Three—make a circle, all of us hold hands, start praying over this man," Marlene ordered. "I'm going inside him telepathically."

"Don't," Shabazz warned. "You don't know what's in him." He covered his mouth and backed away from the horrible stench. He held on to the side of the weapons table and took deep breaths to stave off his own nausea.

Out cold, Jose didn't move, only his chest did.

"He's in way worse shape than we'd imagined, Mar."

Marlene nodded. "I'm going in and we have to get him rehydrated—or he'll flatline."

J.L. bounded up the metal steps to the rack of computers in the room, and took the radio communication to the

Hum-V off mute. "Damali, we've gotta move Jose. He just puked up maggots—and he's out cold."

"You can't go out alone. It's hot out here tonight! Tell Marlene I said stay put," Damali commanded. "I know what she's thinking."

"I know, D, but our boy is . . ."

"Okay, okay—have Marlene call down the white light around you guys. We're going to get Dan, and we'll meet you at the hospital."

"God willing," Shabazz murmured, keeping his gaze on Marlene. "Mar, I'm going to have to carry him, which means anything that tries to breach us as we go into the garage, you and J.L. are going to have to deal with."

"No," J.L. said, looking at the security panel. "I can put on the UVs in the garage to flush it, and then simply leave the systems on and—"

"No," Marlene snapped. "You'll be outside of the van, broken off yourself. The lights might not be enough for what's out there. Plus, if we leave the whole place hot, the generators might be dead by the time we get back, which means the compound could be infested."

"We gotta move this man fast, and don't have time to argue. We leave the compound idle all the time to travel to do gigs, Mar—you know that. Systems are up on normal electricity, then have a generator backup."

"Yeah . . ." J.L. added in, but his words trailed off as the overhead lights temporarily went dead, and then came back up on generator power.

"What just happened?" Damali's shout could be heard in the background coming from the communications panel.

"You guys need us back at base?" Big Mike asked.

"No," Marlene said. "Our direct power got cut and came back up on generator."

"We've never done a night move, or an extraction—and we've never taken a direct power-line hit like this," Shabazz warned.

J.L. nodded and glanced at Jose.

"Stay where you are," Damali said. "We're about two miles away from Dan. We'll pick him up, then head back to the compound."

Marlene reached for the console and put the telephone on mute. Determination blazed in her eyes. She was not afraid to die, a part of her already had when she took this mission. Traffic sounds could be heard coming over the radio. The guardians and Damali were all talking at the same time. She blocked out their strained voices, ignored their entreaties. Marlene glanced around at Shabazz and J.L., ignoring Damali's instructions. It was now or never. Her gaze went to Jose's face, and she spread her hands over his damp forehead and closed her eyes. Shabazz and J.L. stood back as a thin red glow outlined Marlene's hands. Her eyelids fluttered and her lips moved.

Soon every orifice on Jose's body slithered as nightmarish maggots, small black snakes, and tiny beetles fled his ears, nose, and mouth, leaving a sulfuric stench in their wake. Marlene had not moved. Her attention was unwavering. Jose convulsed, but she would not remove her hands.

The boy would not be doomed. She would not allow it! Not another young person in her charge would be lost—or she would die trying. Shabazz was at her side with his arm around her waist as an anchor, giving her his energy to siphon to add to their collective cause. His sensor's touch rippled through her body. Tears of exertion ran down her face, mingling with trickles of sweat. Her clothes stuck to her damp body. She was working. Knew

how to do this. Had been anointed. This was her calling—
a seer, a guardian, a keeper of the sacred sight. She was
the team's elder. J.L.'s hands alighted her shoulders, both
men prayed in a steady chant to protect her as she went
inside Jose's mind.

She had to bring Jose back! She saw past her own
fears, past her own instinct to survive . . . she harnessed
her love for Jose to the light as her mind dove deep into
the dark trying to claim him . . . and then she began to
spiral, connected to his mind, which was locked to his besieged spirit that exited his body—leaving both his and
hers vacant as she chased his soul to free it. She repented
her own transgressions and wrapped love around the
young man as her fingernails dug into his face until her
mind opened to see where a fragment of his soul had been
captured . . . trapped inside a dead fetus, trapped within
Dee Dee's trapped soul, trapped in the realm of pure jealousy, envy, coveting Damali's fame. Secrets and lies, Dee
Dee had envied Damali, it was all so very clear, and that
insidious emotion had made her soul sink when Big Mike
had staked her using his crossbow.

"Release the fetus, it is an innocent and does not belong to you," Marlene murmured. "Jose is a part of that
only," she said more loudly. "It is now dead flesh, but the
soul is not there. You have no claim! Release him!" She
spat out vile slime as it crept up her esophagus, trying to
take root in her, but she gave it no harbor. Jose moaned
and writhed while Marlene worked. Then Marlene saw
her own worst nightmare—Raven.

Marlene's spirit snapped back into her body, jerking
her, depositing Jose's spirit with a twitch. She drew back
her hands and clutched her stomach. Jose's color had improved and he stirred but was still weak.

"I'm going after her," Marlene said flatly, the conviction in her tone clear. The maternal pang inside her fused with guilt, worry, and a host of other emotions she could not define. Hot tears rose in her eyes as she set her jaw hard with determination. "It's time."

"I won't allow it," Shabazz said. "The last time Raven almost killed you!" He stared at the woman whose mind had been made up, defeat claiming him as he fought against a lost cause. The thought of possibly losing Marlene again was nearly unbearable.

"This is non-negotiable, Shabazz." Marlene's voice was firm, yet tender as she prepared to leave. She briefly glanced at Shabazz with understanding, then looked away as she spoke. "Escort J.L. to the hospital to cover him and Jose. The vamps are focused on Damali. While they're distracted, I'll join the rest of the team and be safe."

"Mar, no!"

"Oh, shit, D!" Dan yelled, breaking through the argument occurring in the compound. His shout momentarily stilled the calls for a response from Marlene by the mobile Neteru-guardians who were panicked by the compound's silence.

"Something's just landed on the hood of my car!" Dan hollered. "Help me, help me, oh, Goddamn . . ."

"Start praying out loud, Dan!" Damali ordered. "Now! Anything you remember from Hebrew classes, whatever. Just start saying it."

Shabazz hit the console to take it off mute. "Dan, pray, brother. Hard, like your momma taught you how!"

"I don't remember!" Dan screamed. "I can't remember Hebrew classes . . . shit, something's rocking my car!"

"Then just start an old-fashioned fucking conversation with the man upstairs, dude," Rider yelled. "Like, 'Save my ass, Father. Help! Yo, get this shit up off me!' Don't stand on ceremony—call down spiritual backup!"

"Something's messing with the generators, D," J.L. shouted. "Power's dipping!"

"Give us ten minutes to get to Dan, then we're coming back for you guys."

"You don't have time to turn back, Damali," Marlene hollered. "Jose is bad, we've gotta get him outta here while we still have generator lights! Meet Shabazz, J.L., and Jose at the hospital. I'm going to draw it to me, then you draw it to you, Damali . . . keep it confused."

"Dan, Dan—speak to us," Damali yelled. "Marlene, he's not answering."

They could hear Dan hollering and sputtering disjointed prayers and his car making screeching sounds as metal sounded like it was being grated. Marlene closed her eyes and brought the face she knew too well into her head, drawing it, taunting it, trying to create a diversion.

"We move," Shabazz ordered, hoisting Jose's limp body over his shoulder and snatching up his gun, then thrusting it into his waistband. "Weapons. Start pulling it to you, Damali. Marlene is on her way and has a lock on it."

"Done," Damali confirmed. "Mar, Godspeed. I don't wanna lose you."

Marlene nodded as Dan's remote screams could be heard through the radio. She picked up her stick and a battle-ax as Shabazz also grabbed a pump shotgun, and J.L. took several light wands and a crossbow.

All they had to do was make it to both remaining Jeeps.

"From what I'm hearing," Rider said in a quiet, urgent voice, "we might as well turn back and get up with our team."

Big Mike nodded from the backseat, placing a hand on Damali's shoulder. "Baby, you don't want to find him. We're too late."

"No," she said, her voice cracking. "We go get him, and back up whatever's feeding off of him. At least let his mother be able to bury him in one piece!"

Silence pierced the vehicle—neither the compound radio nor Dan's transmission chattered, only static came through.

"There's his Honda," Rider said, looking around as Damali spun the Hum-V to face Dan's badly mangled car.

"We do this nice and slow," Big Mike warned as each of them checked their weapons and prepared to get out of the vehicle.

Damali nodded, opened the door, and jumped down, swiftly followed by Rider and Big Mike. As they approached Dan's wreck, they could see that both the front and back windshields had been shattered. The top of the car looked like giant claws had ripped it open like a tin can, and the passenger and driver's side doors were hanging ajar.

She glanced at Big Mike, who shook his head, communicating pity for both the lost cause, as well as the fact that he couldn't hear anything lurking nearby. Rider hung his head, and slowly began to shake it, giving her the same silent message.

"Don't go to the car," Rider whispered. "Honey, you don't want to see what they leave. Seeing the remains of a friend is different than seeing a vamp gored. Even with all our losses, you ain't never seen that."

Damali wiped at her eyes with anger and pushed herself forward, braced for the grisly sight. Her second sight was locked on the face that she'd fought in the Chinatown alley. All she could see was the top of Dan's head as she peered through a smashed window. His whole body was wedged down under the steering wheel. She couldn't risk losing her hold on the thing out there stalking Marlene by splitting the focus of her second sight to scan Daniel, nor did she want to. She wasn't sure she wanted to have the image of his death permanently lodged in her mind, so she blocked it.

"Oh, God, they only left his head." Damali jerked her chin up and averted her eyes for a second to steady herself enough to cope with the remains of a friend.

Sudden movement made her grip tighten on her blade as Dan's hand thrust up, holding out and brandishing his gold medallion. Reflexes aimed Rider and Big Mike's weapons at his skull in preparation to take him out. Damali relaxed.

"Get back, get back, get back!" Dan screamed.

The team lowered their weapons and rushed to the side of the car, staring at the trembling hand that held up a gold star. Dan's other hand was covering his head and he was sobbing and screaming.

"It's us, Dan," Damali said, touching his clenched fist. "Are you hurt?"

"Pull him up and slap his face," Rider told Mike. "He's battle-freaked."

Mike nodded and pushed his shoulder cannon out of the way so he could grab at the huddled mass that was struggling to crawl deeper into the small pocket of safety. The extraction took three attempts before Big Mike could dislodge Dan, who swung at him wildly, but never dropped his medallion.

Rider paced over to the fray and slapped Dan twice. "It's us, dude. Relax."

Dan opened his eyes and blinked at the group who surrounded him as Big Mike dropped him. Wiping furiously at his eyes, he scrambled to his feet.

"Oh, shit! Oh shit. I thought one of those big burly suckers had me when that ox, Mike, pulled me up. Oh shit, guys—why didn't you tell me?"

"Ain't got time," Damali said fast. "We've gotta get back—our compound is under siege. Get him in the vehicle."

Rider held up his hand. "This ain't the place to be making fast moves," he said slowly, his head turning as his nose seemed to follow a scent.

"Oh, shit—"

"Shush!" Mike hissed, cocking his head like a hunting dog. "You hear it?" he whispered, gazing at Damali. "Be still, baby. While you was covering Mar, think you mighta missed it." Mike slowly raised his shoulder cannon and spun on the sound behind him and fired.

The bushes lit up as the dirt shell exploded and a screeching mass took flight, circling above. Rider pulled Dan down, dropped to one knee, and opened fire with an automatic, spraying the mass with hallowed dirt–filled cartridges. Reconstituting quickly, the flying mass regrouped several feet away and separated into six forms while Mike and Rider reloaded.

"Give the man a weapon," Damali told Mike. "Dan, we need everybody in the game tonight."

Mike pulled three leather straps from his neck that had vials of holy water at both ends of each thong, and produced a stake for Dan to use from the back pocket of his fatigues. "You read the Old Testament?"

Dan nodded, his hand shaking as he accepted the strange-looking gizmos from Big Mike.

"David and Goliath action, understood, little brother? Watch her back and yours. Don't get nicked. The stake goes dead aim, in the center of a vampire's chest. Get the heart."

Dan put his chain back over his head and stood when Rider pulled him up by his elbow. With Damali in the lead, and the three men behind her, both sides waited in a temporary standoff.

When the six creatures before them parted, a low growl could be heard coming from deep in the underbrush behind them. Damali's blade was before her, every muscle in her tensed and ready to spring. Then two pairs of gleaming eyes could be seen first, low to the ground, as something stalked through the opening the vampires had made. That's when she smelled it, and released her call to it. Marlene had been covered. The things had come to her, the vampire huntress, and it was time to deliver a beat down.

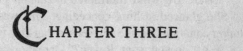CHAPTER THREE

THE GUARDIANS kept their aim steady, but didn't fire as the panther loped to the fore and slowly transformed into a lush, tall, black leather–clad female form.

"This is between her and me," the female entity said, straightening out the triangle of her leather halter-top and then studying her razor-sharp French manicure. "Has been for a long time." She nodded toward Damali, and then glanced at her squad, smoothing out the leather of her skin-tight pants. "You can feast on the others when I'm done—two of them for each one of you—I ate earlier. Italian. But first, she and I have some unfinished business."

"We can't feed on the blond—the one called Dan," one vamp in Raven's group replied evenly. "Remember what Nuit told us?"

"He'll get over it," Raven snarled. "It's a moot point—two minutes, she's dead."

Rider and Mike exchanged a look and glared at Dan, and then returned their focus to the threat before them.

"Later," Big Mike murmured in Damali's direction.

She glanced at him, conceding. This was a part of a larger equation, but she still sensed that Dan was innocent.

"What do you want, Raven?" Damali asked, her voice carrying across the expanse that separated both groups.

"You take my mother, and then my men . . . and you ask me what I want?"

"Damali," Rider said with caution, "she's a second generation, and I don't think—"

Damali held up her hand to quiet Rider.

"Your mother?" Damali opened her mind, her awareness so sharp now that what felt like an electric current ran through her.

Raven laughed, the sound cold and dead. She narrowed her eyes. Damali heard a car approach at a high speed and swerve to a stop, but she didn't turn. Damali kept her gaze trained on her vampire targets. The Jeep door slammed, her guardians glanced at it over their shoulders. Mike raised a weapon in Marlene's direction to cover her from a possible surprise attack. Dan's terrified eyes darted between the approaching guardian and the unbelievable sight before him. Damali didn't flinch. The male vampires tensed, considered the new Jeep and guardian, then glanced at Raven, but didn't move.

The desire to attack the haughty thing that was laughing at her lit a new fire within Damali. However, she garnered patience. A false move could cost a member of her team their lives. She could hear Marlene's footsteps behind her. *Remain in control.* Her odds had just improved as a seasoned fighter joined her ranks, and stepped beside her. She already knew it was Marlene. Damali studied the vampires, her focus on the one called Raven as it laughed even harder.

"Hello, Mother dearest," Raven said softly. Her tone was lethal and her expression was filled with hatred.

Daughter? Damali's concentration wavered. Pure shock gave way to disbelief as she held on to a thread of hope. No. Impossible. She knew vamps were masters of deceit, but something in Marlene's countenance told her to be still. This wasn't necessarily a lie. She watched Marlene and the entity claiming to be her daughter. There was no rage in Marlene, just bitter resignation. The realization made it hard for her to breathe.

"It's over, Raven," Marlene said flatly, her battle-ax raised.

"Fuck you! Follow what you said, or have infinite power, fame? Are you mad? You sound so pathetic, Marlene! It's on!"

"Then, bring it!" Damali hollered, stepping away from the group and Marlene as Raven hissed, and began circling.

"Gladly," Raven said with a snarl.

"Leave her to me, Damali," Marlene said. Deep, incomprehensible sadness made her command sound almost like a plea. "This is something I should have done years ago."

The guardian team glanced at each other. Damali stared at Marlene for a moment. A shudder went through her as she assessed Marlene. Her focus went back to Raven.

"Tell her, *Mother* . . ." Raven taunted from the thicket as she walked, bearing fangs, her eyes now glowing, her vampire henchmen snarling behind her. "You've told so many lies that you can't even remember, can you? But I was your first baby girl."

Damali glanced at Marlene when she didn't respond. Tears glistened in the older guardian's eyes as she stared at Raven. The center of Damali's chest hurt for a moment, and it felt as though her lungs were constricting as Marlene's pain became her own.

"Don't listen to her, Marlene," Damali said, still unable to process what she'd just heard and trying to break the trance Marlene was in. "They lie! Screw with your mind, and get things twisted. Shake it, Mar, and let's do this."

She could hear Rider and Big Mike suck in air hard behind her, as though battling for composure.

"Do her for Marlene," Big Mike said in a low murmur from where he stood. "Mar ain't got it in her. Shouldn't have to put down her own daughter."

"That's right," Raven interjected, her statement dissolving into a hiss. "Marlene never had it in her ... couldn't take care of either of her girls." Then it laughed as Damali's gaze darted between Raven and Marlene.

Suddenly, Marlene lunged forward, her ax held high. Raven ducked. Marlene missed. Now Marlene was trapped on the wrong side of the line. Raven was between Damali and Marlene, with Marlene only feet away from the vamp henchmen, and the older guardian didn't move.

"Me and you," Damali shouted, trying to get an opening to her separated guardian. "I don't know what you're talking about, but you gotta come through me to get to Marlene!"

"No, I don't." Raven laughed. "Be serious."

Damali watched for a strategic advantage. Marlene was not going out like that on her watch! Remembering every skill she'd ever learned, she lowered her weapon and laughed, using the strategy of guile as her mind siphoned the second-generation vampire before her. "What do you have on Marlene? Some petty bullshit? Pullease," Damali scoffed. "I am so unimpressed."

The female creature whirled on Marlene, abandoned her in rage, and took two paces toward Damali. Both Damali and the Raven held up their hands as their male teams tensed to mount a sudden attack. Damali shot Marlene a quick glance. If Marlene would just raise her ax, plant it in that bitch's back . . . C'mon, Mar, what's the problem? She'd take Raven, and then Rider and Mike could get a shot off. Damali kept her eyes on Raven and smiled.

"You're stronger than I thought . . . got a master's skills." Raven cocked her head to the side and smiled. "Then see for yourself, huntress. See if you can deal with this."

Damali had Raven in her mental sight, but was not prepared for the images that careened before her. Immediately pain, grief, emotional agony riddled her. She saw her father go into a lair and become hunted. Her mother was holding her as she wailed as an infant in her arms, and felt her mother's confusion, her rage, her pain of mistaken betrayal. The ritual. Then smoke. Her mother's throat was ripped away, tissue shredded, flesh leaving bone, her mother's face became distorted . . . her father . . . oh, God. Her parents had been turned. She clutched her blade tighter. "Oh, Mom . . . no. It wasn't what you thought—*don't do it.*"

Damali could hear Marlene yelling for her not to look any deeper into Raven's eyes. Needles entered her back where her tattoo covered her spine. She was an infant, Marlene applied the protective emblem . . . a young, frightened, tearful Marlene put the Sankofa symbol on her as she wailed as a baby inside her head. Then Marlene abandoned her.

Swallowing hard, Damali forced the hurtful impressions from her mind. But the truth lingered long after the image was gone. Her parents had been turned. Marlene had given her over to foster care and had not kept her. Marlene's daughter had been bitten the year Damali had been found living on the streets. All this time, and Marlene had never told her . . .

"That's right," Raven said with satisfaction. "She gave your ass up," she said, pointing toward Marlene.

Do her, Mar . . . Damali's mind screamed, as Raven transformed into a large, sleek panther in an instant and made an immediate lunge for Damali.

Madame Isis sent off a chime in the wind as Damali swung it to match a clawed swipe from Raven. Rider's gun fired, knocking one of the beasts away from Marlene. The vampires disappeared as one of their squad began to burn, then angrily repositioned themselves after the shot. Damali swung her blade again, missing Raven, but she heard Marlene yell as a male vampire's fist connected to Marlene's jaw. Big Mike sent cannon fire above Marlene's body to give her time to retreat. They had to get Marlene back in the huddle before the vamps ripped her apart. Marlene swung her battle-ax, but there were too many around her. Yet, the older guardian was not going down without a fight. Marlene took her Aikido stance amid the growling forms. The first one moved, she swung her ax, hit a second with a well-placed kick, and backed another off of her with the blunt end of the weapon.

"Explosives!" Damali called, and Big Mike responded to the threat by hurling a series of holy water grenades at Marlene's feet.

Mike's cover had been just enough to give Marlene a narrow chance to escape to the safety of the team's hunkered-down position, while Rider frantically reloaded his and Big Mike's guns—Raven circling and stalking Damali in a slow threat the entire time.

Using both hands to hold on to the blade, Damali quickly turned to address the threat that was suddenly at her back. The group of vampires dispersed and had her team surrounded—but she couldn't get to them, unless she put Raven down.

"Watch them die," Raven said, her tone taunting. "It's worse than being killed yourself . . . hearing the screams for mercy, feeling their panic."

Anger made Damali swing again, and she nicked the forearm of the thing that reached for her. Raven drew back, her body returning to human female form as she studied the smoldering slice, growled, then leapt. Damali spun away, her elbow connecting with Raven's rib cage from behind, which sent the creature hurtling forward. Fury immediately transformed Raven into the huge panther once more. Landing on all fours, Raven glanced over her shoulder, and as fast as lightning was rushing toward Damali again. Prepared for the advance, Damali spun, her thigh lifting to connect a solid boot blow to Raven's fang-distorted jaw.

But the quick spin made Damali fall—Madame Isis was a hand reach away. Raven leapt, coming down, as Damali rolled away, her blade back in her possession. The split second that Raven tilted her head as though listening for something was all Damali needed to get back up. Raven took human-vampire form, apparently saving her energy.

Good, she must be getting tired, Damali thought as she

heard Dan yell. A holy water vial broke at Damali's feet, making Raven draw back far enough to be in blade range. Rider's gun had stopped firing, but Damali could still hear Rider, Marlene, and Big Mike's grunts of exertion as the team behind her battled. For a second her focus went to those she loved, and a blow caught her in the center of her chest, knocking the wind out of her as Raven's boot connected with her body.

Temporarily dazed, Damali maneuvered herself out of the way of another kick, but realized that when she'd fallen her body had gone in one direction, and Madame Isis had gone in the other.

"Now, whatcha gonna do?" Raven asked through a fanged smile.

Drawing the dagger from her waist, Damali circled the beast. "Kick your unnatural black ass, bitch."

Raven immediately transformed again, using the strength of the shape-shift to her advantage. Crouching low, the panther kept shaking its head as it approached stealthily forward. Damali could feel the adrenaline inside her connecting to tissue, blood, bones, and cartilage. Her hand was on fire from holding the dagger so tightly—the beast's head turned to look into the darkness for a second, which was a second too long. Taking the offensive, Damali rushed the creature, slicing at the paw that spontaneously swiped in reflex, and dropping the animal's limb.

Raven instantly transformed where she was on the ground, holding the bloody stump, screeching, and that gave Damali enough time to reclaim her long blade. The sound of Raven's wails made the other vampires look up for a moment. Rider got one dead in the center of its chest with a short stake produced from his jeans back pocket, and Marlene summarily beheaded it. Big Mike had thrown a sucker-punch, connecting with another vamp—sending it hurtling toward Dan, who torched it with vials that broke around it. Rider ducked as Damali threw the dagger in his direction, connecting to the center of a vampire at his back, incinerating it immediately. Her team was back in control, and it was on.

Raven held the dismembered stub and began to draw away, her spine smacking against a tree. Mike got two more of them in one shot from his reloaded shoulder cannon, while Rider claimed one surrounding Dan with an abandoned crossbow, and Dan hurled his last set of vials. The vials didn't break, but the leather strap tangled around the creature's neck. The vials dangled against its chest and burst into flame, consuming the screeching entity in a slow burn that reeked of sulfur. From out of nowhere, a new vampire rushed Big Mike, but Marlene planted her silver battle-ax blade in the middle of the creature's spine.

Immediately, Raven pushed away from the tree to give flight, but Damali took her out—right in the center of her chest.

Damali pulled Madame Isis out of the wood slowly as ash crumbled and fell away from the tree. Thick plumes of sulfur wafted in the air, and her team—coughing, dirty, and exhausted, came to Damali's side. She studied the blade and then stopped to wipe the black ooze remains on the grass and watched them burn.

"Something was calling her back," Damali murmured. "That's the only reason I had a chance a coupla times."

"Well, who gives a shit why, D? The fine point here, I believe, is that something called her away." Rider picked up the small dagger and gave it to Damali, wiping the muck off it with the bottom of his boot.

Damali nodded as she stood, accepting Rider's simple assessment.

"Might have been guardian angels, li'l sis, who knows?"

Damali glanced at Marlene for a moment and then looked away. "You should have told me, Mar." Multiple emotions zigzagged through Damali's thoughts. Her team stood still, listening to the quiet.

"I know," Marlene murmured. "My second of hesitation almost cost you and members of the team their lives."

Shaking her head, Damali began walking. "No. That's not why you should have told me, Mar. I deserved to know because it was the truth."

They all walked back to the Hum-V and Marlene's Jeep in silence. Damali allowed her thoughts to fuse with Marlene's as she tried to gather some understanding of why Marlene, of all people, would have deceived her with such a lie of omission. Hurt, anger, and disappointment filled her, almost making it impossible for her to summon her gift. But then she focused on the love . . . which became a mother's heartbreak. Marlene had been a young woman, frightened of her gift, and forced into the role. Damali heard Marlene swallow hard, and could see her eyes glisten with moisture in the moonlight as they cautiously approached their vehicles. She could feel Marlene opening her mind, allowing the connection to be made, as images floated through Damali's psyche.

Marlene had wanted a normal life . . . had been in love, was pregnant with Christine—who became Raven after the bite. The elders wanted Marlene to protect a Neteru baby . . . but how did a young, single mother do that without risk to her own unborn child? A choice was made. Marlene opted for safety and ran away. Only to have what she feared most ultimately hunt her down and mistake Marlene's baby girl for the sought vampire huntress—her. Damali released Marlene from the connection. Yes, she knew there was more to the story, but at this moment, she just couldn't deal. Fatigue clawed at her, as did major sadness. She'd trusted Marlene, but could understand. . . . However, that still didn't take away the sting of it all.

"Guys," Dan said quietly, trailing behind the group, "you're not leaving me, right?"

"Hop in, Dan," Rider said with a sigh. "Because of your stupid ass, the rest of our team might be jacked. So, if you're gonna ride with us—shut up."

"Check him out, first," Big Mike instructed. "One of 'em said they couldn't eat the blond. Why not?"

"Probably because they wanted to use him as a decoy, is all," Damali said on a weary exhale. "Remember, when we found him, he was praying and holding on to his star. If he was a vamp helper, they would have used Dan another way . . . Dan was just a lure—bait—they knew we wouldn't leave him to be eaten alive." She shook her head, and motioned to Big Mike. "Ride shotgun with Marlene, please. I'll drive with Dan and Rider."

"We've gotta tell J.L. and Jose about Raven, and the other stuff," Mike said, his expression sad. "It's time for everybody to be on the same page."

"I know," Damali murmured as the team swept the vehicles for safety and climbed in.

Carlos watched Damali pull away from a distance. He now knew what a Neteru was. He'd seen her fight, and understood her disappointment in her family member all too well. Her pain made him ache to hold her.

Intense remorse filled him as he walked through the ashes of the dead. If he'd only known before. He'd told Raven to stay away from her and Daniel! But Raven had been so bold as to amass her third generations to disobey his telepathic order. It seemed other things besides a well-placed blade could make a vampire lose its head; jealousy, the green-eyed monster. So Raven wanted to wipe out Damali and have him battle Nuit—for her . . . foolish.

Carlos shook his head. In order not to blow his cover, there had been nothing he could do to help the guardians ward off the unauthorized attack, but remain unseen and yell for Raven to come to him. By the time he'd arrived, the battle was already under way. He could never let Damali see him for what he was now.

Frustration worked on his reason like a chisel, filing away at him. True, he couldn't say he'd never been told about faith in things unseen—but in those days, he didn't believe. Words he'd heard earlier in the night entered his mind . . . if a man loses faith, then he loses hope. How long had he walked the planet with no faith, and therefore hoping in all the wrong things? Without hope, one cannot love. When Alejandro went down, he'd lost hope, and they got him. Carlos shut his eyes and drifted through the blackness of the woods. But they had also said that if you still had love, the strongest of all gifts, then hope could be restored, as well as faith.

He opened his eyes and followed the Hum-V, watching the red taillights of both guardian vehicles disappear around a curve. The moment that Damali had become seized with worry for her team and electrified by the hunt, her sensations had run all through him. Her breaths had filled his lungs. Her increased heartbeat drummed a rhythm inside his chest. Her tender concern for someone she hardly knew made him taste tears. The sound of her voice made him tremble.

Carlos walked to the side of the road and stared at its vacancy, again closing his eyes, and shuddered when he deeply inhaled the fragrance Damali left behind once more.

"He's with the doctors," Shabazz said quietly as the team entered the waiting room. "I know you're still bent on going, but he won't make it to New Orleans tomorrow. . . . By the time we got him out of the compound, he was almost in a coma."

Damali sat down slowly beside Mike as Shabazz leaned forward with his forearms resting on his thighs.

"We've never sustained a compound attack like that," he whispered, his gaze coming up from the floor to lock stares with each member of the group before going back to Damali. "J.L. almost bought it."

She looked up at J.L. who was pacing like a cat until Mike steadied him with a hand on his shoulder.

"I had to attempt to reboot the security systems to give us enough juice to at least get into the four-by-four and then hope we could get the automatic doors to open . . . I was only like thirty seconds behind Mar and Shabazz—who was carrying Jose, when the generators got knocked out."

"Mar kicked some butt in the dark, second sight—sister fought blind, like a pro. Took a head with a battle-ax, and her walking stick did the rest so she could catch up with you guys. Glad to see everybody made it back in one piece." Shabazz breathed out hard.

"She used her stick to keep them off my back while I

threw a few grenades into the Jeeps to clear them out, and then dumped Jose in—but three of 'em slithered out from under them. They went for J.L. who got one crossbow shot off in the hall. He got one vamp, but then it was on. I almost couldn't get to him fast enough."

"Only thing that saved my ass," J.L. said in a distant voice, "was fiber-optic thread."

The team looked at J.L., and then glanced at each other.

"Me and Jose had been working on a new shark suit design for Damali. We had made these handheld concert lights with the leftovers, trying to think of things we could get mass produced for the audience."

From the back pockets in his jeans, J.L. pulled out two silver-plated, four-inch-long cylinders the width of a double-A battery that had a thicket of nylon-thread hairs sprouting from the tops.

"Looks like the average five-dollar concert trinket, but we put UV bulbs in them. Figured at the big show, we could do an anthem that tells everybody to turn on their light to make sure kids buy them on the way in, and we can sneak them past the vamp crew and any vamp helpers—because they look like nothing harmful. Standard concert junk."

Damali nodded as the group huddled closer, accepting the ingenious decoy with a slow smile. "J.L., you guys are brilliant."

"You shoulda seen him work with 'em though, D," Shabazz murmured, and pounded J.L.'s fist. "Jet Li–type vibe. Brotherman was fighting for his life, running up the sides of the garage walls, leaving a burn with every flip, and backed the two remaining ones up enough for me to get my stake on with Marlene. Then we had to manually open the door—which was not fun."

"You didn't get scratched on the way out, did you?" Big Mike asked, worried, inspecting Marlene, J.L., and Shabazz.

"Naw, man," J.L. said with a breath of relief. "Shabazz and Mar had my back, and I had theirs—we're cool. Was able to get power up, too, from the garage panels."

"So what do we do with Dan?" Rider asked, finally nodding to the one person that everyone had left out of the discussion.

Marlene assessed Dan critically. "You know, if he came running to us under siege like that . . . might he be a new guardian?"

Although Damali agreed, she was notably quiet. There was much to absorb, and now they even had a new person to contend with. She said nothing. Later. Her second sight was ebbing, as were her other senses. She was exhausted, needed to eat and lie down.

"You have got to be kidding us, Mar," Rider said after a hang-jawed moment, and then slapped his forehead and walked away to flop down in an empty chair.

Ignoring Rider, Marlene stood and walked over to where Dan leaned against the wall.

"Dan, earlier you said it felt like something was chasing you before you saw it, right?"

All eyes were on him, even Rider's now.

"Yeah," he nodded, glancing around the group. "I could tell."

"How?" Damali asked, her voice just a weary murmur as she glanced at Marlene—who still could not look her directly in the eyes. "Describe it."

"My skin got all tingly, like the hairs were standing up on the back of my neck. Like an electric current, or something. Then I felt all creepy-crawly—started sweating, and it was hard to breathe . . . I could feel myself panicking, but couldn't figure out why. I'd just been in the Blood Music offices, everything was jaky, they said they would hire me, and the next night would show me the deal—the way they did business—and then I split. I didn't even wonder why I had to meet them at night so late—figured, hey, whatever, they're busy, keep artists' hours, ya know? I was feeling great, just glad to be a part of something for once. But then in the elevator, I could almost feel something in there with me." Dan glanced around the group. "I know this all sounds really weird, like I'm tripping, but I swear—"

"No, you're not tripping," Marlene reassured him. "What else?"

"I . . . I . . . uh, got out, passed the lobby guard, kept thinking I was the luckiest man in the world, that God was good. Soon as I thought that, this woman came out of nowhere—and she was *all that*. Baboom," Dan murmured, his gaze going off into the distance as he made the shape of curves and breasts with his hands.

"I was like, now I *know* God is good, and then she was gone. I stood there for a moment because she had just been behind me, and then the creepy feeling started. I didn't know why, then, but I had the urge to run—so I was trying not to look like a fool in case she was watching me, but I started walking real fast, then trotted, then this terror vibe just slammed me—I said fuck it, and started running headlong toward my car."

"He's got the tactical sensory gift," Marlene whispered, closing her eyes and nodding. "I can see it. His story checks out."

Rider leaned back again with a sigh, as did Big Mike and Shabazz. J.L. sat down and extended a handshake to Dan.

"You're in for the ride of your life, new brother."

"What is going on?"

J.L. shook his head. "Mar will tell you. She briefs all the newbies."

"He's good on the vials, Mar," Big Mike confirmed. "Had dead aim—like a David and Goliath–type capacity. Want me to put him on explosives with me?"

Marlene nodded but glanced at Damali for approval. The team waited. Damali finally nodded.

"That's cool," she said in a distant voice.

"Wait," Dan whispered quickly. "You mean I'll have to hunt more of these things? We're not done?"

"Rude awakening, isn't it?" Rider closed his eyes and leaned his head back against the wall.

"For how long?" Dan's stricken gaze darted around the group.

"For the rest of your life . . . may it be a long one, too," Shabazz said, yawning.

"What!"

"Keep your voice down," J.L. told him in a casual tone. "We're in a hospital."

"Dan, Dan, Dan—always be careful what you pray for, 'cause you just might get it," Marlene said on a stretch as she sat down, leaned on Shabazz, and began dozing. "You wanted the exciting, adventurous nightlife. Hmmmph."

But as soon as Marlene had touched Shabazz, he held her back from him, and then glanced at Big Mike and Rider, and then finally stared at Damali. She just nodded.

Shit, what was there to say? Marlene studied the floor, as Shabazz pulled her against his chest. J.L. glanced at the group.

"Later," Big Mike suggested. "Was hard on everybody. We'll fill you in."

"The exciting life—vastly overrated," Rider commented with a yawn. He glanced at Damali and closed his eyes as though trying to keep the conversation light around Dan.

Good move. Rider did have a lot of sense for a wise ass in the group.

"Get some rest, dude," Damali said quietly to Dan as she stood, patting his shoulder and stretching. "Better learn how to catch forty winks in a chair and eat on the run, literally." She needed space. Time alone to process everything that had happened and she had learned.

"Where're you going?" Marlene asked in a weary voice.

Her expression was filled with pain and worry. Her tone was gentle, no longer having the den-mother stridence it often had. This time it sounded like a question asked to a peer, rather than to a child. That, too, oddly made Damali's heart hurt. She'd just lost the only mother she'd ever known; all she could hope for is that one day the trust would rebuild itself so they could be friends. But that would take time . . . did they have such a luxury?

Marlene's battery had to be on E, just like hers was. She was also beginning to learn that emotional stuff took a toll on second sight. Right now, Damali couldn't see a thing.

"You know where," Damali finally said with a sad smile, trying to leave the door to her heart cracked open for Marlene with the non-sarcastic reply. "To find a hospital vending machine for some chips and orange soda—and I promise to stay inside . . . I'll even take a concert light, and I've got baby Isis in a leg holster—momma Isis is in the Hum-V. Anybody else want anything?"

Dan looked at her in disbelief, covered his mouth, and dry heaved.

"Now you see why we weren't hungry after that gig in Philly? But noooo, you wanted to go get ribs, or Chinese food—noodles—after we'd smelled barbeque already, and splattered guts." Rider chuckled.

Damali walked away fast as she heard Dan hurl into his hands. Rites of passage; the first time out—the guardian team was a trip the way they teased the poor guy, but Dan was now in the fold. For better or for worse, their crew was formed by the happenstance of fate, as always.

Sudden hunger made her hasten her steps while she stuffed a light wand in her back pocket and tried to find the winding path to the vending area that a busy nurse pointed out.

"Hey," a familiar male voice said over her shoulder when she rounded a dim corridor.

She turned quickly, and then relaxed. "Oh, my God. . . ." She breathed out in a rush. "Are you all right?"

Carlos nodded. "I've seen some things, though, in the last few hours that . . ." His voice trailed off and he just shook his head. "I was really worried about you."

"I know . . . you don't even have to tell me—but I'm okay, too. Carlos, I thought . . ."

His expression was so pained that she immediately filled his arms, and his hand went to her hair. He was cold, as though still in shock—just like Dan had been—his lowered body temperature no doubt the reason for the hard tremor that had run through him when she hugged him. She tried to warm him with her closeness, remembering what it was like the first time she'd had her own dark encounter, pouring all the tenderness and comfort she could into her touch. Sometimes that was the only antidote to fear—just human contact, which she now freely offered him, just like Shabazz had offered Marlene.

Her hands stroked Carlos's back and caressed his tense shoulder blades, and she nestled her head against his chest, closing her eyes to absorb the wonderful relief of connecting with him. Her prayer had been answered: Carlos wasn't dead.

Initially, a sensation of profound peace coated him with each gentle touch from her hands, but as her soft skin melted against his, its warmth created a burn that chased away the joyous freedom of feeling alive—replacing it with something else more primitive. Her skin and hair carried a fragrance that was an erotic lure as it threaded through his nasal passages and assaulted his mind. The feel of her locks under his fingers and against his palm awakened every nerve ending in him and permeated him with the desire to explore the other delicate textures she possessed.

When she'd nestled against him, her form fit so perfectly against his body, sending a shard of wanton agony the length of him that made his lungs now battle for air.

"Are you all right?" she whispered, peering up at him. "You didn't get hurt or scratched by anything, did you—that's not why you're here, is it?"

She'd pulled her head away briefly to look at him. Her sudden vacancy left a cool spot on his chest that immediately ached for her to return to it and cover it. His gaze locked with hers; he could feel his eyelids lower, her brown iris stare too intense for him not to react . . . her lips had parted to murmur her question, and the full lushness of her mouth fractured his reason as he struggled not to lower his own upon hers to consume it.

"Something was chasing Dan, and he got away . . . then I found my car, and got out of Dodge." He'd tell her anything to keep her within their embrace, to quiet her possible fears of him.

His words were escaping on stilted breaths as the sensation of her in his arms rocked him where he stood. He held her by her shoulders, allowing his hands the luxury of grazing her skin—the torture of it exquisite.

"After what I saw, I wanted to check some hospital records to see if I could find out what had happened to my family," he lied again. "But I have to wait until the admin offices are open in the morning." *Baby, stay in my arms. Just a little longer, don't go.*

Then she touched his face and whispered to him that it would be all right, baby. She had no idea . . . His mouth found the center of her palm, and it was all he could do not to moan into her flesh . . . Imagining what the rest of her felt like forced his surrender until he completely lowered his lids. Her whisper was the most effective weapon in her arsenal, *didn't she know?* He pulled a deep inhale of her through his nose and opened his eyes. Her face was upturned to his, her gaze seeking.

He could hear the blood rushing through her veins as her pulse quickened. She drew in shallow breaths that made her petite breasts rise and fall under the thin fabric of her damp T-shirt . . . the tips of them now tiny pebbles—he could feel them sting with a request that he couldn't address, not here. The scent of battle and earth was on her. She'd moistened and he could smell it, the faint, fragrant hint of her that splintered his façade of cool, made him swallow hard and start breathing through his mouth. The silence was deafening in this abandoned strip of space and time in the corridor, and it begged him to consider the possibilities.

Intense female energy fused rapidly to invade his will, making him remember exactly what he was, above every-thing else—all male. Her belly, her thighs, her thickening delta was touching him from his waist down . . . and the question that he'd always wondered about began forming in her mind . . . what if?

It ripped at his discipline—he studied her throat with care, and leaned in, allowing his nose to trail the length of it in a heated nuzzle. She smelled so good. She was so soft. Her body was yielding and her mind was issuing a plea, making an offer too difficult to refuse. In her mind he heard her moan softly as he continued to nuzzle her, and he had to fight the urge not to verbally respond. On the edge, he teetered, savoring every moment of her will-shattering temptation. It was a personal brand. Oh, yes, he was marked—she owned him . . . always had, didn't she know?

The pulse of life in her jugular beat an insistent, seduc-tive rhythm throughout his groin . . . blood, life, the mo-tion to create life, friction, heat, it was one . . . and she had no idea how much he wanted to answer her ques-tions . . . had for such a long time. Her mental gasp passed through his skeleton, tensing the muscles in his hips. Even a dead man could remember the ancient dance that made life worth living. She'd only been in his arms for a moment, but right now it felt like forever.

His thoughts penetrated hers, thrusting against her

mind the way he wanted to take her, whispering the answers. *Yes, Damali. I know . . . me, too . . . but I can't promise to be gentle, can only promise that it'll be good . . . and, you, like me, will want more till we both drop.*

When her mind seized upon his and dragged him into an image of a shower, he saw her daydream, the fantasy . . . the premonition, he tasted her fear mixed with desire . . . in the shower she'd caused him to enter her, made it manifest until it had become real before he'd even been turned. He felt himself slipping as his discipline began to give way. Her nails slowly dug into his back. His lips found her ear and he sent a silent message into the hollow of it with his breath. *Stop . . . because I can't.*

She flooded his system. Yes, she was a drug; Neteru. His hands trembled for just one hit. He could feel his incisors lengthening. His grip tightened against her upper arms. Saliva built in his mouth and his jaw tensed in preparation to unhinge, making him fight both needs at once. He dropped his head back as his eyes rolled toward his skull under his lids. She had no idea. . . .

"I gotta go," he said fast, pulling her to him hard and then pushing her away.

"You can stay with us—a lot of stuff is going down . . . and it might be the safest place for you . . . I know you can't understand it all now, but I don't want anything to happen to you," she called after him, making him stop and turn to look at her.

"Is that an open-ended invitation?"

Baby, let me go right now—I ain't no good for you like this.

"Yeah," she whispered. "Any time. *Mi casa es su casa* . . . you once told me that."

So he had . . . when he was a guardian, a living human. *Oh, Damali, you just don't understand . . .*

Knowing that he was unable to restrain himself any longer, he paced farther away from her. He needed to get himself together, and distance from her was the only solution. He closed his eyes and swallowed hard again, fighting to steady his breathing.

"If I'm invited, I promise you, I'll take you up on the invitation . . . after I handle my business."

He had to turn and walk from her, the emotions she visited upon him were haunting. Forever now felt like a split second that gouged his body with want. "Live well . . . I'll be back . . . maybe on your birthday—stay safe, and say your prayers at night."

She nodded, closed her eyes, and held up her hand, spreading her fingers like she was touching one side of prison glass. He felt her remote palm through his back; it made him turn to face her and match her motion from across the hall. One more moment like this and he'd lose all control. Instead, he pulled away. He had to before he couldn't, but he made a fist to hold the sensation of her hand within his—and was gone.

When she felt the abandonment of his touch, she wrapped her arms around herself in weary consolation. The fire that had been lit inside her was so all-consuming that for a moment she couldn't move. She had actually felt him across the room, and when her body had melted against his, she'd almost cried out it had felt so damned good. Guilt immediately assaulted her—what was she doing? Her teammates had been attacked, she'd just come from a vamp battle, the compound had been compromised, and yet she'd fallen into his arms and he'd made her get wet . . . dear God in Heaven, what was happening?

Still, to know that he was alive, safe, had made it through one more night just before dawn would crest through the large hospital plate-glass windows, meant there was still hope, still time, no matter what he'd done wrong before.

Every instinct within her told her to trust him . . . she'd practically felt the man's soul through his chest. It was as though they breathed as one. His thoughts had seared her, and the rock-solid length of him had brought on sudden delirium. Six feet two inches of all male . . . she'd needed to touch his back to keep from running her fingers through his hair . . . had needed to find his shoulder to keep her lips from finding his . . . had willed her thighs shut to keep them from wrapping around his waist . . . didn't he know? Her skin still hurt, ached from where he'd grazed it . . . branded it with his caress.

The way he'd breathed a hot trail of desire against her throat had lit the ember that had always been there for him. The brief encounter simply made the fire burn hotter. It was as though her body was producing a secret river to put out the flame . . . she'd almost followed him when he walked away.

She stroked her cheek with the warmth of her palm, still able to feel where he'd kissed it, where his hand had covered hers from a distance. . . . Heaven help her, she could still feel him everywhere on her skin.

Damali closed her eyes again, pulled by the sensation . . . she'd wanted him to kiss her so badly that her mouth had watered. She brought her hands up to her neck, needing to touch the frustrated place that had been left wanting. Whatever this thing was between them, it was so intense that it had left her trembling in the middle of the hospital hallway. She had to get it together, get some chips, and go back to the group. She took in several quick pants, then tried to breathe deeply to let out a hard exhale.

"Wow . . ." she murmured, running her fingers through her locks. If a hug could do all that . . . then . . . *dayum* . . . what if? That had always been the question—their question.

When she turned to find a machine, the sight of Marlene made her nearly jump out of her skin.

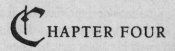

CHAPTER FOUR

HE'D WALKED as far as was necessary, beyond human suspicion, before hurling himself to a quiet place, under the streets, a dark cavern of cement sewer tunnel that would give him shelter from the sun when it came up. This was no way to live . . . and the irony was, he wasn't alive.

Carlos placed both hands against the cool, damp, concrete wall, standing back from it, leaning on his palms as his head hung and he considered his fate.

He had to get Damali out of his thoughts, out of his nose, out of his skin, his bloodstream, and his mind. His fangs wouldn't even retract as he thought about her and shut his eyes. He'd come so close. He could still feel her lacerating him with her softness. His breathing hadn't steadied, nor had his pulse. The ache for her was becoming so unbearable that he threw his head back, let out the moan that he'd sheltered for the duration of her embrace, and punched the wall in frustration—crumbling cement to leave a crater.

"It's a real bitch, isn't it?"

Spinning on the intruder, the fact that it was male redoubled his strength in preparation for instant battle. When he recognized his adversary, he knew it was a perfect night for Nuit to die. But Nuit just laughed, kept his distance, and circled him, cool.

"Why don't you go eat and relax—you've got less than an hour before daylight, and this is no way for a man to try to sleep. Too late to go to New Orleans . . . the women are fantastic there, and the food excellent—blood alcohol levels are high, the cattle eat fantastic cuisine . . . a little wine in your system might help you drift off easier, but alas. Maybe another night."

A combination of fury and humiliation gripped him. Carlos snarled, and rolled his shoulders.

"That's better. You've got to pace yourself. I've heard a hit of Neteru will do that to you. . . . You broke her off from the herd, didn't you?"

Carlos growled low in his throat. "You never gave me a name."

"Did I have to? You said name any one of them. I just did."

Nuit smiled and circled him, breathing in deeply. "I can smell her on you. Amazing . . . you got close to her, but had the presence of mind to remember our deal. I would have been able to pick up the scent if you'd violated her, too." Nuit relaxed. "Very good. I won't have to kill you."

Carlos narrowed his focus on Nuit, wondering which limb to tear from him first—not answering.

"Now I better understand the block to my calls to you

all night . . . if you had that hunt rush pumping through your system . . . yes . . . makes sense."

"Then how did you find me?" Carlos paced back and forth, adrenaline spikes hard to shake as Nuit stoked and toyed with his anger.

"Your agony could be heard for miles. I began to worry that you'd just been staked." Nuit laughed at his own joke, his guard seeming to become more relaxed.

The two vampires stared at each other. Carlos analyzed the information contained in Nuit's statement, and immediately realized that it had opened an advantage— something he'd temporarily forgotten. One of his deals had made good. Nuit was blind to him, but didn't suspect the Vampire Council or the Covenant. Nuit assumed that the blocks to his calls had been produced by interaction with a Neteru's strong telepathic ability overriding his mental clarity. Perfect cover. Carlos almost smiled. Yeah, he had slayer in his system.

He needed to play this to the bone. To kill Nuit now would be premature—two masters in a death struggle would go beyond dawn. Nuit needed to believe he had the advantage in order to open another opportunity to get to the cocky bastard when there was more time. It was all about power and control, as well as perception, illusion. Who had the power . . . and who believed they had the power. Plus, Nuit had eaten, he hadn't. Right now, Nuit possibly had the endurance advantage. Carlos carefully weighed his options. Even though he had the rage advantage, this would be a long fight. But if he garnered patience, another opportunity could be created to bring Nuit down. Carlos studied the situation, and put the roulette wheel in motion.

"I got close, and couldn't raise anybody from our territorial pack by telepathy," Carlos finally said before Nuit became suspicious. "My focus was totally compromised . . . maybe overwhelmed is a better description," he added, feigning submission.

Nuit looked at him hard, and then grinned. "I guess you did get close to her, or you wouldn't be down here in a sewer losing your mind. But, odd . . . it requires a master's patience, will power, and discipline not to have just taken her in public, which is where I can only assume you found her. Unless you do have some deference to your maker . . . hmmm. I bet it was positively torturing you not to have been able to—"

"Fuck you!" The wound was too fresh for Nuit to dig his claws into it with a snide remark, and it was impossible to stop the visceral response. Carlos walked away from Nuit, but kept on his guard. The only thing that helped keep him from going for Nuit's throat was the fact that Nuit's comment exposed an important variable. Nuit didn't know he was looking at another master vampire.

Nuit returned a cruel smile, taunting him with a slow, seductive response designed to stoke Carlos's rage. "Fuck me? Ahhh . . . Anytime, but not tonight. What happened to Raven?"

"She went after the Neteru and got her ass kicked."

Nuit studied his nails. "That's a damned shame—she was good pussy. Well, you can always go make more."

Carlos stared at him, disgusted. He would kill this motherfucker.

"Oh, that's right—you're a second generation, and can only make thirds." Nuit laughed. "All right, all right, I know—you need me to make a female second to be on your level. We can arrange that. Just pick her out, since

Raven misbehaved. I had also told her not to do the Neteru—*ever*. Just so you know, you and I are on the same page. Women can be so jealous at times. Foolish."

"Yeah, well, she almost botched the delivery by sending six vamps after Damali's team, and then by going after the huntress herself."

Nuit stared at Carlos hard. "The guardians are always expendable."

Carlos shook his head. "Not if you want the huntress to feel safe and come out of hiding on her own."

"That *is* brilliant . . . You do have a point."

"You told me to bring her to you, untouched. Correct? And, that she had to comply of her own free will, or some shit like that, right?"

Nuit nodded, no longer nonchalant. "You can get her to come to us freely?" Excitement exuded from him and he licked his lips, and then rubbed his jaw with his hand.

"Your fangs are showing," Carlos said evenly. "Chill."

"She'll do that to you. Forgive me," Nuit said on a deep breath. "Just one question . . . how in the hell did you back away?"

The question gave Carlos pause, because in all honesty, he didn't know.

"A sense of self-preservation," he finally replied, casting a disparaging glare toward Nuit. "I may be new, but I know better than to go against my maker . . . or a master vampire. If I chill, well, then it's all good."

"The ability to govern such restraint is laudable . . . and very wise. Maybe making you wasn't such a bad decision after all." Nuit studied him for a moment and rubbed his palm over his jaw. "But you've never come to me to feed from my kills."

"I ate from Raven, remember . . . and had a guard along the way," Carlos said quickly, trying to keep the ruse going. "Then, I went after the Neteru like I was told to—after that, I really haven't had feeding on my mind."

Nuit hesitated, then came near him and wiped at the sheen of perspiration still on Carlos's brow. "Understandable," he murmured and put his finger in his mouth. Carlos snarled and Nuit backed away with a smile.

"She's even in your bloodstream. I can taste her in your sweat." Nuit sucked in a low hiss with a gulp of air, closed his eyes for a moment, and shuddered. He ran his finger over his lips and his head tilted as he inhaled deeply. "But she had a white bath—a damned prayer chastity belt! How did you get past it to even sense what she'd be like?"

Carlos could feel his jaw beginning to unhinge at the sight of another male demonstrating such open desire for his woman. He ran his tongue over his incisors, sending them back into his skull. Not yet. The night would come soon when the game would be over. In that instant he made up his mind that there were only two pending offers to consider—the Vampire Council's or the other side. Nuit was a dead man walking.

"Because she trusts me. That's the only thing that will render her prayer guard ineffective. She has to willingly breach it and we have to draw her beyond it, remember? If I bring her to you struggling, you still won't be able to get past it—so let me work her."

Carlos leveled his gaze at Nuit. "You just sampled the product, and it opened up your nose, didn't it? I told you I had the goods. Don't fuck with me. Not tonight."

"I'll make you a second female, quickly. No man in my territory should have to suffer like this—unless he crosses me." Nuit gazed at Carlos and held him in an intense stare. "What was she like?"

So, Nuit had taken a hit . . . liked the product and was damned near strung out from just a taste. Everything he'd learned in the streets collated in Carlos's mind, and he leveraged his advantage, messing with Nuit without mercy. Let the bastard twist.

"I can't even discuss it," Carlos said, the truth of his statement not lost on Nuit. That was the best part of it all, he could tell the truth, and the credibility would come through in his tone. Carlos watched his enemy nearly writhe with impatience, and a deep sense of personal satisfaction took residence within him. To the victor go the spoils.

"I'll bring her to you, Nuit. Then we can deal with my options. For now, she looks like she's very close to doing the concert—maybe even signing with your label," Carlos lied, just to add more lure to the game. "I've been in her ear and in her mind, because she trusts me. We go way back; I can sway her . . . she doesn't even know I've turned—so don't blow my cover. That's how I got past her guardians and her radar."

"Are you serious?" Nuit leaned against the wall as though he now needed it to hold himself upright.

"She never even saw my fangs," Carlos said with pride. "It was smooth."

Both vampires looked at each other. Nuit was almost trembling.

"That's why I said to stop flushing my hunt," Carlos went on, relaxing as he felt his guile take root within Nuit. "That guy, Dan, he's a wannabe . . . but Damali cares for him. The kid got her to consider it, first, when one of the Minion threw the bait out for him to hook up with Blood. I was working on the huntress from a business perspective. Everything was cool, until Raven went after Dan, and her thirds attacked the compound. You have got to pull your people back, or make sure none of the other seconds are moving on your kill. I thought you had this territory locked down, man? There are breaches everywhere, and it's bullshit. We don't have a lotta time."

Nuit pushed himself off the wall and nodded. "No one has ever gotten us this close to her physically, or to shifting her will—from there, breaking her spirit is only a matter of time. And *none* of the others have ever been this loyal."

Carlos nodded and walked closer to Nuit. "You want to feel this agony?" He leaned in toward Nuit to let him smell where Damali's head had rested against his neck, then quickly backed away. "That's pain, *hombre*. My jaw almost unhinged—but I remembered the family."

"Shit . . ."

Nuit tried to come near him again, but Carlos held up his hand. You always had to give them just a taste to make them hunger for more.

"*Sí*. So you understand the sacrifice—however, I don't have a lair, the sun is about to toast both of us, I got motherfuckers creating havoc, and I really am not in the mood to sleep in the sewer my first night out—and not after being this loyal. I need my rest, and I deserve—"

"A fucking throne and a harem, Carlos. The females I'll send to your lair as part of the package are insatiable. Yes. I completely agree. I'll make some territorial adjustments, and you can have one of the other dons' lairs."

"Give me the Dominican's joint. He and I go way back, and he did a few of my boys a while ago when I was making space for my own in the streets. Some shit never dies—territory is territory. As above, so below."

Nuit nodded. "Take his villa in Beverly Hills. He has a sumptuous vault in his basement. I'll do him myself, will explain to the others that it was just business. After a taste, I need one more body for the night, as it is."

Carlos chuckled. "I hear you. Then imagine how I feel."

Nuit laughed. "He might even have a third generation female already in there who might still be awake—might help take the Neteru edge off? You want her?"

"Naw, I'm cool, man," Carlos murmured. "Give whatever female you find to one of the other dons. I just ain't in the frame of mind. In fact, I might just hit a blood bank and take a few pints to bed. If I go hunting this late, I might forget what time it is and wind up on the Neteru's trail again. Could fuck around and sun bake myself by accident. I'm telling you, man, this slayer is *all that.*"

"It is intense, isn't it . . . but so much so that you don't trust yourself to hunt?" Nuit rubbed his face and shook his head. "Absolutely amazing."

"She's equivalent to a master level, Nuit," Carlos said quietly, lacing the truth in his game to make it even more credible, but perhaps offering more than he wanted to, the pull of Damali still a toxin within his system. But at the same time, he had to drive a convincing point that would assure her temporary safety.

Carlos let out a long breath that made Nuit carefully watch him. He closed his eyes and projected images of Damali to Nuit in slow motion.

"She can hunt better than Raven ever could—you should see her in action, man . . . the adrenaline, the stamina, the very perspiration on her after the hunt reeks with the Neteru hormone . . . one whiff and you're intoxicated . . . she can see in the dark, almost like us." Although baiting his prey, the memory made Carlos inhale and have to pause. The game was rough, but he had to play it.

Carlos sighed. "I'm not talking myths and legends. I've seen her . . . held her. The woman is a telepath, a tactical sensory—her skin literally comes alive under your hands, she has the nose . . ." He pressed on. "Can project thought, and has a will of iron . . . can you imagine what she'll be like when she turns?"

Trying not to smile as Nuit's knees buckled, Carlos opened his eyes and glanced away.

"She's beyond awesome . . . think of what delivering that first break of skin will be like—especially if she turns her throat to you with her panties wet and begs you to take both her neck and her—"

"Stop." Nuit's fangs glistened in the darkness. He couldn't even pull them back. Water dripping from overhead provided the only sound that echoed between them. "Two more evenings—you just used up one . . ."

"That's why I said, back off with the random hits. If you kill her, or she gets hurt—or one of her people gets jacked, she will go into deep mourning . . . she'll never come to you for years."

"Whatever you want—work the strategy to bring her to me like that. If you can get inside her head, inside her compound . . . can get her to follow you to me—then do it! What else in the territory do you want? Name it."

Nuit stalked back and forth running his tongue over his incisors, trying to regain his composure. "Three thousand years since they made a female Neteru—and we thought they wouldn't make another one. Since that time, they've only made males." He held Carlos in a furtive gaze. "Do you understand?"

"Hell yeah, I understand what jonesing for Damali is like." Carlos chuckled, an earnest one from his core.

"You want the first daywalker female off the line?"

"Is that a rhetorical question, or are you playing with me?"

Nuit laughed with Carlos. "Done."

"Appreciate it, man, 'cause I'm all fucked up—don't trust myself to even run from the sun . . . 'cause I wanna sit outside her window so bad. I don't want anything you find at the don's when you clean out his place. Can't go there after getting a Neteru in my nose. You feel me?"

Nuit walked toward the tunnel exit nodding. "Yes. I definitely 'feel you,' and I imagine it is difficult to step down when you've been so close." Nuit paused and gave Carlos a furtive glance. "Fifteen minutes, and the lair will be yours. Bring me more word and scent of her next evening. I need to smell her again."

"Done." Carlos leaned against the wall as Nuit vanished.

Information was knowledge, and knowledge was a powerful thing. In the disgusting exchange, he'd moved up in the ranks, took out an old enemy, scored a plush lair, and bought Damali and her crew a valuable, temporary off-limits marker. Baby might have a coupla days of peace. But would he? Regardless, he had inadvertently become a triple agent by making alliances across three borders—Nuit, the Vampire Council, and possibly with the invisible DEA—the forces of light. Question was, how to play it.

Still, not bad for the first night on the job.

The stricken look on Marlene's face chilled Damali. If Marlene had seen them . . . Humiliation made her cheeks warm, and it was hard to hold her gaze.

"Big Mike told the others about what happened out there with Raven," Marlene whispered. She cast her gaze out the window as she spoke in a quiet voice that trembled. "I should have told all of you that she was my daughter . . . but . . . I couldn't deal with it. I wanted to put the fact that she was once my child out of my mind. I loved her, Damali," she murmured as she swallowed hard.

Marlene's eyes held such pain that Damali was almost forced to look away. "Carried her in my body, and put her to my breast. She was my baby . . . and Nuit took her when she was your age. She was like you in so many ways . . . beautiful, talented, headstrong, and fearless. Thought nothing could happen to her that she couldn't handle, and that I was just Mom who didn't understand the 'happening' new world. She wouldn't listen to me, wouldn't heed my advice, and the streets took her, and then *he* got her. She was wide open, and vulnerable . . . maybe that's why I was so hard on you. I was afraid that I was watching history repeat itself."

"Mar—"

"I know I didn't do right by you, child," Marlene said fast, cutting off Damali's words quickly and wrapping her arms about herself. "God forgive me . . . I just couldn't take care of you both, and I thought if I gave you to people who had resources, and if you were hidden . . . I just thought that maybe we'd all be spared. But he came, not knowing I was pregnant when I ran, and thought my Christine was you . . . then he turned her into Raven. The joke was on him, though. She wasn't a Neteru. You were safe, and that was my consolation for a long time. It's all good. I have to believe that, or else I just won't be able to go on."

Two large tears formed in Marlene's eyes, and Damali went to her. Although it had been a relief that Marlene hadn't witnessed her intimate exchange with Carlos, she didn't want a telepathy block from pain like this to be the reason Marlene's second sight was down. She was also sorry she'd been the one that had to kill Raven with the sword Raven's own mother had given her . . . and now, holding Marlene in a tender hug, she felt all the reasons Marlene kept things from her.

Yes, she could understand. How would a young, pregnant woman in love explain vampires to a lover? How would a young woman cope, in that day and age, with being left to bear a child alone, predators all around her, and no momma or family to help her because she had to run away and hide in order to protect them? How was Marlene to care for an infant that would bring vampires constantly sniffing, and still protect and provide for a baby, as well as her unborn child or herself, for that matter?

Damali closed her eyes, holding Marlene tighter. Oh, Marlene . . . Yes, she'd seen teenage mothers in the street with no support, no skills, no money, no education, no parenting skills, and preyed on by guys who'd just stop, drop, and roll them. Yeah, she'd witnessed how that struggle ravaged the hope and potential from so many young girls. It had been the thing that had kept her straight—seeing with her own eyes, and maybe having unknown second sight, at that time, had helped her make wiser choices. There but for the grace she went. She could have gone out like that, too. Marlene had been practically a child herself . . . young, alone, afraid—with no money, no real skills or education, no defenses, and had to live by her wits and her gift. God in heaven, what would she have done if she had to walk a mile in Marlene's shoes?

Damali stroked Marlene's back as she held her, hoping that the aging guardian still had enough sensory battery left to feel the healing of her touch and be able to sense without words the forgiveness being transmitted to her. Yes, it was so true. The things Marlene had taught her were right . . . *judge not, lest ye be judged.* You never know what scars another person carries deep within them that causes them to act the way they do. She remembered Rider's story, and the things Big Mike had said about his own childhood. Then there was Jose's pain. She knew Shabazz carried his secret hurts so deeply that no one on the team really had the full story about what had happened to him. And Lord knows what J.L. had experienced in Laos.

Her thoughts drifted to Carlos, and she wondered what scars he'd carried that had made him choose the life that he did. They all had long stories . . .

"Mar, I am so sorry I had to be the one to . . . release Raven's soul," Damali murmured into her hair. She couldn't even bring herself to call it what it was. She couldn't describe Raven's demise in the crude terms the team normally used to verbally distance themselves from what they had to do. How could she say "put down," "drop," "stake," "take out," "roll," "splatter," or "gut," when talking about the loss of Marlene's daughter? Marlene had been right about that, too. Words had power. Vocabulary was important. Maybe if people called it what it really was, then the very thought of "doing somebody" would give them pause, and they'd think twice about murdering another human being. But that's just the thing, Marlene's daughter wasn't human, which is what was breaking Marlene's heart.

"I'm so sorry," Damali repeated. "Oh, Mar . . . I won't even claim to know how you feel."

"No, thank you, baby," Marlene said on a shaky sigh. "You just put my daughter's soul to rest. I couldn't have done it. I didn't have it in me. That's why I hesitated in battle. I'd keep seeing her face when she was a toddler . . . I'd think about how she'd climb into bed at night with me so we could read stories, or how proud she was of her first little gold star in school." Marlene drew a ragged breath. "As a mother . . . you think about all the good, and wonder how it could have gotten so bad, and you lacerate yourself wondering where you went wrong . . . how could I have let her get taken by evil . . . and they call me a guardian? I couldn't even protect my own child."

Marlene's shoulders shook as Damali held her and rocked her for a long time. The sun peeked out from behind the deep gray haze of clouds as the sky gave birth. All Damali could do during the transition was stroke Marlene's hair and let her cry.

"We have to get back to the group," Marlene murmured. "None of us has really slept, the compound is breached . . . and I can't see. I was already weak from laying hands on Jose, then the fight to get out of the compound, and then . . . Raven. I'm totally blind, Damali. I'm no more good to you. My second sight is just blackness. I can't get past the pain to concentrate."

When Marlene pulled away, Damali held her by her shoulders.

"Marlene, you're worth more to me than your sight or ability to guard. Don't you know that by now?" Damali's hand went to Marlene's face and she caressed her cheek as she spoke. "I love you, Marlene, and understand why you gave me away. You just need some rest and some time to heal. This was hard, I know. Why don't you let me guard you for a change, and take care of you a little bit for once?"

"Letting go, and seeing your children grow up . . . and accepting that, is probably the hardest thing in the world to do," Marlene whispered, wiping the tears from her face. "I respect your choices," she said, nodding. "I'm proud of you . . . thank you for not hating me."

"Hating you?" Damali shook her head slowly. "For being human? For having a life and for wanting some joy of your own? No."

The two women shared a slight smile, both understanding each other within the unspoken exchange.

"C'mon. Let's get back to the team."

They walked the corridors in silence, Damali's arm about Marlene's shoulders as she guided her to where everyone else was sitting. The expressions the team held said it all. Hope was edging away from the group. Profound loss was taking its toll. They were exhausted, battle weary, down a good man, and on the run.

Damali helped Marlene to sit, and then she walked in front of the group, choosing her words carefully. "Listen, everybody. We need a break. Last night was . . . It was worse than we've ever had to deal with."

Rider and Big Mike nodded. Shabazz took up Marlene's hand as J.L. rubbed her back. Dan's face held such empathy that Big Mike slung an arm over his shoulder.

"Okay," Damali said on a long breath. "We need to post a couple of men here at the hospital to stay with Jose. Maybe even Mar can stay?" She glanced at Marlene who only nodded and looked out the window. "He needs your prayers, Marlene . . . even if you can't see."

"She can't see?" Rider whispered.

Damali shook her head and Shabazz lowered his gaze.

"Grief," Shabazz murmured. "Let me stay with her and Jose, here."

Damali nodded. "J.L., Dan—I need you guys to go back to the compound and work on getting all computer systems and security operable, as well as develop some new weapons for the concert. We need the generators stabilized, and electric lines—"

"You are not still thinking of doing the concert, li'l sis?" Big Mike ran his palm over his bald scalp and let out his breath hard.

"Yeah," Damali said evenly, feeling pure rage fill her. "After what just happened to Jose, and now Mar, not to mention the others we lost . . . we have to go to New Orleans today to scope out the lair in the daylight . . . and if we don't find what we're looking for, we'll need to do the concert to get on the inside of their operation. It's the only way to bring Jose fully back to us, and to bring back Marlene's sight. Maybe even put the other souls lost from our team to rest."

Rider pushed himself up, and nodded. "Better have me, you, and Big Mike go into the compound and sweep it for J.L. and Dan, then get on a flight."

"Yeah. That's where I was going," Damali said in a quiet voice. "Once the compound is safe, if Jose gets released again, Mar and Shabazz can bring him back and seal it before nightfall. While we're gone, we're also going to need some slamming material—three songs, Dan said, right?"

Dan nodded. "Yeah, and you have to be back in enough time to do some of the promo I've got lined up— by three P.M. at the latest so they can tape you."

"All right, we've got a full day ahead of us, and a lot of work to do. The three of us can scope out the last known lair, and get back in way before it gets dark."

"Sounds like a plan," Big Mike muttered. "Never went in without a seer to guide us, though. I mean no disrespect, li'l sis, but sometimes your sight is on, and sometimes it's not."

"I hear you." Damali gazed at him, her self-confidence eroding moment by moment. "You'll have to trust me, then. I'll be able to see."

Dan, like J.L., had been quiet except for one comment, and his line of vision swept the group, and then dropped to his hands that were folded between his legs. "I still feel awful, though. If they got the guy who saved me . . ."

"Carlos is fine," Damali said. "I just saw him."

The group stared at her and a mild electric current passed between them to settle upon her.

"When?" Marlene asked cautiously.

"A few minutes ago, just before you walked up. He was in shock, looking for hospital records of his family, trying to make logical sense of what isn't logical. Said he needed to come back when the admin offices opened this morning."

The group visibly relaxed.

"I gave him sanctuary to stay with us . . . like we gave Dan—if he gets hunted."

Again they stared at her, but didn't speak.

"We cannot leave an innocent man to get fed on by the dark side."

"Rivera isn't just an innocent like Dan. He's a drug dealer, darlin'." Rider began pacing. "Or, did you forget what he does for a living? Vamps ain't the only thing we gotta worry about—try a drug hit, drive-by to settle a score, the police, being brought in as accomplices to his shit, whatever. There are a whole lot of ways to die, sister."

"He's still human, and obviously not a vamp helper, and the sanctuary is only temporary until we wipe out the vamp line chasing all of us—then he can go back to whatever he chooses to do . . . He saved Dan's life, and that counts for something," she argued. A rush of defensive anger throttled her ability to remain calm. "Plus, if Dan hadn't made it out of the parking lot, and if they hadn't chased Dan to where we found him, then we wouldn't have been able to take out a second generation female, Rider! Everything happens for a reason—everyone has intrinsic value in this war, or did you forget?"

In their outburst they had momentarily forgotten Marlene's pain, and both Damali and Rider hung their heads when Marlene covered her mouth and stood, and then paced to a window.

"Mar, I'm sorry," Damali whispered.

"Oh, Marlene . . . listen. I'm sorry," Rider murmured.

Marlene kept her back to them and only shook her head.

"Go do what you have to do," Shabazz told them in a sad, quiet voice. "I'll stay with her and Jose."

"Pssst," a voice called to Carlos in the tunnel. "I have three minutes to give you this information before it will become too dangerous for you to travel. Dawn approaches."

Hesitant, Carlos waited, monitoring the heat of the environment around him. The pull of the dawn made everything around him feel like an oven. It sapped his strength, made his senses sluggish, and he could only hope that he'd have enough energy to travel to the Dominican's lair.

"Say whatchu gotta say, fast," Carlos replied, his chest heaving as though he were having an asthma attack. "I don't have much time."

The blue-clad knight stepped out of the shadows. "I took a risk. I'm not supposed to be here—but the warrior angels gave us word that you helped the Neteru defeat a second generation . . . and we saw you fight your vampire nature when you had our huntress in your arms—you even told her to pray! You could have violated her, but you didn't. There is a *major* conference about the whole situation now at the levels of mercy. Your love for her gives us hope."

"State your business," Carlos said, wheezing. "I'm running out of time." Pain began riddling his body; the air was becoming thick and polluted by slivers of light.

"We want the maps."

"I don't have them, yet. What else? One minute, and I'm out."

"Bring us the head of the master vampire who hunts her. When he falls, it will be easy for us to wipe out his line. That will also free the Neteru's parent's trapped soul. We'll be able to destroy many of the vampires, as well as the demons they live with."

"Easy, was already on my agenda. Talk fast, *hombre.*"

"We'll give you ten minutes of amnesty to deliver the maps to her once you have them in your possession. I am a seer, that's why I guide my battalion, and chanced this meeting close to dawn. We'll clear a way to allow you to get the maps to her, but under guarded conditions."

Too weakened to argue, Carlos siphoned the remainder of his reserves to change shape, and drifted toward his new refuge in the Dominican's lair. The density on the planet was crushing. With his last burst of energy, he hurled himself back to safe darkness.

Rider slapped a newspaper across Damali's thighs as they sat and waited to board their flight to New Orleans in LAX.

"Have you seen this?" he said as Mike also gathered close. "Read it and weep. This is who you gave sanctuary to last night."

Damali stared at the headline. Carlos Rivera's car had been found in the North Hills, still running, with a silver briefcase filled with a hundred thousand dollars, a leather briefcase filled with a million dollars, enough artillery to stop a small army, and his handgun weapon fired into the ground. And, there was a high-ranking Dominican drug czar missing.

For a moment the threesome just looked at each other.

"You know what line of work Carlos is in, right?" Big Mike put his hand on Damali's shoulder. "Even if he's not a vamp, or one of their human traitors . . ."

"If he went out there at night," Rider said, agitated, "the sonofabitch got nicked, trust me. Rivera isn't the type to leave one-point-one mil lying in the dirt. Something's wrong."

"No, he didn't get nicked," Damali insisted, tossing the newspaper on an empty seat. "It takes three days to turn a vamp—and . . . He just didn't get nicked, I know that."

Tense silence drew and quartered the conversation to a halt. Damali could feel her pulse race with worry. Heaven help Carlos . . . what had he done? He was in so deep that they must have tried to ice him. Rider was right about one thing: vamps or the mob, both were dangerous predators that could have a man's life hanging in the balance—how many times had she tried to tell Carlos this! If a war was on, then the team's concern had merit—she couldn't let him in the compound . . . but she also couldn't let him get eaten alive. *Choices*. But at least, for the moment, Carlos wasn't a vampire. If he were, she'd be frying right now.

"He didn't get nicked," she murmured again, more to reassure herself than to convince Rider.

"What makes you so sure?" Rider finally asked in a sarcastic tone as he studied her.

Both Big Mike and Rider stared at her as Rider's question stabbed at her. She found her gaze slipping away to watch the planes through the glass.

"Because I hugged him—and I'm still sitting here in the sunlight."

"Oh, that's just fucking great!" Rider shook his head and pushed himself back in his chair. "We fight six vamps and their ringleader, have the compound invaded, a man on a stretcher—and a guy with a possible nick in his system gets up close and personal with our vampire huntress—like in jugular range? Why am I following this woman to New Orleans—to a lair, in the middle of known vampire country, huh? Just answer me that!"

"You should have seen the look on his face," Damali said. "He was like Dan. Freaked out. Confused. Maybe he did see something in the woods, and got the hell out of there—which is why the money was left behind. Or maybe it was a drug deal gone bad and he made it out before he ran into Dan. He might have shot one of them and took their car. Or maybe he was delivering a bounty for his family—knowing Carlos, that's what he was doing, because he still can't wrap his mind around this madness.

Can you blame him? Did you, when you saw your first set of fangs?"

Rider continued to sit back in his chair with his arms folded, appearing grudgingly mollified.

Big Mike sighed. "We aren't going to get anywhere arguing amongst ourselves. That's always evil's strategy—divide and conquer. They did it with the religions, cultures, nations, and it's happening now with us. Unify. Respect each others' points of view . . . and have compassion for each others' weaknesses . . . and squash this bullshit—now!"

Both Rider and Damali nodded, but looked off in different directions with their arms still folded over their chests.

CHAPTER FIVE

"TELL ME again why we just took a flight from L.A. to New Orleans at seven-oh-five in the morning, with no sleep, no *real* weapons—because we have no *real* luggage, other than a duffle bag with some lights and disguised stakes and shit—which has put us in New Orleans, by way of Dallas, in the middle of mosquito country, at two nineteen in the afternoon . . . *and,* we only have an hour to spare, traffic notwithstanding, to go back home? Huh? I'm just curious why we headed east to lose two hours of precious sun, when the light is two hours to our favor in the west—on a wild goose chase, I might add— please, somebody tell me?"

Damali kept her eyes focused on the expressway, monitoring the signs on I-10 as she pushed her foot down on the gas. "First of all, it's still just a little past noon back in L.A., Rider, which means we'll fly into the light and out of the dark. And, Dan is handling the interviews—gives him a chance to get some media hype . . . he gave them my photo and a statement for the interviews I'll miss. So just relax."

Rider glared at her and then took up his argument with Big Mike, who only shook his head.

"We are in a Budget rental car, not a fortified Hum-V—and we are heading northwest to the Lakefront area—which just so happens to dead end, literally, at a cemetery."

Rider folded his arms over his chest, imploring Mike with a glance to take up his cause. "So, I ask myself—*self*, what is wrong with this picture? Why would a reasonable man—who has been on starvation monk rations—pass the renowned French Quarter and all its daytime beauties, give up the best poker and gambling in the country, not hit a liquor store in the city that never closes its bars, to go, practically unarmed, into a *master* vampire's lair on a hummer?"

When Damali continued to ignore Rider, and Big Mike would only chuckle, Rider's pleas became more fervent.

"I also ask myself—*self*, why . . . for *the love of God*, would I go to a place that got its start in very shaky historical circumstances of double-crossings, royal crown incest, and war . . . where six thousand people just *coincidentally* died of cholera, twelve thousand more of yellow fever . . . where it was so bad that the dead wagons would roll down the streets and the local authorities would shout, 'Bring out your dead!' Huh? We are going to a place where fires burned the city down however many times—and they have cities of the dead *within* the city—where there're swamps and alligators and snakes and hurricanes and floods *and* because the water table is *so high*, tombs are *aboveground*, not *buried*, like in most urban environs, in these mass-tomb cities . . . is *anybody* feelin' me? It's the vampire Big Apple, *okay?*"

Big Mike laughed and pounded Rider's fist. "I feel you—the vamps got a point. The women are fine, the food is good—crawfish and po-boys and jambalaya, red beans and rice, jazz . . ."

"Yes," Rider snapped, not amused. "In the *daytime,* Mike. In the damned daytime! I do not want to have bouillabaisse or a well-seasoned roux sucked out of my neck by one of the thousands of topside grave dwellers who might still have a penchant for fine dining! Do you hear me? I'm trying to live the quiet life—I'm re-formed—we already did a Mardi Gras together, you and I, remember?"

"Yeah . . ." Big Mike drawled. "I remember."

"Remember? That's putting it mildly—how about a mental tattoo, for chrissake? A hundred thousand women in the streets, most of them inebriated to perfection and willing to part with their bras and panties for *mere* plastic beads—and what did we wind up with?"

"Two of the finest, biggest-assed, worth-your-jugular, rock-da-house female vamps in the world, Rider . . . aw man," Big Mike sighed and closed his eyes. "It was awesome—I love New Orleans! Damn . . . I remember like it was yesterday. Sorry for the vivid recollection, baby sis, but Rider just took me back."

"You have to get him out of the compound more, Damali. I can't take it!"

Rider opened his arms when Damali began laughing and he pretended to stake himself in the chest. "Do you see what I have to contend with? Big Mike ain't been right since he got blasted by gris-gris voodoo!"

Big Mike peered up at Damali and winked.

"But she was *fine,* man," Big Mike chuckled and shut his eyes again, still laughing. "Part Choctaw, part Creole, part Caribbean-African queen . . . and she could cook. Have mercy, brother. You don't know what you missed."

"Missed? Big Mike, let us not forget," Rider said, not believing his ears, his voice rising with every word, "she had one little character flaw, dude—fangs!"

"Yeah, but she was *all* that. Still get the shivers thinkin' about her."

"Mike, listen to yourself, brother!" Rider moved his arms wildly now as Damali and Big Mike laughed.

"Do you hear him, D? Do you hear the man? He's delirious, delusional . . . he's getting a nervous tic from being locked up in the compound too long. I can't take it. I just can't take it. Pull over and let me out—I'm going to a bar, then heading back to L.A. on the next thing smoking."

By now Damali was waving her hand for them to cut it out. She couldn't breathe from laughing so hard.

"*By law,* they close the tombs for a year and a day— did you know that? Why? Because pestilence was once so rampant—and Mike keeps telling me the woman was fine!"

"She could make a gumbo to die for, and—"

"You almost *did,* you crazy sonofabitch. Marlene had to take your ass to some Doctor Buzzard shaman to get the spell off of you!"

"But, damn, man, you have no idea—"

"The only reason you're alive is because you're packing fourteen inches, and she didn't want to take that rare natural resource off the planet!"

The two guardians stopped the debate midstream and looked at each other, one swallowing a smile, the other so embarrassed that he couldn't fuss anymore and had been temporarily rendered mute. Damali glanced at Big Mike and Rider. She couldn't help it, and it took everything in her to keep her jaw from dropping. *Fourteen inches?* Get out of here! *Go, Mike* . . . She shook her head.

"Fellas, that was *way* more information than I needed to know." She tried not to laugh, or let her expression change as she'd made the statement, but her mind was still trying to cope. Nah. Bullshit. Rider always exaggerated and talked smack. Fourteen . . . ? Dayum, compound, bro.

Big Mike looked out the window and swallowed another chuckle. Rider scowled, shook his head, and sighed.

Try as she might, she couldn't stop giggling from time to time as they made their way to the Lakefront area. But as they neared the cemetery, they all became more focused and the mirth dissipated.

"All right—first we go check on the vault that he once occupied, then we cruise by his mansion on Lake Pontchartrain. We get a floor plan so we can come back with the full team later, if we can get inside, and then we go back home. Very simple."

"Well, at least his joint is lakeside and not on the Mississippi—closer to the swamplands," Big Mike said in a very cheerful voice that made both him and Damali smile while Rider grumbled.

"The only part about this I like, is the part about getting back on the plane—it's so damned humid out here you can cut the air with a knife . . . and let's not even begin to discuss the mosquitoes—New Orleans in the summer, in a graveyard and an abandoned vamp's mansion, ain't my idea of the quiet life."

Big Mike and Damali ignored Rider as they got out of the car and began walking toward the vault in the area that Marlene had identified. They passed rows and rows of the ten-foot-long white structures, their footsteps making quiet shuffling noises against the soft, grass-covered earth. Wet was the only way to describe the environment—in New Orleans nothing ever seemed to totally dry, Damali noted, remembering her own brief experience there as a child.

"They covered the bricks with white plaster because the damp air crumbled the bricks. Mar said Nuit's tomb wouldn't be white, though, but some type of marble . . . and he's in the black Catholic Creole section in the back. He was black blueblood. Said that's how her posse had found him twenty years ago."

"Whatever, Damali," Rider sighed. "All I know is, I'm worried about what might be still kicking inside the waiting wall—that section over there where the bodies go and have to wait until a real tomb can be opened."

He shook his head and spat. "Nasty, I tell you. We are in a place where, if the tomb was already locked for the one-year ordinance they'd dump a body in that very unsecured-looking waiting wall safety-deposit-box area—so the remains could be cremated by sunlight and heat . . . then just push whatever maggoty mess was left off the vault slab into a three-foot cavern behind it—*within the vault,* ladies and gentlemen, to make room to slide the next casket in. That is what we are about to walk into—in this insufferable heat!"

Rider slapped his neck and flicked the offending mosquito off his hand. "Even the bugs drink your blood out here!"

"Rider, please shut up," Damali said, exasperated. "You are not making any of this easier."

"Oh, please forgive me," Rider said with a wave of his

arm. "My bad. Let me not cast a negative vibration on this *fun* excursion."

They walked a while longer in silence, only Big Mike's occasional private chuckles to himself breaking the barrier between them. When they came to a halt in front of the dark-gray marble tomb identified as Nuit's, Big Mike turned to Rider with a wide grin.

"*Laissez les bon temps rouler*—let the good times roll."

"Mike, did that female vamp tell you that? You are getting on my nerves, dude. Seriously."

Mike laughed. "Yeah, she did . . . over, and over, and over again. Iron lace and criminals . . . God, I love New Orleans."

Rider frowned and was about to speak, but Damali held up her hand.

"Fellas, please. Break it up. It's showtime. I need to concentrate if you want a seer." She needed to steady herself and hoped they wouldn't notice. Since her brief encounter with Carlos, she'd also been practically blind. It was as though holding him sent such a current through her that it had literally blown her mind like a fuse. Then, she had absorbed all of Marlene's pain right after. She was emotionally exhausted, and had trouble focusing on anything except Carlos's current location and safety. She was drawing a blank, but didn't want to shake her team members' confidence. Half of winning any battle required having one's head right. If you believed, had confidence, you could conquer anything. "You guys ready?"

Disgruntled, Rider finally nodded, glowering at Mike's happy expression.

"Pestilence, plague, those were the weapons of Nuit's era, D. Don'tcha think we should consider the fact that disease is still a standard way to off somebody?"

"There hasn't been a member of Nuit's line alive to bring back the plague or go in here in a long time," she argued.

"My point exactly."

"All right, Rider, listen. We get in, see if this is where he sleeps—then we're out. It's early afternoon. What can happen?"

"In the dark, with his last ounce of strength, the bastard could sit up quick and rip somebody's heart out." Rider glanced at Big Mike who was now serious. "Ain't funny, is it, Mike? Obviously you *do* remember some of the other aspects of New Orleans not in the 'must see' section of the travel guides."

Mike nodded and let out his breath, adjusting the duffle bag on his shoulder. "Two minutes—everybody hold a stake, I'll move the lid."

They passed a strained glance between them as Rider and Mike pried the tomb open. Thick cobwebs blocked the entrance and something unseen skittered in a dark corner. They covered their mouths against the musty, dank smell. Within minutes, Big Mike had broken the coffin covering off with a drum anchor and chime chisel. Bones and frayed pieces of fabric greeted them once they removed the lid, but thankfully nothing moved.

"Y'all, not trying to be funny or nothing, but, this is no place for a guy with a sensitive nose." Rider had his hands over his nose and mouth, a stake clamped under his armpit.

"This isn't his lair," Damali murmured. "He's too smart for that—we should have known. I don't smell or sense him either."

"Okay, then, let's go. I'm convinced—curiosity is satisfied. Let's go home now."

They walked out of the vault, this time not arguing with Rider's insistence that they get the hell out of there. As soon as they cleared the crypt, Rider hawked and spat again.

"Have you any idea what places like this do to an olfactory sensor?"

"Yeah, I do, but can you stop with the hawking? Dag, between the toilet seats left up all the time, and the spitting thing, eeew," Damali said, finally taking a real breath.

"Like I said, we all need some personal space." Rider shrugged. "We each have our little foibles, but did you smell anything? My nose is full of stinky shit."

"I didn't smell a hint of sulfur in there. Probably will be like that in the mansion, too—if it isn't a tourist stop, or sold to a family or something. Before my dad hunted him, he might have kept residence here—but knowing Nuit, like all vamps, he moved his operation to high ground when he came back. I really should have thought about that part more."

"But, Mar said that Blood Music owned this property—so something might be up with it." Big Mike walked a distance away, got still, listened, and then shook his head.

"Yeah," Rider conceded. "I guess we had to check. We'd all look pretty stupid if we hadn't, and the bastard was so arrogant that he'd gone right back to the most obvious place—faking us out because we wouldn't think he'd be here. Fine, people. Let's do this fast."

After a short walk, they found the rental car and climbed into it again.

"He probably willed the mansion back to himself, so that he could still keep it, like all his other holdings."

Damali's grip tightened on the wheel. "There's something about this place, though. It's nearby—I can feel it. Gut told me to try. I don't know." She finally sighed, turning the key in the ignition and pulling off slowly, thinking.

Big Mike nodded. "That's why they need helpers—people to do their dirty work for them, to file bogus birth and death certificates, move property around . . . Yeah, let's go check out the mansion and see who's home."

This time as they drove, there was no raucous laughter, no teasing, and no fooling around. Instinctively they all knew that going into a mansion was more dangerous than opening a vault during the day. In a house, there were many interconnecting rooms, plus places to get trapped with nowhere to run. Windows could be sealed against the light, and tunnels could lead anywhere, particularly darkness.

"Looks empty—no activity," Mike murmured as he listened for sounds at the property's perimeter.

Standing on a lush carpet of golf-course-quality grass, the team stared up at the impressive whitewashed, six-columned mansion that had two levels of sweeping verandas running the length of the house, which was complete with multiple wings and an arched carriage port. Mature trees bowed and swayed in the breeze, draping Spanish moss as though it were made of ladies curtseying with hoop skirts at a Krewe masquerade ball.

"Not bad for a freed black sugar plantation owner back in the day . . . but, why is it white? Thought Nuit wouldn't stand for it. They normally don't like that color," Damali said in a quiet, concerned voice.

"At some point, he obviously had to fit in," Rider said,

staring at the mansion. "Couldn't be too blatant in an era that still burned people suspected of witchcraft in town squares, now could he? Ingenious bastard."

Damali and Mike's eyes followed Rider's line of vision. Strange symbols had been etched in the black wrought-iron railing in front of the verandas, and on the shutters. To the unaware, the designs would appear to be simple artistic license to add beauty to the home. Some of the subtle markings looked like a family crest woven into ornate curlicues, but there was no doubt in the team's mind that it represented a vampire crest for Nuit's territory. Money, power, fame—Nuit's trinity.

"Thought they couldn't deal with iron?" Big Mike muttered, still studying the house.

"That's witches, not vamps—get your lore right," Rider said.

"All right," Damali said in a weary tone, "Mike's bad. Let's go around back and do this fast."

"Summertime is ripe with thunderstorms, D," Big Mike said as they all looked up at the darkening clouds.

"You have *got* to be kidding me." Rider sniffed the air. "Now our flight could be delayed. If my nose wasn't all jacked up by the crypt I would have smelled rain coming. Damn!"

"It's summertime in the storm belt . . . floods here, too."

"Well, Mike, I just suddenly feel better!"

"C'mon, guys. We're wasting time."

On Damali's command, they crept to the back of the expansive three-level structure and found a small back window that led into a stone pantry at the ground floor. She nodded, and Big Mike pried the wooden door open, breaking the L-shaped iron latch. As they stepped into the dark terrain, she noted that the windows weren't covered, and Rider motioned to silently suggest that they take a quick look upstairs. If too much light were evident, that usually meant a house wouldn't be occupied by night-dwelling inhabitants—which also meant that they'd just broken into a private home.

Stealing up a narrow flight of brick-and-stone steps, they stood in awe of the fully furnished, very clean, functional interior. Damali, Mike, and Rider glanced around at the expensive period furniture, Damali noting that the place had the color scheme of New Orleans king cake—purple for justice, green for faith, gold for power. Stained glass was set in the main doors, which opened to a *Gone with the Wind* staircase. Light poured in everywhere. She shook her head, as did Rider and Big Mike. Nothing came up on their internal sensors. The vampires' helpers often inherited from vamps, or kept their establishments running in their absence, but this place had too much light for a vamp to fall through.

"I don't think so, either," Damali said quietly, keeping her voice to a near whisper. "Even in their lairs, Marlene said, if the houses are flooded with too much light, it's almost like a battery drain while they're in-state."

"Right. They usually block off a whole wing or a corridor, unless they do the old-fashioned graveyard burial thing." Rider nodded and sniffed, and then shrugged.

"I'm told, by reliable sources," Big Mike said with a wide grin, "that the dirt thing is passé. They do underground condos, or subbasements in mansions. You are talking Dracula era, before indoor plumbing."

"I will not venture to ask how you came about this deep knowledge," Rider said with a testy voice. "But, that is pertinent information. Let's roll."

"Wait a minute," Damali said. "Does the inside of this house look smaller than the outside did to you?"

Rider and Big Mike glanced around.

"Oh, shit." Rider sighed. "You know, if you're wrong, I believe breaking and entering is a felony worth up to five to ten years in the state pen—which will make the compound seem like a vacation paradise. You cannot just break into a real person's house and explain to the maid or butler that you came to exhume a body from the basement—at least you have to have a permit!"

"Yeah, I know," Damali said. "But if this was once his lair, and it has so much light now . . . Doesn't make sense. Why would he keep it? Yeah, he could have moved, but he's in the high-rent district in New Orleans, and this is mecca for the North American vamps. Hmmm."

With her hands out before her, she closed her eyes, walking and making a small circle the way Marlene had once shown her. "I don't feel any energy coming from the western side of the house."

"The sun sets in the west, their dawn. Makes sense to me, D." Big Mike shrugged and started walking. "Hit it from the sub-level—the ground floor . . . since they don't have formal basements because of the waterline. Let's see if there's a false wall down there."

"This is such a bad idea, folks," Rider complained as a strike of lightning flashed outside through the huge bay window of the parlor. "The storm just ate up daylight, and we're going into a known lair, trapped in a stone pantry—which in my mind is the same as a basement. I am not liking this."

Regardless of Rider's protest, the small group made their way back down into the pantry area, passed through several rooms, and began feeling the western wall.

"Look around this room," Damali said after a few minutes of their efforts and having made no headway. "No windows. We came in on the east side that had windows and the door Mike opened, went through a middle section," she said, motioning to the room they'd just been in, which had one teeny window. "Now, in this section, there's nothing in here but dust and old wine racks. The bottles on the shelves are filled. Something isn't right. I can feel it in my gut."

"Want me to light it up in here? I can do that," Big Mike said, "but we were trying to keep on the DL. The little bit of gray coming from the other room gives us cover—just like it was necessary to park the car out of sight. Understand?"

"Yeah, Mike, but I want to get behind one of these racks to check the wall."

Mike nodded, and moved forward.

"Hold up, and this time I'm not just making idle complaints," Rider said, his tone serious.

The group gave him their attention.

"You smell something, Rider?" Big Mike asked, studying him.

"Yeah."

"I do, too," Damali said.

"You got blood in your nose, don't you? Rider, you always get this sick look when you do." Big Mike folded his huge arms over his chest.

Rider covered his mouth and pointed toward the bottles. "Take one in the other room so we can check it out before Mike lights a UV torch."

Working fast, Damali extracted a dusty bottle as the group paced quickly behind her. She held it up to the gray

streaks of light and wiped off the dirty label; they all
stared at the crest.

"Arrogant sonofabitch has his own private stock."
Rider was about to spit, but changed his mind when
Damali shook her head.

"Okay," Damali sighed, handing the bottle of black
liquid to Big Mike. "Time to light a torch."

Rider groaned as the threesome again made their way
into the darkness and stood back while Mike set down the
bottle and unzipped his duffle bag. He produced a small
battery-powered stage light and handed Rider and Damali
each a long, concert light wand.

"Everybody hold a light and a stake," Mike murmured,
passing out the equipment. "Just to be on the safe side.
Might want a few drum anchors in your pockets, too."

They nodded as Mike flicked on a lamp and shined it
against the bottles and stone wall and stared. As soon as
the light hit the targeted area, the wall started giving way
as though a crumbling illusion. The center of the solid
mass simply burned where the lamp first struck it and
peeled back. It was like watching a photo catch flame in
an ashtray, the middle of it smolder, then blacken, and
then curl toward the edges of the frame to reveal a new
image.

"Oh, shit!"

"Rider, man, what is this?"

"The light," Damali whispered. "The light is burning
away the illusion!"

Stepping back fast, Damali's light wand inadvertently
touched the floor, which also started vanishing from the
point by her boot where her wand had connected with it,
creating a cavern that began swallowing her feet. She im-

mediately scrambled, trying not to drop into the yawning opening. Rider yanked Big Mike by his shirt to fall against the eastern wall, but wherever their lights fell seemed to make solid structure evaporate.

The floor was disintegrating so fast that she lost her balance. "Hit the lights!" she yelled as her wand fell into the opening pit around her, along with the duffle bag and some of the unpacked stakes. Floor space kept edging away from her and the team, and she caught herself from dropping into the abyss by holding on to Rider's legs while he and Mike scrambled to anchor themselves to the dissolving door frame.

With one hand, Mike was able to switch off the bright lamp and grab on to the wood frame with the other. Rider's wand had been swallowed beneath him. He was clinging to Mike's waist for dear life, as Damali precariously dangled by his boot.

"Hang on, Damali!" Rider yelled. "Pull up on my leg, sweetheart, then take my hand. Mike, move back, slow and easy. Get us out of this, and I'll never rib you about being a big, lurchy motherfucker again! Pull!"

She wrapped her arms around Rider's boot and pressed her face against his pant leg. She could hear Mike's grunts of exertion as he used his raw strength to draw her out of the hole, using Rider as a human rope. Dirt and rock bit into her forearms, scraping her skin, but she could feel progress—then something grabbed hold of her legs.

"Something's got me! Hurry," she yelled. "I can't shake it!"

"If you're scratched, they smell blood, baby—give me your hand!"

Kicking and twisting, but trying not to lose her grasp

on Rider, she could feel icy, sharp fingers snatching at her legs. Panic made her struggle wildly at first, hindering Rider's efforts. Then she stopped fighting so he wouldn't lose his grip on her hand, and she tried to keep her body still for a moment to also make the thing about her legs grow confident. She needed to trap it against her to use its own position against it. Her lips murmured a prayer. She let one get a good hold on her legs as the snakelike thing slithered between them. Damali snapped her calves shut, bent her knees, and forcefully brought her shins and the creature's snakelike head forward against the jagged cavern wall.

Immediately, whatever had her dropped away, and she used her remaining strength to push her boots against the wall to climb to safety up Rider's leg.

"We're outta here," she said, panting.

"No argument," Rider said.

"I think we found the lair, li'l sis. I'm good if you are. Let's roll."

"Roger that," Rider said, coughing from the dust that had been kicked up in the struggle, as they all stood and began to run.

They bolted to the adjoining room, and then fled through the next, until they were outside panting and running in the torrential storm, leaving snarling sounds behind them.

"Ain't got nothin' to sweep the car," Mike said, out of breath as they approached it. "Could be infested—the cloud cover and rain don't leave much light."

"Fuck it, dude," Rider said, huffing air. "We're in the car, and we motor!"

"Some things gotta be addressed the old-fashioned way. If it's infested, we kick its ass." Damali flung a car door open and jumped in, brandishing drum anchors as a weapon.

The others jumped in behind her, and they all peered around the car interior as she started the ignition, shifted into gear, and pulled out.

"The flight is going to be delayed, judging by the weather."

Big Mike nodded his agreement to her observation, but was clearly still too charged to speak.

"We're not doing New Orleans in a thunderstorm, at night, after opening a lair with no weapons. That's out. Don't even consider it."

"All right, Rider. Suggestions, then?" Damali glanced at him hard, and kept driving.

"We're in Lake Ponchartrain—which ain't far from New Orleans Lakefront Airport," Rider said slowly. "I've got an old buddy from 'Nam who's out of his natural mind, and he'd fly us in a small charter, direct to Dallas where we can connect to get to LAX . . . if the storm dies down a little. He's insane, which is no more than what we just did."

"In a storm, Rider?" Damali shook her head. "I'd feel a *lot* better in a jumbo seven-forty-seven. Okay?"

"Oh, so *now* the lady is concerned about the principles of safety. Give me a break. A floor just dropped out from under us with Hell below it, and you are worried about crashing in a storm? I would think that would be the least of your worries, Madame Huntress."

"He's got a point, D . . . By the way," Big Mike said in a very quiet voice, "you nicked?"

"No," she snapped. "But thanks for asking." She softened her voice and patted Big Mike's arm. "Thanks for the bail-out. They were demons. Not vamps. Had to be.

Vamps deliver a bite when they attack. Plus, Mar did say that she only thought demons had taken over Nuit's old lair—guess she was right? Just like she and her team had found years ago."

"Somehow, li'l sis, that does not make me feel better."

She continued to rub Big Mike's arm. "I know. But now you sound like Rider." She tried to chuckle unsuccessfully. "Shit . . ."

"Wait," Rider said, his tone slow and cautious. "Demons do not guard vampire lairs. In fact, the two species are in direct opposition to one another—will try to eradicate each other on sight." He sat back and wiped the streams of water off his face. "Then why would Blood Music, known to be owned by vamps, still have ownership of what we've confirmed to be, the hard way, a demon portal?"

Everyone looked at Rider, and he ran his fingers through his drenched hair. "If demons had somehow jacked this place from him years ago when he got staked, that I could accept. But the fact that he still owns it today makes me wonder. Something fishy is going on."

Damali turned up the defrost blowers in the car and cleaned the window with her fingers, making a small circle so she could see to drive. The comment stilled her, and she let it roll around in her mind as she wiped water from her eyes with the back of her hand. She allowed Rider's statement to sit with her for a while before she spoke. "That's just it. Marlene told us my father got bitten, and my mother went after him. Then," Damali said in a sad, far-off tone, "my mother staked herself to keep herself from one night going after me."

The interior of the car was so quiet that only the blowers made a sound. Hard rain pelted the vehicle, its metallic drumbeat fusing with the swish of the tires against the wet road. Occasional traffic crept by, throwing a rush of water against the rental car.

"Nobody ever staked Nuit," Damali finally murmured. "When Marlene's team learned about my mother's intent to cast a spell and came to the mansion, they used a counter-spell on him and he vanished. A demon-ridding spell . . . because that's what they thought he was. But they never found the vampire that had bitten my parents. They assumed that what had attacked my parents had been just one of New Orleans' regulars, a demon—not vamp, and moved me and their team to Gullah country in South Carolina. Marlene didn't suspect Nuit was a vamp until he came for, and turned, Raven."

"If demons are guarding Nuit's entrance to his lair while he's not in it, then this thing is real big." Rider glanced at Damali and Mike, and rubbed his hand over his jaw.

"Right," Mike chimed in.

"My point from the get-go."

Insatiable hunger propelled him up off the black, silk-covered futon. Carlos sat up and glanced around the pitch-dark of the bedroom he'd just acquired. He stretched, then yawned, regaining his orientation. Night two—now what?

First order of business was to take a leak and then bust a grub. Then he remembered and slowly stood.

"You didn't eat enough your first night," a voice in the shadows hissed.

Carlos started, his night vision sharpening. He then relaxed when he saw the messenger's hooded robe and red eyes.

"Did you bring the maps?" Carlos walked across the marble-appointed room, searching in the old Dominican's closet for something to wear.

"Yessss . . ." the courier hissed again. "On the nightstand. Once you read them, I suggest you burn them. Too precious. Could fall into the wrong hands. Be quick. We have also sent your clothes."

"Good," Carlos said, casually. "The old Dominican didn't have much taste in rags, and was shorter than me by half a foot." Ignoring the entity, he walked into the vault-like closet and found a pair of black leather pants, a black silk shirt, and a pair of black alligator boots. He took his time, actually enjoying the impatience he sensed from the messenger who hovered just outside the closet door.

"We have been concerned," it said when Carlos came back out of the closet. "We lost contact, and the Vampire Council wants assurances that you have located the Neteru and haven't been compromised. And . . . there was a registration of the loss of one second-generation female vampire and eleven male thirds last night, before we lost a don . . . thirteen in all. That is a lot of activity. As I said, a concern."

"My mission was to break Nuit's forces—reason enough for the high number of vampire kills."

The entity nodded. "Impressive . . . I will duly communicate your progress in that regard."

"Tell them not to get in my way. I'm hooking up a smooth strategy here topside."

"They need to be informed of some of the more intricate aspects. I am sure you understand."

"C'mere," Carlos ordered. Hunger was making him lose patience with this courier, but he allowed the disgusting creature near him. "Take this scent back to the council. Tell them that I was on sensory overload. Now, I need to eat."

The two gleaming eyes inside the robe momentarily disappeared and then flashed again. Carlos could only assume that the thing had closed its eyes, when it nodded and emitted something resembling a sigh.

"They will be very pleased. I will courier your response, and this very special demonstration of loyalty. Hunt well, tonight."

As soon as the entity vanished, Carlos began dressing, and then stopped—realizing that if he wanted to shower and wanted to dress, all he had to do was think about it. He laughed, and quickly dispensed with the task. Almost immediately, an awful clawing sensation began burning his insides.

"Oh, shit," he murmured into the quiet. If he didn't eat, any extra resources he used, like projection or shape-shifting, even movement, would steadily increase his hunger and sap his strength. He would only be strong when he fed. "Sonofabitch!"

Beginning to panic, he walked across the room, opened the door, and ascended the stairs. Maybe, just maybe. He made his way to the kitchen, opened the refrigerator, and stared at the food. Had to be something for any of the human helpers that kept the house. Sniffing the lunch meat, he cautiously bit into a piece of sliced ham. An acidic taste immediately filled his mouth, making him retch and heave bile into the sink. "Damn it!"

The exertion had made his hands tremble. He had *the shakes*? This was bullshit! A new level of panic ripped through him, and he ran from room to room in the four thousand square feet of the first floor. The gaudy gold fixtures, the gleaming red marble, the velvet and gold furniture—everything the color of ruby red made him want to holler. He tore around the corner and rushed up a spiral marble staircase, searching room by room for thirteen rooms for anything in the house that might take away the pain. He could smell it. Blood was in the house. He stopped moving, forcing himself to be still and concentrate.

Sensing his environment with his mind, he roved over every inch of the lair site. Of course. The vault. Tearing back down the steps, he dashed through the house, and back to the hidden black marble stairs that opened behind the false fireplace in the den. He almost tumbled down the steps; he couldn't get there fast enough. Once in the bedroom, he spun around and saw openings to other rooms.

He passed a sunken living room with all-black leather appointments. He stood in the middle of the room, quickly glancing at the wall stereo system, HDTV, art— was the thing that would quench his hunger in a safe? It was there, so close, but behind what? Again he summoned calm and the scent wafted from deeper within the underground chamber. He passed several more rooms and found, of all things, a kitchen—with a walk-in freezer. Half afraid to open it, the hunger made him reach out his hand and pull the heavy black lever on the black matte-finished appliance. Sections of human bodies hung from hooks and occupied racks. Carlos slammed the door, and pressed his back against it. Oh shit . . . what had he done? He wiped his hand over his mouth. He was drooling.

"Okay, okay, okay, man," he whispered to himself, walking in a circle. "You can tough this out. One more night, maybe two." All he had to do was make a choice, and one way or another the pain would stop and he'd be able to get to Nuit. But he was *not* going out like this. Eating bodies like a freak? Oh, hell no!

Another intense convulsion stabbed at his intestines, and he began to move in a serpentine resistance to the mere thought of denying himself the sustenance he needed. But he smelled blood—not just meat. Saliva was building in his mouth. Even his sight was dimming. He leaned over the sink and dry heaved again, and turned on the tap to splash his face with cold water—and hit ruby gold. The tap ran blood.

He drank from his hands, but he couldn't get enough of it down his throat fast enough. He turned his head, putting his mouth under the faucet—and he stayed there until he was so gorged that he could barely breathe. He came away from the sink, wiping his face on a crimson towel, and then burped.

Perplexed, curiosity made him bend to look under the sink. A fresh tank, like a spring-water cooler, gurgled and bubbled from the forced siphon. Deep. Nuit had probably ordered it as a gift to repay him for the Neteru sample. Cool. Made sense. Had to keep him fed to keep him on the Neteru's trail. Yeah, fair exchange was no robbery.

Steadier now, he glanced around and spied a wine rack, immediately recognizing the crest on the dark glass. Carlos laughed out loud. "Private label? Get outta here!" A hundred questions slammed into his brain as he checked out his new environment more slowly. How did they keep the blood from clotting? How often did he have to eat? How did they bottle it? Then he became still. Who paid the price for this gift of life so they could live? He slowly approached a bottle and pulled it out of the rack.

How many kids . . . women . . . children . . . brothers . . . fathers . . . how many to make a good bottle?

Full, but far less exuberant about his find, Carlos slowly went to the upper levels of the house. He had work to do, and although he felt much restored, he was deeply disturbed. An aftertaste registered on the back of his tongue, and he stood in the middle of the palatial villa trying to figure out what it was. He closed his eyes. Anticoagulant. Carlos wiped his mouth with the back of his hand. He needed answers. A small voice in his head told him to just ask.

The mental conversation was becoming more disturbing than his recent panic attack. It was as though he could understand this new life by instinct—then he remembered. The line retains the knowledge of the line. Now he knew why blood from the tap tasted different than when he'd drunk from Raven, and why he needed so much of it. A fresh kill was always better. It was more potent. He didn't need as much because it carried the adrenaline and hormones of the victim. So, if he raided a blood bank, or drank it out of the tap, he'd need three times as much.

This could not be happening. A kill a night . . . If he lived for years, the body count would add up to a personal war. Or, if he just fed off of multiple victims per night, but not enough to totally drain and kill them, they'd eventually get sick, finally die, and turn. Now the Vampire Council's policies made sense. If too many vampires were feeding topside, at any given time, and without population limitations, they'd wipe out the human food supply within a couple of years.

Carlos studied the wine rack. Discipline. Masters had discipline, and had access to fresh blood from willing human donors without siphoning it from a bite, in exchange for material gain. Carlos raked his fingers through his hair. People would put a needle in their arm, or even their momma's, for money.

The old vampires were ingenious. He was sure they also had emergency backup provisions.

Now he understood why the Vampire Council was so appalled by the number of humans Nuit had turned. With the demon influence, his mutated seconds mangled their victims—maiming, nearly destroying them. They ate as much as a master, and one bite could cause a turn—fucking up the vampire ecosystem. Yeah, he could dig it. He'd seen them at work.

Thoughts of his brother tore at him, as Alejandro's death became vivid to his mind's eye. He breathed out hard, feeling his face grow sticky and crusted with dried blood. He walked up the stairs and found a bathroom—deciding to wash up the old-fashioned way.

Coming out with a towel over his head, he went back down into the vault to find another black shirt—this time pulling out a sleeveless T-shirt. Damn, this was crazy. All right. Start again. He trudged back up the steps and went to the front door, but stopped and glanced down at the newspaper that had come through the slot.

A newspaper delivery at night? Interesting, but definitely a message. There was a black-and-white photo of his car in the woods with the door open and two suitcases on the ground plastered on the front page. Carefully he assessed the situation. He needed a plan—a new plan A, B, and C if the ones before it didn't pan out. He knew the vultures were circling and couldn't afford to have his resources jacked, even if he was supposedly dead. His mother and the rest of the family had to be taken care of no matter what.

It wasn't about just showing up at the police station one night with some long story about why he, of all people, had left a cool one-point-one mil sitting beside his car, and illegal firearms next to two butchered FBI agents. They'd lock his ass up and hold him without bail, if the cops didn't take him in the back room and shoot him first for doing one of their own—then he'd have to play dead and vaporize to escape, and the shit would get really ridiculous. Would send his mother and grandmother through more heartache. No. He had to lay low and somehow get this rap pinned on somebody else. Somebody else who was already dirty and the authorities would be all too happy to close the case on. The Dominican don fit the plan perfectly. Maybe he would call the cops to set up a meeting. He could propose a trade, information for immunity.

The maps! Carlos tucked the newspaper under his arm and hurried back downstairs, collected the maps, read them, and left them to burn in the fireplace. They immediately caught flame and turned to ash. Okay—now to search the Dominican's lair.

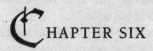CHAPTER SIX

"RIDER, JUST chill! You've been complaining nonstop for the last six hours. We've been over this crap a hundred times." Damali flopped down heavily on a stool in the compound's weapons room and let out a hard breath. "I'm just glad Marlene, Jose, and Shabazz got back to the compound all right, and that Dan and J.L. didn't have to deal with any problems while they were here alone."

"You sure Jose is okay back there, Mar?" Big Mike looked over Marlene's shoulder and peered down the hall.

"Yeah, poor guy. His fluids keep dropping and he gets all disoriented. They pump him intravenously to rehydrate, and then he perks back up only to do it all over again. I'm not sure how much of this his system can take before something major goes wrong."

"It's hard on his liver and kidneys, not to mention his heart, the doctors said," Shabazz warned. "Gotta figure out how to put this bastard, Nuit, down fast—and hope he's the one, at that."

"I know." Damali glared at Rider and dared him to speak. "We'll find out soon."

The fact that their team didn't know much more than when they had started out only made her feel worse, especially given Jose's weakening condition. She roughly towel-dried her locks in frustration, walked across the room, and flopped down on the sofa. Her nerves were still fried from the harrowing ride in a prop to Dallas, and then the ensuing drama to get their flight moved up. It felt good to have on clean clothes and to have clean skin and hair again. The whole misdirected adventure had made her feel grimy, tainted, and she'd spent a half hour soaping Nuit's environment off of her.

Rider paced, still piqued about the whole New Orleans fiasco and walking around fussing despite Damali's command for him to drop it.

"Look, man," Big Mike sighed. "We've explained everything to Marlene and the fellas—right, Mar? So why beat a dead horse?"

"Me and Dan were able to come up with some pretty cool stuff for tomorrow night, so you won't have to go in there like you did today." J.L. stood and stretched. Dark circles were forming under his eyes, the strain of the last twenty-four hours taking its toll on him as well.

"Yeah, and I took care of all the PR stuff so people would just think you were booked elsewhere—the interviews went great. Everything is copacetic." Dan rolled his shoulders and leaned his head back, massaging his neck.

"Need I remind you all that this happened in the day— so I can only wonder what could happen at night!"

"Rider," Marlene said on a long breath, "you are workin' my *last* nerve. Shabazz and I are tired, Jose is sleeping, J.L. and Dan have been wracking their brains on wild new designs—and Damali has *got* to get some rest . . . or she won't be any good for the concert tomorrow. Not only does she have to be in top fighting form, but the girl also has to perform in front of a worldwide audience. Not to mention, it will be her birthday—and it would be nice to do something fun . . . but we have this other very un-fun thing to do. We're all maxed, in one way or another. We all need sleep. So cut it out."

Damali yawned at the mention of rest. It was pure reflex, and the hot shower hadn't helped. "I haven't even worked out my routine, figured out which pieces I want to do—and I'm a little nervous to do the old stuff . . . seriously, that was good for local crowds, but going overseas with the message . . ."

"My point exactly. And the music team, plus lights and sound, need to be tight. Dan gave the Blood crews basic info—because their people are handling *all* the setup. So, if there's a switch in any aspect of the performance, it will have to be done right on stage."

Everybody yawned their agreement as they nodded in response.

"What's the layout, though, Mar?" Damali asked through another yawn.

"Concert starts at nine P.M. our time and runs till midnight. You get introduced as the last act, and will be the only female performer. At eleven thirty you have to jam your butt off for less than a full half hour, because of the group-change lag time. They're doing this nonstop, six artists—commercial bumpers in between each group change—but at midnight, they're going to do this Blood Music, *Raise the Dead* ceremony . . . which means our people have from an hour before showtime until eleven thirty when you go on, to do our thing."

"Well at least we know that the five artists aren't vamps, maybe just traitors, because they've been on every talk show and interview circuit hyping this event for about a month. Plus, anybody on stage and getting broadcast live isn't a vamp." J.L. sat back down and dropped forward, working the kinks out of his back.

"I'm so exhausted I can barely think about it, guys. Seriously." Damali brought one fist into her chest and pulled her elbow with the other hand, trying to stretch the stress-tension out of her blade arm. "My concern is that it will be night and we'll have two and a half hours to do this thing—they'll be strong, right now we aren't, and we'll also be distracted . . . plus, there will be a lot of innocent people in the equation. I just wish I knew what the bigger picture looked like."

Rider finally sat down. Damali found herself pulling her legs up beneath her on the sofa. It felt so good just to put her head down for a few moments. Everybody had eaten, replenished their bodies, all members of the team were present and accounted for, and they had done all they could do. They knew what Nuit's mansion and vault looked like, but what good did that do? It was wasted time and energy. The rest of the plan they'd just have to make up as they went along. Dan hadn't gotten inside long enough before he had to run for his life, so he brought no real info. She just wished that Carlos wasn't out there solo, running around and in harm's way.

"Look at her," Shabazz said in a quiet voice. "The girl is wasted—we all are. I wish that for one night we could all just turn in, shut off the lights, and go to bed without worrying that something might come crashing through the doors. Now we've got demon legions to add to the mix."

Yawns made the rounds again throughout the room as each person found a corner that had a comfortable chair, a love seat, a bench, anything that would allow the human form to lie prone and be still. Even Rider begrudgingly found a place to recline without discontent.

Detective Berkfield glanced out of the unmarked sedan nervously as his partner took a drag of his cigarette. He studied the opening of the small alley that led to a row of expensive, North Hollywood shops. Pedestrians casually milled up and down the streets, stopping to chat, or to go into yuppie cafés or ethnic gourmet bistros. The area was populated enough by educated bystanders that, if this thing with Rivera went down wrong, there'd be witnesses. He had to give it to Rivera. This wasn't some deserted dock at the wharf handoff where anything could go wrong.

"You think Rivera is bullshitting?"

"You got the call," Malloy said, allowing the smoke to slowly filter out through his nose. "How did he sound?"

"On edge." Berkfield yawned. "Wasn't like his old arrogant self. Think that botched hit on him might have screwed our boy's confidence."

Malloy nodded. "He's moving."

Both detectives watched Carlos Rivera exit a small opening from between two buildings. It was like the guy had come from out of nowhere. The detectives glanced at each other as Rivera leisurely strolled by their vehicle while he took his time and advanced on the other side of the street, crossed another, and kept walking without acknowledging them.

"The bastard is smooth."

"I'll say. But give him some maneuvering space. Rivera said to drive around the corner and pass him as he dropped the Dominican drug files in the Dumpster, then let him keep walking. After a minute, we can go collect the info—it'll be in a folder."

"He's a bold sonofabitch," Malloy muttered, engaging the gears to pull slowly away from the curb. "Think he'll do the witness protection thing?"

"Said he was already a dead man walking." Berkfield let out his breath hard as the car crept around the corner but kept an easy distance from Carlos.

"Then what does he want? He said they already tried to set him up, so he had the Dominican don whacked—they won't sit still for that bullshit in their territory. They'll hunt him down until they wipe out everybody in his family."

"That's the thing. Except his mother and his grandmother, Rivera says they already did his whole family, so now he's a man with nothing to lose."

Berkfield and Malloy glanced at each other again.

"A man with nothing to lose is a dangerous thing to have running around inside an organization."

Berkfield nodded, but kept his eyes trained on Carlos's progress past an alley opening. "Yup. The fool is going after the Jamaican's records tonight, and said he'd dump them for us tomorrow."

"Shit. Why doesn't he give us the Russian, Italians, and Asians, too, while he's at it?" Malloy chuckled and shook his head, wiping the fatigue away from his eyes before flinging his cigarette butt out the window.

"Know what that crazy bastard said when I asked him? You know I had to ask."

"What?"

"He said he'd deal with them in due time, but he liked the Caribbean and Brazil—so those two had to go first. Now, I ask you, Paul, why would a man give up info that could have him blown away, and then go to those places where all the friends, family, and organization members of those people you dropped a dime on could come for you? Either he has a death wish, or a real slick agenda."

"Think he's using his own product?"

Berkfield rubbed his face as Carlos returned from the alley and kept walking.

"Hard to say. He doesn't look as rosy and on top of the world as he used to." He laughed as his partner rolled the car forward at a slow, creeping pace. "You know, Paul, now that you mention it, in the last twenty-four hours, his product has been drying up—like somebody turned off the tap . . . maybe that's what's got him ready to commit hari-kari. Either that or he snorted up his wholesale stash and wigged."

"He leads a stressful life. Will sometimes break a man. Especially a young, ambitious one on the move too fast."

"Yeah, but he said all he wants is his house, his car, the money, and the club—all the rest of the assets can be seized. Crazy bastard even put his warehouses on the disks he's dropping—giving us his drug locations, and his other illegal operations, as long as we attribute the find to the Dominican so his legit personal property won't be seized."

"That has to run through channels."

"Think about it, Paul. Fifty bodies from the wrong side of this war are going to go down because one Carlos Rivera is tired and wants out. You know how much we pay SOBs to do all sortsa shit, Paul. This guy has lost his marbles, because he told me—his mouth to my ear on the phone, and God as my witness—he just wants his mom and grandmom, and some chick named Juanita DeJesus, to be able to split up everything—and to bury him right. I'm startin' to feel sorry for this guy—can you believe that? Fifty top kingpins all across the country!"

"From what you're telling me, those disks and the names in that black book he's gonna leave us hold enough information to solve about twenty-seven homicides, and bust the inner core of the Dominican L.A. ring . . . months of police work."

Again both detectives glanced at each other with a smile, checked their weapons, and hopped out of the car to walk down the alley.

"Me, myself," Malloy said coolly, "I don't care if the bastard is having a nervous breakdown, has become a junkie, has a die-with-honor death wish, or if Jesus came down off the cross and baptized him for salvation. May he see the light. Whatever. Point is, we just hit the mother lode. So, keep the bird on the wire talking, and dropping regular presents. Did you mention this to anybody yet?"

Berkfield laughed. "What, and tell people that Santa Claus is a twenty-three-year-old millionaire? Are you crazy? Not yet. I wanted to savor the power of information for a bit before going in to haggle a deal to keep him on our side, and alive, if possible. He's no good to us dead."

Berkfield reached up with a grunt and fished around in the Dumpster, his hand connecting with garbage and greasy things he didn't want to consider as he made a face. "You get the next holiday package under the tree, Malloy."

"Gladly," Malloy chuckled, lighting another cigarette.

Carlos watched from a dark corner within the alley. Something wasn't right. Berkfield's partner had a different tint to his skin that created a thin, dark aura around him, but it wasn't vampire. If he was vampire, Carlos would have immediately been able to sense it, but he'd never seen this trace around a human before. Marked? The answer to his mental question was answered immediately. That was how his kind invisibly identified their helpers. Interesting. He'd learned something new. For a moment, he wondered what the seal around his mother and grandmother looked like. No matter, as long as they were off-limits.

This delivery had to go down smoothly, so he'd purposely drifted back to manifest unnoticed in order to watch it transpire without a hitch. Carlos inhaled, still appraising the detective with the strange aura. It wasn't a demon trace, either. Marked—and not Nuit's. Hmmm. So the Vampire Council had set him up in the news. *Very* interesting.

"Got it." Berkfield huffed from the mild exertion. "Paul, we just got ourselves a promotion right here, buddy, if this stuff checks out. Maybe we can work a deal with Rivera, you know . . . keep him on the street, feeding our team info, undercover-like as a source. We do it all the—"

Richard Berkfield stopped talking and looked at his partner, confused. For some odd reason, Malloy had the safety off his gun, it was in his hand, his trigger-finger was readied, and the weapon was pointing in his direction. What the . . .

"Hey, buddy, you wanna put away the nine? What's the matter with you?"

"You are about to fuck up a very nice lifestyle, Richard. Let's not be hasty. Hand me the package and let's go take a walk."

Materializing quickly in the shadows, Carlos moved silently toward the two officers, using Berkfield's stunned focus on the barrel of his partner's gun to roll up behind Malloy and catch him off guard.

Carlos tapped Malloy on the shoulder and Berkfield's eyes widened.

"Not a good idea."

"Where the hell did you come from?" Berkfield stepped back, glancing at Carlos and Malloy, as Malloy whirled around.

As expected, Malloy immediately fired, and Carlos felt the blow like a close-range punch, but not the burn of the bullet penetration. There was a hole in his shirt over his heart, but he watched his skin seal beneath it. He chuckled. This was so cool.

"I made a courier drop, and I intend for the delivery to be honored." Carlos held Malloy's gun. "Pull the trigger and you're a dead man."

He sighed when Malloy pulled the trigger again, and he watched the bullet discharge in the wrong direction, whir past Berkfield's shoulder, splattering the already stricken detective with his partner's guts. Carlos took a whiff of the remains as Malloy fell, a look of horror on his face. Carlos grimaced with disgust. Marked kill were tainted with a repulsive scent layer and not very appetizing. Now he further understood why they got passed over as dinner.

"You can see you've been infiltrated," Carlos said coolly. "Watch your back—you've been splattered, and an alley isn't a safe place for a man dripping blood."

"But, but, but he shot you point-blank range."

"Kevlar," Carlos said as he turned to walk away.

"Bullshit!" Berkfield yelled, but Carlos strolled ahead of him. "Since when do they make Kevlar T-shirts? The bullet went right through you and over my damned shoulder!"

"I gave you a gift, saved your life, now you owe me. My assets—you keep the drugs, and you might want to keep some of this to yourself . . . good career move, in my opinion. Tell them your boy had a fucking nervous breakdown from working too hard. Only his prints will be on the weapon. I assure you."

"You came out of nowhere . . . and . . . oh shit, what the fuck?"

"I'm going back into nowhere, until I drop my science on you another time. Say your prayers at night. Be thankful for small gifts. And, believe in things unseen."

Carlos turned the corner that led into the street; he could hear Berkfield running to catch up to him, and then watched from an overhanging fire escape as the poor man spun around three times searching for him, wiped at his clothes, crossed himself, and called for backup.

Time was of the essence. He stood outside Damali's compound on the dark side of the road and willed the phone inside to ring. A male voice answered, and sounded weary.

"It's Carlos. I need to speak to Damali."

In the background beyond the mute channel that had been engaged, he could hear mild pandemonium break out as she came to the phone.

"Carlos, where are you?"

He looked down at his T-shirt and sealed the gunshot hole in it, and glanced at his hand, dissolving the image of Nuit's ring. "Close by. Want to take you up on that invitation to come in. There's a lot going on, and I have some info."

"We can come get you . . . uh . . ."

"Tell the team I am not being followed—but I do need you to kill the exterior lights for a minute so I can come in."

She'd put her hand over the receiver, and then had hit the mute button again. An argument was under way. He let out his breath hard. Time was ticking, and tonight would be the last night he could really help her. He called her in his head. *Get back on the phone.*

"We don't turn off the lights," she said quietly.

His mind wrestled with the obstacle, trying to work around her team's resistance. "Tell them to lower their guard—a knight of Templar visited me, and left the newspaper. I need to get info to the group for tomorrow. He gave me some maps that I didn't understand."

She paused, and then began a flurry of words back to her group. Good.

"Just ten minutes, then I'm out—I have other pressing business going on in the streets. Tell them, okay?"

Again, her hand covered the phone and he could hear her battle for him. She didn't even hit the mute this time. Real good. The knight hadn't lied.

He closed his eyes, already invited, just blocked by the damned contraptions they had everywhere. He was not going through the door double-lock process—he'd fry. He hoped that nobody would panic and hit the hall sprinklers. This was bullshit. But on the other hand, he was glad she was so well fortified . . . it just bothered him that, at the moment, he was on the other side of her world.

"Tell them," he added, slowly, "not to blast me when I come through the door. I've got maps that will burn in the ultraviolet light, the knight said—now I don't know what the hell he was talking about, but—"

"Bring them in. We won't flash you."

He could hear the team murmur agreement, and he relaxed as the lights around the compound went out. But he hesitated for a moment, scanning the terrain to be sure he'd be the only guest, while another part of him became mildly concerned. *Baby, do not panic and toast a brother—cool?* Everybody just chill, no lights, crossbows down, everybody just take it easy.

Carlos kept the mantra in his mind as he crossed the road, hoping that the lights wouldn't suddenly come up. But when he reached the door, Damali and two of her male crew were there. She was unarmed, they weren't. But he crossed the threshold nonetheless, received a quick hug from her in the dark, and immediately she pulled away from him and led him to the inner rooms with the two henchmen at his back.

The hug had destabilized him a bit, but he shook it off. Had to stay focused. This was business. It was about her safety. But in the dark . . . *man.* Okay. Think.

Slightly taken aback, he surveyed the extensive weapons room as an Asian guy at the computer panels flipped a master switch and he could feel the entire compound heat up like it was a tin can in a microwave. This, he hadn't anticipated.

"Shabazz—"

"Save the intro, Damali. Me and Carlos know each other, or should I say, we remember each other. Lotta guys in the neighborhood did time for workin' with him, or got shot."

Carlos nodded to Shabazz. What could he say? There was no defense. It was what it was.

Damali let her breath out hard and extended her arm, moving it slowly as it swept the room. "Rider, J.L., Dan, Big Mike, Marlene, Jose is sick—but will recover. There. You've met everybody; everybody, meet Carlos—or re-meet him, whateva. The man came to help. So chill."

"Speak," the one pointed out as Big Mike said. "Now."

"Wait," the tall guy with spiked hair interjected. "A formality. My name's Rider," he added, picking up a crossbow. "They call me the Nose. And, while I can't put my finger on it, the scent ain't right. So . . . How the hell did you know where we were? I don't like it."

"He saved me, guys, remember?" Dan said fast. "This guy put everything on the line, fellas. Seriously." Standing, Dan's expression held an apology.

"Rider, stop. Put the weapon down, okay?" Damali shook her head and stood in front of Carlos. Although fatigue had dimmed her sensory awareness, common sense still prevailed. If Carlos were a vampire, or vamp helper, no religious guy would have let him know their location. The Templars weren't that sloppy.

"If a Templar sent you," Marlene said suspiciously. "Then?" But Marlene pulled back a bit and folded her arms. "How about if you stay on that side of the room, and Damali comes this way and stands with us . . . just till we get comfortable. We don't get many visitors at night around here—none that don't bear fangs."

"You know, Mar, now that you mention it, the hair is standing up on my arms." Shabazz bristled and picked up a weapon, glancing at Big Mike and J.L. who gave him a nod and flanked him. "Damali, come on over to this side of the room."

"No! Would you guys stop? Carlos, show them whatever it is you came to show us."

"Thanks, D," Carlos murmured. The fact that she had remained on his side of the room was not lost on him at all. The Templar had made good on both parts of his agreement; he'd get him into the compound and would try to surround him with enough mercy that the guardians wouldn't sense his vampire status. But he only had a few minutes. Damali and her team, although weary, had keen sensory ability. He had to talk fast and get out.

"I got a newspaper shoved through my front mail slot, and inside of it were some drawings I couldn't understand at first . . . until this guy came and told me to choose wisely—then rolled. It was the weirdest thing. Said something about New Orleans, and bullshit going down at the big international concert. I figured one of two things—either the guy was whack and could pose a threat, so you should know, or, it had something to do with all this bizarre shit we've seen lately."

One by one the stances before him relaxed, and Carlos kept his attention roving over their expressions. It was a definite standoff, and the monitor behind the guy J.L. disturbed him. It was flashing like wild, but he'd been able to mute the sound. His attention was divided between too many things at once. It was sapping him to project, cover the hole in his shirt, conceal the ring, keep the alarms from sounding, stand away from any unusual lights on the table; the smell of holy water and incense was wearing him out, as was Damali's fragrance. The joint was a freakin' oven, he had to materialize maps, and hope the guardians would heed the tunnel layouts before daylight came and the illusion of the maps torched . . . and the big guy named Mike kept tilting his head like a bloodhound, like he could hear something, and the hunger was beginning to come back—the energy drain was kickin' his ass. He'd need to feed again after all this.

"Look," Carlos said, tossing the maps out for the guy named Mike to catch. "I don't know why I bothered. Turn off the lights, and I'm out. No need in jeopardizing you all—I have a lot of people looking for me. Dig? I want to slide out of here cool like, and not get sprayed when I roll."

The attention of Damali's palace guards went to the maps, and the blinking monitor no longer made the huge brother keep tilting his head. They descended upon the information like vultures, but he was curious—Damali hung back, near him. Deep.

"Where did you really get that, Carlos?" She'd whispered the question so quietly that she'd almost mouthed it instead of speaking.

The complexity of her question, and the way her voice had murmured, made him step closer to her than was advisable. The nearness was working on the wrong side of his brain, gnawing it away from cool logic.

"Now is not the time, but you have to trust me."

She nodded, and put her hand on his arm. He stood there glancing at her team as they absorbed the information, trying his best not to breathe too much of her in. The heat of her hand was melting his common sense. He needed to get out of there. Now.

"Do you know what this is, dude?" Rider walked around the table and saluted.

Shabazz and Big Mike gave a grudging nod.

"Looks like these things can open up a portal at will—big change," Shabazz muttered. "Not good."

"Apparently, there was an alliance formed," Carlos began with caution. "We're in the last days, the knight said, and key sectors of the demon realms have joined with a major sector of the vampire empire. Evil is concentrating, gaining force."

"A vampire-Amanthra hybrid . . ." Marlene whispered, making the group stare at her. "I didn't think it was possible, because the two species are enemies. But now it all makes sense."

"That's what the superstitious guy said." Carlos allowed his statement to sink into the wary team around him, and just pointed toward the maps without crossing the invisible boundary that had been drawn between the sides.

"He went on and on about how it used to be that the vampires could only come up through lair sites—burial sites, where they kept their coffins, and had to have human helpers move their coffins from place to place. But, under Fallon Nuit, he made a pact with the demons, and can use demon transport levels to move underground without human support—like high-speed train zones through the third and fourth layers of Hell. Like I said, do what you want with the info. He was talking some crazy shit. I need to go."

"Man, you mean these things can just take a Concorde up from Hell and exit at any demon portal? Or they can jet underground and come up through any of Nuit's or his vampire line's lairs without aboveground movement?"

"Gone are the days of having Igor move a vamp's coffin in a horse and buggy and stow it in a basement, I guess," J.L. said with sarcasm. "This is the era of the global economy, brothers."

Carlos nodded to confirm the answer to Rider's question and to add weight to J.L.'s statement. Things had changed, and it was better that Damali's squad knew that, and didn't underestimate what they were dealing with.

"That's what happened in Philly—it was like sound got sucked right out of the air in a vacuum, then vamps came up. We'd seen 'em manifest before, but not with the total absence of sound." Mike let his breath out and just shook his head. "This is problematic."

"Understatement," Rider muttered.

"The absence of sound is a result of the speed and the matter displacement. Demons move in silence—as do ghosts, but the vampires have more density, which is why they hold their form . . . unless they will a transformation into something else." Marlene shook her head. "It's all so clear. But I don't know how to block a moving target."

The team passed nervous glances between them. Carlos struggled as much with his desire to tell them more in order to give them a fighting chance, as he did with the oppressive environment they had him now trapped within. But he needed to get them to understand before he got out of there.

"Other master vampires cannot use the tunnels—Nuit was the only one who formed an alliance . . . the religious guy said." Carlos shrugged, trying to seem blasé about the whole thing, but they were staring at him hard. "He said those zones are heavily guarded by very militant elementals that were marginalized by the vampire empire. The shit is getting ready to be on, from what I understand. You have the old vampire guard who can't maintain unilateral power for business as usual, you have the new guard who don't know how to utilize their power without running amuck—and neither side can keep a lid on the chaos. There are side deals and pacts being made everywhere."

"You seem very well-versed—if not intimate, with the whole issue at hand," Shabazz said in an even tone as he slowly looked up from a map.

"I ought to be," Carlos admitted, shaking his head. He had to think fast on his feet. He'd fucked up, had told them way too much in his urgency to protect Damali. He and Shabazz were from the same badlands in the past, and the bottom line was that a brother from the hood could smell bullshit a mile away—sensory gift or not. Shabazz wasn't even one of the noses, but he could feel shit.

Carlos passed his line of vision over the group in a slow, serious rove. "They did my brother, my cousin, my two best friends . . . you read how they found them—their mothers couldn't even bury them right. So, maybe that's why the Templar dude, being of the cloth and all, had some mercy and filled me in. That was cool of him, given that I was on a rampage to find out who did it. Maybe they just didn't want me to snuff somebody inno-cent and start a damned war."

"You're starting to believe this stuff, aren't you?"

Damali's question hacked at him. If she only knew. Believe? He'd seen both sides: a slice of Heaven and a whole lotta Hell. If he could just draw her into his arms and explain how this crazy bullshit had gone down . . . and why it was now so important for her to trust him—if it was the last thing she did . . . even if he was mixing truth with the evasions and lies now—it was coming from a correct place in his heart. He tried to send it by thought, but gave up, afraid to chance it. Not now. He was already spread too thin.

"I'm starting to see things that I never understood before," he told her truthfully. "I don't know what to think, or what to do, so I came here. That's all I can tell you."

"I know exactly where you are," she whispered, and briefly looked away.

When her line of vision broke its hold on his, the absence of those deep, brown orbs of understanding made his chest cavity constrict from the loss. *I never want to hurt you, baby . . . that's why I can't stay much longer.* He had to get it together. Pull out of his own thoughts. He'd lapsed, trying to talk to her from his mind. But that was pushing the envelope—he had to focus to keep all illusions intact.

"What's in this level three tunnel, man? Or on level four? A demon grabbed at Damali today, and I'd like to know what we're up against if we have to go after it." Rider had set down his weapon to hold an edge of the map, but kept sniffing, and then appeared to shake off a disturbing scent.

Carlos glanced at her. "You all right, baby?" He could feel possessiveness riddle him. Who'd attacked her?!

She nodded, and he looked up at the team.

"I'm okay," she murmured, and came closer to him, burning his shoulder where her hand landed. "Don't worry."

Carlos remained very, very still. He had to. He simply looked at her as she'd touched him. It had seemed like she'd extended her arm in slow motion, and he could see her pulse beat in the delicate inside of her elbow, right where the forearm connected to the upper arm, and beneath her bronze skin a faint blue-green vein hid . . . moving life through her. The motion was mesmerizing, as was the scent that the shifted air carried when she'd reached for him. And she wanted him to stay tonight for his own safety . . . to sleep in her room, love her hard and fast, then tender, so she didn't have to think about tomorrow. Had she any idea?

"I know you got a torch for my baby sis and all, brother, but you need to check them heat-seeking looks toward her while she's got six Glocked-up brothers and a momma who can fight, staring you in the face."

Whoa, bad slip. Way out of order. The big brother had bristled, rightfully so. All Carlos could do was nod and wait for the ruffled feathers to settle. Shit, he had to get out of there. Damali was a telepath—even if he wasn't sending, she was receiving, and it was messing with his cool. *Baby, please stop.*

"Mike, please," Damali whispered. "Can we stick to the matter at hand?"

This situation was getting confusing, and way too tense. Carlos let out his breath hard and raked his fingers through his hair.

"Listen, man, here's the deal—all bullshit aside. On level one, you have your average run-of-the-mill ghosts, haints, souls that died with a grudge in their hearts, issues, and whateva. Level two, they get a little more trippy—like the poltergeists and the kind of mess that can possess somebody to do some whack shit in one second, then make them all of a sudden wake up from the daze, and not know anything about the three bodies in the room with them."

"Keep talking," Rider said. "The man is making sense here."

"All right," Carlos pressed. "I'ma say this one time

like the guy told me, then I'm out. I've got things to do. He said, the further down you go, the less ghost-like the demon becomes, and the more solid it becomes as the density gets thicker—it compresses the soul weight and creates these hideous deformities, and the souls that were once within those things are jacked and stored to be fed on within the levels, twisted like the demon's bodies are. The third level is where vengeance creatures come from and their territory is so wide it overlaps a part of the fourth level . . . So you've got your recipe for the garden-variety demon. By the time you get all the way down, though, now you are in a very sophisticated space. These are the things that take on the original form of man. The longer the being can hold its human form, the more sophisticated—like the difference between werewolves, a level five, and vamps—level six."

J.L. nodded, appraising the maps. "It's like a deconstruction/reconstruction pattern. First the body dies, the soul leaves—if it goes down to level one, it remains this floating, unformed negative energy. The further it gets pushed down, based on the weight of the sins on its back, depends on what level it clocks in at. Then there's the crossover zone," he added, pointing on the map that three people held.

"Yeah," Carlos said, pleased. "Level four. From there the physical matter starts trying to come back into its original form for reentry into the world. As above, so below. From above it is a very cool process—that's where babies come from."

Carlos chuckled, and Shabazz and Big Mike gave him a lopsided smile along with Rider.

"But," Marlene said in a quiet voice. "Coming from

the other direction, the birth process is backward. It spews up fully formed, already corrupted, and at the end of its life horrible entities—instead of innocent, not fully formed, growing, at the start of its life beauty."

The group fell quiet for a moment, and Carlos studied them, remembering Marlene's loss, and his own. He could have sworn that Damali visibly cringed as Marlene had spoken. It was as though her hand had mentally reached out to touch his face, but then retreated. Maybe it was just the bitter agony of hearing himself described as a creature of the night that had made him believe such a foolish thing. Maybe it was simply knowing that a mother stood in the room, remembering what her baby was like before it had been turned. Although they were blind to him, he could pull from them, and both seers barraged him with truths that hurt too much to think about. Now all of those emotions crushed in on him. But he could still swear that Damali had reached out in her mind to stop the pain.

"What's on level seven?" Dan murmured.

"The exact opposite of what's in seventh Heaven," Damali said softly, "and we don't even name it in this compound."

"Okay," Rider said on a long breath. "So. If Nuit's gang can use the demon high-speed-line, and won't have traditional aboveground coffins, how do we find them?"

Carlos put his hands behind his back and began to pace to keep from touching Damali. "His spot in New Orleans has a door."

"Been there, seen it, done it, not going back," Rider said emphatically, shaking his head.

"It's light sensitive," Mike added. "Breaks up illusion."

"Thought projection," Carlos replied, and then caught himself as the group stared at him. "The church guy said to bring down the light or let the light shine, some shit like that to dispel the illusion. Truth works the same way—all that religious rhetoric—*the truth shall set you free*. Makes as much sense as the rest of the stuff he said."

Again, he could feel the group relax one by one. Another close call. Damn.

"Nuit has a mansion in Beverly Hills under an assumed name—that's a possibility, and he owns a significant share of the high-rise that the Blood Music offices occupy, and we could place a safe bet that he'll open a channel in each of these five concert locations. If I was a betting man, and believed all the hype some sword-carrying priest told me, then I'd put my money on that as a sure thing."

"So," Damali said, going over to Carlos to touch his arm again, "if time wasn't so tight till the international thing, we could have tried to get invited to perform at one of his major concert locations. That way we could have gripped up and blasted it with light, hit 'em with some serious spoken word of truth, and we would have been able to open up one of his holes—then find the coffin, and stake this bastard. We're already locked in to do your club as a venue, so I don't think we can get to do the big stadium portions at this late juncture. But we know all the locations of where major sections of their concert will be held, so at least we can go back later."

"We only need to take out the head to get to all the second-generation vamps that need to be eliminated, which takes out the thirds, and the fourths, and so on. We can cover all under Nuit with a salvation prayer, and when we take the head of the hydra, the rest of them will perish," Marlene said with a strong voice. "I've gotta do it for Raven."

Carlos didn't say a word. They didn't understand. One had to *individually* name each soul one wanted to claim back. Not to mention, the only reason it seemed that the seconds and below got dusted, had much to do with territorial realignments. If there was a master to step in, those lower levels weren't going anywhere—unless that master wanted to build from the ground up. But that was way too much detail to drop on an already wary group. So, rather than further indict himself, he just nodded. Later, maybe, he'd explain to Damali.

"It's like an implosion bomb, the empire starts collapsing from the inside out until a whole line dies with one stake to the master's heart." Big Mike folded his arms over his chest. "Judged you wrong, Carlos. My bad. Was serious science you dropped."

"It's cool," Carlos said quietly.

Just listening to the way they described the wipeout, he wasn't sure why it tugged at him, but it did. Plus, what that big brother was talking about were fairy tales . . . unless a territorial harvest was turned down—which just didn't happen. And Damali's second touch was still seriously messing with his cool. His equilibrium was off by a long shot. His ten minutes was closing in on him. Marlene was looking at him real strange now, and Damali had come up to him, he could feel a hug pending and that was not the thing for her to do right now. It was time to jet.

"Look, I told you as much as I know, and I know you guys think I'm crazy. I just figured I'd pass on the message. But right now, I need to handle some business in the streets. Hit the lights, and I'm out." He was babbling, and realized that he wasn't making sense. The temperature had kicked up, and that UV border . . . with Damali calling him from deep inside her head. *Oh come on, baby, cut it out.*

She filled his arms and hugged him, closing her eyes as her head found the center of his chest where it had been the night before. He could feel tears inside her heart as it thudded in anxiety against the cavity that held his dead one. She breathed life into him by sheer force of will, her grip tightening as her mind tried to get him to understand.

Magnificent, glorious warmth entered him and radiated out. Didn't she know that she was trying to use her body as a human shield to protect him from outside harm, and yet he was the very harm that she was grasping so tightly against her breasts? But she held him, her eyes siphoning a decision as she looked up, slaying him where he stood, in front of others who would never comprehend. Beautiful vision, they had named her correctly . . . Still believing in him so much—and he couldn't promise not to manifest everything she abhorred.

"I wish you would just stay and be on our side."

"I can't. Baby . . . listen—"

"It's so crazy out there and I keep seeing you hurt bad in my head. Don't leave; please . . . don't go back out into that madness. If a Templar of the Covenant came to you, then it's not too late."

She closed her eyes and tilted her chin up and breathed deeply while shaking her head no, don't go. He raised his chin higher than hers and tried to fight the urge to close his eyes, too, and lost. Her protective squad had every right to just waste him on the spot; he knew it, didn't care. Because at the moment, he couldn't resist breathing in her hair, and there was no force on the planet that could have stopped the tremor that she'd sent down his spine with her hand. He'd take a silver bullet for her—or whatever else they had for him, as long as it put him out of his misery.

"I gotta go," he whispered to her, ignoring the very concerned team in his peripheral vision. They were moving farther and farther away in his mind as her face tilted up toward his again and her lips parted.

"Why, Carlos, has it always been like this? You know you have been dancing on the edge of disaster all your life, and this time, I think you're in too deep. Didn't you see the maps of Hell? Or if you don't believe, then look at what's in the newspapers. Isn't that enough? Where does all this lead?"

He couldn't answer her as a power within Damali—greater than fear, greater than self-preservation, greater than caring what others might say—exuded from her and began seeping into his pores, and it was this thing called righteous conviction. She'd held her ground against him for five years on the point, and yet here he couldn't last five minutes in her arms . . . not even with her team looking anxious and holding weapons. She had him trapped by her spoken words—truth. And he was bound by every other gift she'd been blessed with, and it began unraveling his instinct for survival, right at the foundation level . . . and replaced it with the next one up on the primal rung.

He'd opened his mouth to urge her to let him go, and she'd filled it with her own. Just like that. Right there. No argument. Her brethren were left dumbfounded. The lady that was like her mom stood paralyzed, wringing her hands. It happened so fast, a split-second reflex. Had been a long time coming—but still blew him away.

That's when his inner foundation snapped, discipline

uprooted, logic vanished, and his fingers became tangled in her hair, despite the throats that cleared in the background, while his hand slid down the center of her back, and they'd hit a wall by the door with force, the seal between them unbroken. He had thought he'd crushed her spine, somehow, until she gasped, and that had only made him kiss her harder, swallowing the sound, her desire in his throat, his lungs, sending back his own deep reply, fueling a double-edged hunger which she answered with a hard rake down his back. Right then and there, as her nails scored his flesh, he felt himself lose it. He pulled back when his gums began to rip too fast. He took out the frustration on the cinder block wall next to her. His cover was blown.

"One of you hit the lights and let me get out of here!" He pushed away from her and stalked down the hall, waved his hand, using his power to hold back the sprinkler system, and then a moment later cut their lights. They were taking too long! The building immediately cooled.

Fuck it—it was too late to burst into flames anyway.

CHAPTER SEVEN

"AN IN-YOUR-FACE breach! I don't believe it—we're history!"

Rider was standing on the weapons table raising a crossbow at the vacant doorway. J.L. was freaking out as cold-body alarms suddenly went off, like the hallway sprinklers did—after the fact—after Carlos had released his hold on them and cleared the building. Their lights had gone out and come back up. Shabazz and Big Mike were stomping on flaming maps of Hell like madmen, Marlene was walking in a circle brandishing her stick. Dan had a Glock nine frozen between both hands as he stood near the computers with his mouth open . . . and the only thing Damali could do was gently wipe her lips with the back of her hand, savoring the taste of Carlos as she studied the wall. Time started slowing down.

She closed her eyes and put her fingers in the deep

grooves Carlos's nails had left. The tremors that ran through her were like waves of aftershocks she couldn't control. She didn't care. Unable to move, she glanced toward the holy water sprinkler systems spraying the hall, alarms sounding very distant, the team's voices muffled, and breathed the last trace of Carlos into her—almost following it, she could feel him pull her, and his dilemma was hers, too . . . she could literally smell him. Yes, like her, he was torn to shreds between that rock and a hard place decision. Not just torn, it was much worse than that, this ache. It ripped. Filleted all judgment till she had to catch her balance.

What was everyone babbling about? If they would only shut up, she could hear him! She couldn't regulate her breaths. Her skin was on fire. Her hand covered her neck, and his moan that she'd swallowed sent a new coating of heat inside her belly. He was calling her, still, if they'd only shut up! He was standing across the road on the other side of the border of light, summoning the strength not to break down the door. She could feel him getting stronger. The shudder of need that ran through him quaked her even from that distance away. She closed her eyes and told him the truth—that she wanted to be with him right now more than he could ever know.

His response was immediate. The fantasy carved images of him and her into her brain . . . she could feel each delicious detail as she stood very still. Something in her snapped, and rather than retreat from the forbidden pull, she transmitted full-blast everything she had always wanted with him. *Didn't you know, since way back when, how many nights I nearly lost my mind?* She couldn't help it, unvarnished truth spilled out silently, privately, and the echo in her mind was his burning reply. *If I had known . . . trust me, I would have never let you go. Had I known tonight, I would have carried you past the lights to my lair. Just come to me!*

Oblivious to the chaos around her, she connected beyond the compound perimeter to mentally meet him.

Instinct told her not to, cautioned her not to go there or open up a return response, but she found herself tilting her head, opening herself fully to him. She bit him, and nuzzled him in reply, kissed him hard, and scored him again with her nails. She felt his intense shudder through every cell of her body. He made her crave his entry with such force that her hand reached out to hold on to the wall once more. She felt the rough-texture cinder block, and in her mind she slammed him against it, kissing him harder, wanting to take more of him deeper. *It's all yours, baby . . . just get me out of here, I'm guarded.*

Just as quickly as she'd hurled the thought, something powerful, razor-sharp, scored her throat—it didn't hurt, but shards of light exploded behind her lids and a tremor ripped through her body, morphing into a convulsion. Frustration imploded, sent her next response to him as a dare, a challenge with the image of her room, her in it, and what she'd like him to do, then she bit him harder within the vision. *All night,* her thoughts whispered, *till you fear me more than the sun.*

A howl in the distance fused with his moan, welding his desire to her spinal cord, tearing through her vertebrae, and leaving her breathless. In her mind she could hear her voice cry out like it had its own will, the effect of it making him take her harder—she wasn't forming words, just deep, honest, uninhibited chants of ecstasy . . . harmonic expression, hitting notes way outside of her range—and now he couldn't catch his breath, was begging her not to stop. She smiled, telling him the cold-blooded truth. *Yeah, I hear you, baby, been needing you like this for a very long time.* She'd been trying to explain, but he never would listen.

He put up his hand to the prison glass of invisible distance that separated them, and she met it, raising her palm, spreading her fingers—it left a pang that traveled. The sensation was so raw that she continued to brace herself so she wouldn't fall. With her eyes closed she could literally see him exactly where he was standing in the thicket, washed with moonlight, total energy, shoulders bare, her mark on him, sharing adrenaline, needing to hunt, needing her more, his chest expanding and contracting, breaths were now coming faster, he sensed her locking in to feel him again, to hunt him. His deep, intense eyes said it all, his expression pained like hers. There was only one answer she could give him—*yes*. She could dig it. They needed to stop playing with this!

He'd caught her reply like a hard blow to his jaw, and it made his head snap back. Yeah, he'd heard her response loud and clear. What? Don't play with *him*? Who was playing right now? Then his summons became a command and transformed into an urgent request as he dropped to his knees in the tall grass outside. *Please come to me, come outside, I can't take it, baby.* Her mind wrapped around the fervent message and stroked it as she sent it back. Watching his chest expand, taut with muscle as he battled for oxygen, sweat running down his temples, arms outstretched, the blue light of the moon making every surface of him glisten, his Adam's apple bobbing with each ragged breath that he drew, the answer became so clear. His voice was an insistent refrain for mercy, telling her what she already knew: *Damali, come to me. Now! I need you.*

"I do, too," she said out loud. She started for the door. Whatever her guardians said, she was leaving. She had to. "Turn off the lights," she heard herself say.

Suddenly she was shaken hard. Dazed, Damali looked around. Marlene's grip tightened. A pair of wise eyes held hers; an aging hand touched her damp face, and broke the spell. Damali leaned against the wall and breathed. The need to go after Carlos made tears well up in her eyes as she resisted his call. Her team stood momentarily frozen—she couldn't address that right now. Her goal was too singular; her focus unwavering. The voice in her head was escalating, panicking as her attention divided, telling her: *Baby, don't listen to them—this is about me and you!*

The guardians would just have to back off, and deal with her decision, and let her out of there. Never in her life had her body ached for a man like this. This wasn't a democratic decision, something the group had to vote on—she was out.

And even with Marlene standing squarely before her, she could still feel Carlos losing his mind from the same fire that burned her. Every second of lost momentum to fill his arms—she suffered.

"I've gotta go," she whispered, hoping Marlene would understand.

"Right now, he'll hurt you." Marlene blocked her and her lips began to move quietly.

Slowly, but surely, she could hear the rest of the group speaking in panicked chaos. Only when Damali could push herself away from the wall and stand unassisted, did Marlene move away. Time immediately snapped back and picked up the pace.

There was no way to tell if she'd been locked to him for a few seconds or a half hour. Disoriented, she tried to focus her attention enough to gather conversation. But every now and then a wave of desire would ripple through her, and she would brace herself till it dulled and passed.

"I couldn't even get a shot off," Rider hollered, his crossbow still leveled at nothing. "If I did, I would have got both of them . . . Shit."

"We had a flat-out *weapons room* breach," J.L. was yelling, "right in our own backyard! I can't believe it!"

"A breach? Motherfucker, this was a full-scale invasion!" Big Mike stomped the ashes, which had long been out, and then started beating them with a stake on the floor. "I'm gonna stab that slick bastard, Carlos—watch and see, I'ma blow his ass up—bringing maps of Hell in here to our girl like he was bringing flowers—ain't that some shit, Shabazz?"

"Maaaannn . . . I know some people that know some people that know *some* people—feel me—I'ma have the motherfucker seen. I'ma kill him up good!"

Dan's gun barrel jumped as he continued to point it at the wall. "Look at the freakin' wall!"

The group stared at the five evenly spaced, inch-deep drags down the wall and fell silent.

"Big Mike, no offense, but that's a strong SOB—even you might hafta just blow his ass up. Long distance. Period. Fuck this crossbow." Rider jumped down off the table and shook his head. "We're history. Been fun, gang. I'm going to go get a drink."

"Wait, Rider," Shabazz said, making him stop. "This is

some valuable info, dude. If we have to go up against one made before Rivera, and at the top of the food chain—we just learned a lot about how this predator functions, man. Rivera rolled in on us like he was a goddamned master, brother! Rivera just got made—which means he's either a second- or third-generation vamp. You dig? We just learned how strong they get when a female Neteru . . ." His voice trailed off and he looked away. "We learned a lot. Need *much*-improved weapons. For real, for real."

Silent horror mixed with a violating sense of humiliation fixed Damali's gaze to a piece of crumbled cinder block on the floor. Oh, my God . . . this was the new chant in her skull. Heaven help her, she almost went out there. Two seconds, and it would have been over. The guys ranted on, while she tried to become invisible. If she didn't die of the bite, then she would definitely die of shame. She closed her eyes. Please, God; don't let them have seen anything that had gone through her mind. Oh my God. It was beyond personal; in fact, strike the request to the folks upstairs—even they didn't need to see that. She wrapped her arms around her waist, and pulled in small sips of air.

"You got a point," Rider muttered, oblivious that she had zoned out of whatever they were talking about. "An inch-deep slice into cinder block, times five fingers, done with his bare hands—and waltzed right in our front door, chatted, kissed Damali, and rolled? Blocked our alarm systems, too? Oh, no. This is over the top for me, fellas. We are talking about something that could cross every barrier that we've rigged. Thought I'd seen it all."

"Deep part was," Shabazz said very slowly, "he wanted her so bad you could feel the electricity in the air—it's still cracklin' in here. But he didn't bite her.

That's real strange. You could see it on his face; he was trying to show respect, but lost it when she went to him. But he didn't nick her, that's the thing, or pull her out of here, when he could have. Something's up with that—we need to figure out why, especially before tomorrow night."

"Why didn't you hit the lights, J.L.?" Big Mike stood and drove a stake through the table and snapped it in half, and then cast the remainder across the room.

"I did!" J.L. was at the console, his fingers a blur as he checked and double-checked his failed systems. "What the hell!"

Jose walked into the room and everybody started.

"Shine some light on dude," Rider said, jumping back.

"Yo, y'all, sprinklers is going off and shit, what the—"

"You missed Mardi Gras in here, Jose. It was deep." Rider was walking in a circle as Big Mike blasted their teammate with light and Jose covered his eyes.

Marlene pointed at Mike's stake in the table and on the floor. "Get that light out of Jose's face—it was the adrenaline in Rivera's bloodstream! He blew out all systems, just shut 'em down and walked! Why? Because he's no second generation—he's a *master*. He did it because he'd crossed the threshold, got close to the power sources in here, and close to her. It's like having a top-of-the-line vampire in here on PCP. They flip. You fellas ain't gettin' this, are you?"

"I know," Damali murmured. It was the first thing she'd been able to say since the mayhem broke out.

The room went immediately quiet.

"You all right, girlfriend?" Rider asked quietly. "Like, these lights in here ain't bothering you, or nothin', right?"

Damali didn't have the energy to respond to Rider's

sarcasm. Instead, she wrapped her arms around herself tighter and faced the wall. The sadness in her was lodged so deep within her chest that she couldn't even cry.

"I felt it when he kissed me. His jaw unhinged and his incisors dropped . . . and I could hear him in my head . . . but I wasn't afraid." The rest of what he'd made her feel, she buried deep within herself and just let her breaths continue in small sips of air.

"Oh, baby . . ."

She could feel Marlene's arms wrap around her, and she allowed the hug, but needed to pull away. The maternal touch just didn't mix right with the one she'd just experienced, and oddly, she didn't want the first one to vanish just yet.

"Gentlemen, lock up the compound, repair the equipment, do make yourselves useful—but don't say a word to her right now. Please."

"He's turned, Mar," Damali whispered. "They got him."

When Rider opened his mouth to give Marlene a smart reply, her glare closed it.

"Not a word," Marlene said in a near hiss. "Not a mumblin' word. Her heart's been injured, and it's a mortal wound. C'mon, let's go talk."

Thankful for the extraction and female company that would allow her to grieve, Damali numbly followed Marlene down the hall. Truthfully, she really didn't care what was up anymore. He'd turned. The full monte. And she knew when it had happened. The pictures in the newspaper—it had happened in the woods.

Marlene sat quietly beside her for a long time on the edge of her bed. She didn't touch her, or ask her questions. The two of them just sat.

"I don't even know what to say to you, Mar," Damali murmured after a while.

"You don't have to say a word. I've been there. My lover . . . Raven's father. It cut to the bone when I found out, and I thought I would die. It's a soul wound that never heals."

"Why did he help us? Regardless, what he'd told us was the truth, I could sense it, and so can you . . . that's why I didn't think he was a . . ." She whispered, her voice trailed off as she looked at the window that was now covered by steel. More and more it felt like a prison, not a sanctuary any longer.

"Because . . . he loved you, once, I think. And if he'd wanted to hurt you, he would have, in the hospital—if he turned when we both guess that he did. One day he will, though. We both know that."

It was the last part of what Marlene said that made her cover her face with her palms and lean over so far that the backs of her hands touched her thighs. The wail of despair that came up from inside her was from somewhere so core that even rocking as she released it didn't stop it from ripping at the cloth of who she was. This man that she had prayed for, hoped for, saw the good in and knew could change . . . had the will and the intellect, and had fallen. And not just fallen to the things of the world, like a gun, a lock-down, no, but he'd fallen so deep into the abyss that there was no bringing him back. Yet much of it was his choice.

She'd tried to tell him, a long, long time ago . . . when they'd sat on the beach, when they'd argue street politics . . . when he'd smile and say, "Baby, I got it all under control." But he never would listen, thought life was a game, and it could be played to the bone, but some shit you just didn't fuck with, the dark realm was one of those things, to name a few. Machismo, male drama, he'd rolled out every day dangling by a thread between life and death or worse—half-life. Oblivious, until something deep moved on him, and then it was all over. And she'd seen so many fine brothers, just like him—leaving people to wail and pray after their souls . . . now even that within Carlos was gone.

Although she knew life wasn't fair, was a grown woman, a vampire huntress that they proclaimed had some invincible, powerful, unstoppable vibe within her—and could bring it, in this very private moment of personal defeat—she wished so desperately that it could be fair—just once. What if? Basic reality and life was kicking her ass. Watching a person come so close to making the right choice, and then watching them become too entrenched and afraid to step off from the old and into the new, and then watching them drift back to their old ways like it was a comfortable sweater, and watching, helpless, unable to do a thing about it all when time just decided to run out on them, felt like unparalleled defeat.

And an old sister of her soul, the warrior queen, proud with head high, sat beside her, just rubbing her back and rocking with her, probably crying inside her own heart for those same losses like that to the world. Marlene knew. Now so did she.

Even being a baaad-sister didn't stop this type of shit from hurting. Mar had tried to warn her. Said it wasn't a flesh wound, wasn't nuthin' to play with, couldn't be sewn up with stitches . . . couldn't be set in a splint—but eventually she would have to set it straight to survive, not being able to breathe from the pain. It was a rite of passage—stepping off, leaving the dead in body, mind, and spirit, and moving on. But Heaven hear her cry, this one really hurt.

Bitter sobs wracked Damali, and Marlene petted them up through her bent spine to help her system flush itself of pain. All women knew this magic, the ancient art of healing through touch—the shamans didn't own province over it, this was female power at its best . . . compassion, letting hurt just run its course, till disappointment magnified to screaming wails, but it was the thing that brought back sanity after the storm.

Every loss she'd sustained purged with the tears, and now she knew why Jose was dying from the inside out. There were things worse than death, watching a loved one fall and slip away was one of them, and she cried for every mother, every father, every child, every brother, every sister, every lover, every grandmom, every spouse, every anybody who had to sit and weep and watch and witness their prayers go to hell in a handbasket.

Crazy part was, her spirit hurt so bad that, after a while, she just stepped it out of her body, and watched her whole drama of rocking and crying from a remote place in her mind. That type of decision had to be the brain's safety valve, a thing that happened to people when their sobs got too intense, she imagined. She sat beside herself, helping Marlene, wondering when her well of tears would run dry. Because she didn't go there—had never truly allowed herself to just lose it. So what the fellas had gathered around the door, and for whatever reason, that only made the tears fall harder. Perhaps the worst part of it all was that she didn't even trust herself anymore.

She had quietly loved this man who'd been her knight

in shining armor, had loved this street warrior gone rogue who'd rescued her from foster care—*she had loved him* . . . so much for so long . . . didn't he know that even turned, they still had a bond? She'd known he'd crossed over, way before the kiss—but had lied to herself, hoping. Didn't want to believe her instincts. Wasn't sure which line got crossed in his dark path, general life or something harder. There was just no denying it; she still wanted him, turned and all—regardless of what she might do. Didn't matter if she walked away, like she knew she would. There'd still be the marker for him where the brand landed a long time ago. Some truth was so deep that she couldn't even say it to herself. Seeing him in the shower now made so much sense, his eyes, then eyes she didn't know—both were his, the light and the dark side of the same man—it had been a premonition.

So she cried until she just had to lie down and sleep it off, which was better that way—at least she didn't have to keep telling herself the awful, hard truth.

Marlene shut Damali's bedroom door, walked down the long hall, entered the weapons room where the team gathered, and glanced at Big Mike.

Mike tilted his head to the side and nodded. "She's not stirring, Mar. If you're not picking anything up either, we can talk."

"When are you going to tell her, Mar?" Shabazz asked in a tense voice. "She'll be shark bait on her birthday, and we might not be able to stop it. You just saw what happened."

Jose nodded. "I've been trying to design something for

her ... something that can keep her from even being scratched. When I was knocked out at the hospital, I saw it in my head. Got the idea from the light wands."

Without Jose having to tell him, Big Mike brought over Jose's sketch pad, and he flipped it to the page that held a new pencil drawing.

"Looks like a shark-resistant wetsuit," Rider chuckled.

"It is. Reinforced silver-threaded fabric sealed to a thin layer of Kevlar with fiberoptic threads running through it. Covers her from head to toe, but looks like it's concert worthy ... shows the curves, fits like a glove, but won't let her sustain a bite or a scratch—except in the face ... but she won't let them nick her face. Madame Isis covers her front, and will back the vamps up. Doesn't keep her from broken bones or internally hemorrhaging, though, should one of them really land a hard blow. If she gets bitten in the shark suit, the jaws of a vamp deliver the force of a great white. So she can still get hurt, but at least their virus won't get into her bloodstream."

"By the time her birthday rolls around," Marlene said quietly, "the likelihood that she'll be killed from a bite will diminish. That's not their objective, to kill her."

"Precisely," Shabazz murmured. "But, the suit is extra insurance, and is da bomb, Jose."

Jose smiled and dropped his open book on the table, even that small effort appearing to have drained him.

"How long does the suit battery last?" J.L. murmured, glancing at the fatigue in Jose and getting up to look at the design closer. "This is awesome, brother."

"Thanks," Jose breathed in a rasp. "Wanted to still do my part. The battery lasts about four to five minutes, but if she gets surrounded, or they take her into a dark lair, she'll leave 'em smoking."

"That makes me feel a little better, after what we just saw." Rider sighed.

Big Mike smiled. His fingers drummed the edge of the table serving a funky beat, trying to lift spirits, and working hard to calm his own frayed nerves. "Jose, man, we're connected. You did your thing. This is the first time in weeks I started feeling my rhythm again. Words are pouring into my head."

"Let spirit speak," Jose said with a weak chuckle. "We all need a positive word after what y'all told me."

Big Mike grinned. "We gonna have Damali's back, and blow that concert wide open."

Mike waited for the others to nod in agreement. The group needed a confidence boost. They couldn't just go down like that, and Damali needed something to give her new energy, too. Her sobs had broken him up. He'd never heard her sound so sad. As an audio sensor, he knew her crying would stay with him for weeks, maybe longer. The only thing he could do was to replace it with something else. Perhaps that's why he loved his music so much. It cleared his head, blocked things he didn't want to hear. He glanced at his team. They smiled. They understood. They were his family. He started a beat on the table again. Words came to his mind, chased away Damali's tears, and rushed past his lips.

"She leaves 'em smokin'—on fire . . . baby got da high beams for any desire. She's hot, burning with emotion— passion so deep, she ain't jokin' . . . she ain't playin'— will beatcha down. Betta step off, or hit da ground . . . She's running wit da big dogs, stay on the porch—this ain't no game, baby's got da torch, *'cause*—"

"She leaves 'em smokin'—so watch your back! Nighttime's coming when creatures attack. She'll drop a body,

dead or alive. She works da rhythms like a nine to five."
Rider laughed, making J.L. join in.

"Go, Jose, get your energy on, my brother," Big Mike
teased.

"Ain't scared of nothin'," Jose said with a smile, picking up from J.L., "ain't worried 'bout a thing. Baby's
locked and loaded when she steps in the ring. The wise
will tell you, ya betta step off, *'cause*—"

"She leaves 'em smokin'," Rider repeated. "All day
and all night. Li'l sis ain't bluffin', check her stance.
Fights fire wit fire, the only chance. Baby owns the high
road, ain't kickin' it low—"

"Will huntcha down, so act like you know." Big Mike
picked up the tempo and winked at Shabazz. "I ain't lying, just ask her friends. Hunts like a panther to the very
end . . ."

Satisfied that his medicine was working, Mike laughed
hard. Even Dan was tapping out an offbeat rhythm,
though his spastic ass couldn't rap. Everyone on the team
laughed except Marlene and Shabazz as the others kept
the beat, and each freestyled a verse, adding to it, releasing tension.

"Smoking." Rider jumped in again. "Watch your back.
Baby got da high beams, don't lose track."

"Smokin'—hear what I'm sayin'? Smokin', I ain't lying, *smoking*, leaves 'em cryin' and dyin', smokin' like a
house on fire, smoking, and your only chance, betta—"

"Enough!" Marlene yelled, bringing an end to beat-
box revelry. "You guys think this is a joke?"

"Naw, Mar, it's a great concert entrance song to go
with her new weapon outfit. Screw it," Rider said with a
nonchalant chuckle. "If we gotta do this, then let's do
this. You wanted new music, we're all fucked up, every-

body's head is twisted, and we have to get a show right before tomorrow. But, *no,* we don't think this is a joke. Trust me."

Jose shrugged. "Look, we're in the business, we're all artists—need new material to come out *smokin'.*"

J.L., Big Mike, and Rider looked at him and laughed, and started beating on the edge of the weapons table in percussion harmony again.

"You're awful quiet, brother Shabazz," Rider said with a sheepish grin as Marlene stormed from the room.

"Do you know what the significance is of the seventh trait that you guard? The last thing that will happen to our girl on her birthday?"

The team fell silent and gave Shabazz their attention, casting nervous glances between them. Finally Big Mike shrugged. "She'll get stronger, the hunts more dangerous, she'll have to ward off a master who might be sniffing around her, like Carlos, getting hopeful—we're just having a little fun while there's still something to laugh about. You and Mar need to chill."

"On her birthday she becomes a vessel for both sides. Every seven years a female Neteru can either produce another vampire huntress, if made with a guardian—or her womb can sustain a vamp. Her antibodies against vampirism don't kick in until her birthday, didn't you all hear Marlene before?"

Shabazz finally nodded when satisfied that their expressions were suitably terror-stricken enough to produce reverence for the issue.

"Shit," Rider whispered. "Like, man, I thought we were guarding her coming into some Zen-master-slayer state or some shit like that, I mean for real for real, so I wasn't really all that concerned, given our girl was getting stronger and shit, you understand the shit I'm saying, right? Holy shit!"

"You're babbling, Rider. And watch your mouth, like Marlene has been telling us for years."

"Fucking A, I'm babbling, Shabazz. Damn."

"You think Marlene would be all freaked out just because Damali is getting stronger, and might get a rush from killing a vamp? Stronger, able to draw them out of a lair—that would be a good thing, right? Think about it. It's the vulnerability that Marlene is rightfully trippin' about."

"This is too deep." Jose slumped over the table, leaning on his elbows, and shook his head.

"Profound is a better word," J.L. murmured. "Like the bullshit of legends."

"I'm still not following," Big Mike said, ignoring the group's dismissive glances of impatience.

"What the *hell* is not to understand, Mike?" Rider was walking around swinging his arms wildly. "One of them does her, and it's all over."

"No," Mike said, shaking his head. "Why now? At twenty-one? Talk to me, Shabazz. She's like my baby sister."

"It has to be a guardian that sires, or—"

"Aw, shit, we do not need that level of complexity in the group, dude." Rider began circling again. "Aw, man, aw, man, aw, man . . ."

"Relax. She has one hundred and forty-four thousand guardians on the planet to choose from. Remember? Nobody in here needs to worry or get their hopes up—the chemistry would have already been identified by now, and he would have been led to her . . . and he hasn't been.

Correction, he was, but that's history. His choice. Shit happens."

"That's cool," Rider said woefully. "Okay. I can live with that. But, just for the record, anybody know who Prince Charming was?"

J.L. slapped the back of Rider's head. "Listen and learn so we can do our job, man. It was supposed to be Rivera, but he chose the dark path."

"Ow, fine. But don't try to act like nobody else never thought about it."

Big Mike grabbed Rider by the shoulders and sat him down hard on a stool. "Shut. Up. Rider. And listen."

"Vampires can't breed . . . their seed is dead, and in the females, the wombs are dead, right? Nothing ages on or in them beyond the age of the host's death." J.L. rubbed his face with both palms and then began walking. "They make more of them through the bite. Period. I don't understand how a Neteru—"

"You're right, except if a Neteru willingly gives vampire seed a host—that's *the choice*. Not whether or not we sent a hunting party to New Orleans, or to do the concert. Please!"

Now Shabazz was pacing. "On her birthday, our Neteru's sensory patterns will lock in and her body is going to change again to add the seventh sense—which uses all senses, and she's going to have to fight a craving that's as bad as the vampire thirst. She'll be in here like a damned junkie. On the positive side, if a guardian gets to her, or the initial fertility season passes, then we have no issue, and we're cool for another seven years. But, if the vamps get to her, then we've got a serious problem. There's a one-month window when her system, for lack of a better term, reboots—old antibodies flush, she's susceptible to the vampire viral infection, and it takes a month for her to be restored."

"They'll try to turn her, right? So we just have to be on red alert during this first one-month vulnerability window?"

"No, Jose. **Were** it just that simple. If she gets bitten *and impregnated* before her full tolerance is set, which is synergistic to the vampires' romantic proclivities—biting is an integral part of their passion process, all lusts are involved when they . . . You get my drift. She'll only have enough antibodies in her system to keep *her* from turning, but not anything else in her body. It takes a month from her birthday, till her next cycle—her first full cycle after her birthday, for her to be in the clear. Are you hearing me?"

"Talk to us, Shabazz," Rider murmured. "If there aren't enough antibodies flooding her system when it's virally infected and she conceives, the cells will first ensure the host, the Neteru, is not endangered? The antibodies won't help the fetus if there aren't enough in Damali's body to assist both, is what you're saying? *Everything* about the way she was created is meant to keep her fighting?"

Shabazz let his breath out hard. "Yeah, Rider. Plus, if she gets into a telepathy lock with a master, she'll *want* him to bite her, like a dare almost, to draw him to her. It's her hunting instinct. But the possible backfire is, within the lock, she'll also be feeling his urges as strongly as if they were her own. She can transmit, and she can receive and feel him—has to in order to locate him. The right guardian will be led to her the same way one day. That's the double-edged sword of the telepathy gift, though. A master vamp will be trembling to bite her. She'll feel that primal desire, too. But she won't have a natural fear of it, because instinctively she knows it can't hurt her—and that's her vulnerability—the fearlessness. It'll kick in all of her hunting instincts, which are a real turn-on for the male vamps. Gentlemen, consider the reality of a huntress that was genuinely afraid of a vampire bite; do you think that human entity could repeatedly go into harm's way where she could be bitten?"

"No," Big Mike murmured, his expression one of stricken awe.

"Right," Shabazz said evenly. "And trust me, fellas, if she has that master vamp in a mind lock to be able to track him, her instinctive goal will be to always get to his lair to terminate him, but she will transmit her first flash of competing desires back to him—and he'll oblige. It's a dance. She lures him, he steps to her, she pulls him harder until he can't stand it and stops hiding from her. Then, it's on. Whoever is stronger, wins. Think back on those roiling emotions of your first time, huh?"

Big Mike walked in an agitated circle and began wringing his hands. "Oh, brother, brother, brother. That's some powerful feelin's. You ain't scared of your momma, your daddy . . . will walk through fire to—"

"Mike, why do you think me and Mar have been a nervous wreck? She's grown in human terms, but in Neteru physiology . . . Damn. Look, problem is, poor baby girl does *not* understand that she could host a daywalker. Her protective instincts would never allow us to drive a stake into an infant vamp when it comes into the world bearing fangs . . . then they'll have her. She would flee to be with them, if for no other reason than to protect it. She'd hide in their lairs, they would provide her hybrid child food, amnesty, teach it their ways, and it would be daywalker royalty. And our Neteru would willingly agree, once humans attempted to eliminate it, because what mother doesn't want her child to belong to a society that accepts and protects it and gives it opportunity to thrive?"

"Basic instinct," Jose whispered, his tense gaze fixed on Shabazz.

"We thought Mar just didn't want her to go to New Orleans because she'd try to rush a master's lair when she was too young, before she was strong enough to hang. Didn't know they could do something like that to her." Mike scratched his bald head and looked away.

"Damn . . ." Dan whispered. "This whole experience is so freakin' deep . . ."

"You ain't seen nothin' yet," Rider said, giving Dan a disgusted glance. "She's just vulnerable for this first time out, though, right, Shabazz?" He searched Shabazz's face for confirmation, growing more alarmed as he talked. "I mean, after this one, then she's cool, right? Can handle herself . . . like Marlene said?"

"My brother, Lord have mercy," Shabazz sighed. "While that may be true, if they get to her on any of these ripening cycles, they'd take very good care of the huntress queen in the den. She'd be the only productive female in the line that could keep siring more daywalkers—because the master male vamp would risk his very existence to protect his empire builder . . . which means she'd definitely become his woman. We'd lose her from our topside family for good."

"Damn, Shabazz," J.L. whispered. "Imagine, a Neteru, with mother instincts and warrior capacity, thinking she was protecting the ultimate innocent—one that she'll be telepathically connected to from the moment life sparks.

Brothers, a normal human female gets superhuman strength when her young are imperiled. Women have lifted cars up to get their babies out from under a wheel. Wanna do that times ten, and go for a Neteru's child? And we just witnessed what the potential daddy can do."

"Now we are on the same page," Shabazz breathed out slowly. "Worst part is, if one of us does get to that vamp progeny, assuming that we even could . . . her spirit would wither. She'd never forgive the forces of light. She'd lose hope, faith, love, and she'd die."

"So, this seventh sense thing all boils down to . . . basic, natural . . . Wait. You mean to tell me that—"

"Don't even say it, Rider. Yeah. We're guarding her honor on her first time out, so to speak."

Silence held the group hostage. For a moment the team just passed stricken glances between them.

Shabazz walked away from the table. "You saw her morph in the street, yourself, Rider. You couldn't stop her. The second-generation female vamp set it off and marked a territory—that vamp wasn't telling Damali she couldn't have DeJesus, the body in the morgue. She was talking about the head vamp, Nuit. Raven was made by that master vamp. *She was a second generation,* and probably Nuit's present, but sterile, queen. . . . Raven was strong—was made by two guardians, and gave off heavy DNA-generated scent when she was abducted and then bitten. But she wasn't the real McCoy." Shabazz rolled his shoulders and closed his eyes.

"Wait," Big Mike boomed. "I thought you said it had to be a choice? Raven got abducted, and that wasn't a choice. Plus, she got bitten. Probably not her choice either."

"They'll look for a Neteru before it comes of age and will try to inculcate that huntress into the vamp lifestyle, topside, by placing the poor kid within human vamp-helper reach. When it's time, by then, a Neteru will comply of his or her own free will—after years of brainwashing by darkness. But when they grabbed Raven, and sniffed her out—once they were sure she was a decoy, she was history. Marlene never really came to terms with that."

"We need to go easy on our boss lady," Big Mike murmured, and received a nod from Shabazz. "She's on our side, too. Don't get it twisted. All this is deep, y'all. I don't know how Marlene dealt with it."

Shabazz nodded. "Right about now, since the ranks seem to be closing in, Nuit can probably pick up Damali's scent, or has a conduit to pick up her trail—that's why Mar was guarding so hard lately. She had reason. And now we know which new second-level vamp he'll use as a conduit."

Rider and Jose looked at each other. J.L. whistled and then sighed. Mike just shook his head. Dan's shoulders slumped. They all spoke as one. "Carlos."

"No wonder baby girl was crying so bad . . ." Again, Mike just shook his head. "Damn. She loved that fool, anybody could tell. Even I prayed he'd get his shit together, straighten up his act and fly right. Now, can't nobody cure them blues. Her hope just died. She's gotta ride this one out by herself."

Rider blew out a long breath of frustration. "Been there. Wished she didn't have to ever visit living Hell. Ain't love grand."

"That's where Mar was coming from," Shabazz murmured.

"Let's stay on the point," Rider said with a weary tone. "We'll know when the exact ripening hits, right?

Twenty-four hours of a birthday window is a lot of hours where anything could happen." Rider's gaze tore between the members of the group and finally settled on Shabazz. "I mean, after all, the team trackers . . . We should be able to—"

"No, unless you're her 'destined pair' guardian, even you guys with the noses won't be able to pick it up when the exact ripening starts."

"All right," Rider finally said. "Then, what happens if we just hook li'l sis up on a blind date, with a *regular* guy—one that we *all* approve of, one that *she* likes . . . and then go from there? Huh? That sounds like a plan."

"He wouldn't make it through the night."

"What? She'd rip his throat out or something?"

Rider looked at Shabazz, his eyes wide, but the others had the same expressions on their faces as well.

"No. The male master vamp would. He'll hunt for her till he finds her, and will fight to the death to claim her. Even if her first season passes, he will look for her until she's no longer reproductive. He's got a one-month window every seven years. She's twenty-one, that means we keep vigil for at least another twenty-five years."

"Twenty-five years?" Rider was walking again, shaking his head and mumbling to himself.

"Jesus," Big Mike whispered on a long breath. "What about her having other normal kids and—"

"She can have them, if she picks a regular guy . . . But the vamp that desires her'll perpetually hunt her—and the worst part is, he won't stop till he finds her. That's why we have to put this sucker down, permanently, so the girl can have a life."

Shabazz walked around his teammates, becoming frustrated at their lack of comprehension. "Don't you guys get it? Don't you read? Don't you know that the female being was always sacred? A strong woman, Neteru or not, can birth leaders of nations! She can be poor, of the humblest means, but her energy, her beliefs, her prayers, her values—what she teaches those that come from her can change history. The dark side is breaking our backs up here, compromising the strength of so many possible vessels of change!"

Shabazz held out his hands to the group, his words becoming more impassioned as he spoke. He walked in a circle, his arms sweeping now, as he tried to impart what he'd learned, what he'd witnessed.

"Gentlemen . . . from the great queens of the Nubian Empire—from Eve herself . . . she was made as the second prototype, after man, when the Heavens perfected the model. The human female was smarter, had more of the gifts from On High of mercy, compassion, understanding, love, trust, healing . . . wasn't warlike, and could produce life."

He opened up his arms and let his head fall back. "That's why she graced temples and was called a goddess—and then when evil had compromised enough men and gained a foothold, they erased her from the scriptures, from temple walls, and made her a second-class citizen—a breeder. *That was not the divine design.* But unprotected, no longer cherished, stripped of resources, the earth gift called woman becomes vulnerable—as do her children. More women and children reside in this poverty as the darkness hunts generation-by-generation, nation-by-nation, to find a weak vessel. They've been looking for a female Neteru for thousands of years."

Big Mike stood wide-legged, taking a battle stance. "The dark side knows this, the light weeps because of the abuse, and a woman's womb holds the possibility of nations, like our brother said—this is a serious matter. Shabazz, you are telling this group that for the first time in three millennia, since you and I did Kemet together, like Marlene's past life visions told us, we have a female Neteru to protect, and she could go down by a male vamp? Never. Not on my watch!"

"So, now, we're battling some horny Drac—"

"No, Rider!" Shabazz cut in, disgusted. "It's not just that. Damali is the *first* Neteru born that crosses two millennia since they made them. She's the strongest one the light has ever crafted! In the past, only a few females were made, because they posed such a risk—but after eons of the male vampire hunters being unable to protect a normal human female carrying a Neteru heir, and with this era being so in need of one, they cast Damali as the millennium bridge. The Covenant came to Marlene and gave her the word, that's how we located the girl after she was lost in the system for a while. We are to form a ring of protection: Damali in the middle, our core, then us, then the Covenant guards our back, the warrior angels guard theirs. This is serious, man!"

"Shabazz," Big Mike murmured, "she's young enough to have an heir every seven years, if I'm hearing you right, and that means four to five possible Neterus in her lifetime, flooding the new millennium."

Shabazz nodded and looked away, breathing hard. "For the Armageddon, brother. Damali, plus five, and the ultimate One who will come again from On High as a lion not a lamb—is six warriors of light, plus the Son, the Seventh, and ultimate warrior to lead during the twenty-first century."

"And, if she's compromised," J.L. whispered, "it can

be six on the wrong side of the war, plus their top gun, who will remain nameless in this compound."

"I understand now why Marlene wants her to be able to discern who to be with, man. She's got five windows of vulnerability. Plus, she can't lose her confidence her first time out in this huntress transition, 'cause we might not always be here, or there may be a time when our guard post is breached like it was tonight, and she has to know how to pick up a false reading on her own." Jose blew out a long, weary whistle. "Marlene must be spazzing out."

"Daywalkers, Shabazz . . . what exactly can those things do, man? All joking aside," Rider whispered. "What are we up against if our girl makes the wrong choice?"

"Neteru crossed with vampire makes a daywalker. Topside chaos. All the dark powers of vampires, and all the evil, able to live on anything we eat, their preference for blood notwithstanding—with no daylight shield to protect us. Plus, we just learned that Nuit's line, the ones seeking Damali, are hybrid—mixed with revenge demons. I can't even fathom what that combo unleashed up here will do, brother."

"Shit . . ." Rider spat on the cement floor again, wiped his mouth with the back of his hand, and sat with a thud.

"Damn, man, we told you—give that nasty habit a rest." Jose pushed himself up and began looking at the table, rubbing his chin. "Daywalkers. If a brother and a sister were made, and connected . . . ?"

"A brother and a sister? You have got to be kidding me! That's, that's eeeiiilll—yuck! God, we've gotta drive a few stakes very soon, fellas, 'cause the mating habits of vamps know no bounds!" Rider was on his feet again, and this time Big Mike didn't shove him to sit down.

"That's the deal," Shabazz sighed.

"Why do you think there were rumors about this being done in some of the lines within the old human dynasties? Hell, it happened in some of the Indian empires, and amongst the Incas, Mayans . . . the Romans and Egyptians, Europeans, Chinese—name an empire," J.L. said in a weary tone. "They all wanted to keep the bloodlines intact, in the family. Cousins, siblings—it was all about maintaining absolute power . . . topsiders trying to break this Rubik's Cube of DNA code, and a lot of the rulers from the vampire-human traitor ranks, empire leaders, have been trying to break this code since the dawn of time for the vamps. They were close to it, but didn't have both Neteru or guardian halves."

"Fucking genetic engineering the old-fashioned way." Rider sat again on his own accord and just simply shook his head.

"If it goes down, it'll be the beginning of the end of life as we know it," Shabazz whispered. "The daywalkers have eternal life, can reproduce indefinitely, as well as bite and transform a normal vamp to give it a viral immunity to sunlight . . . they can essentially bring all their nations topside, and the reigning sibling king and queen would be at the very top of the food chain, but still beholden to their father—the master vamp in their bloodline. Power unlimited. That's what Nuit is after, and he's about to open the gates of Hell on Damali's birthday, on five continents. Do you understand?"

"They've already found our Neteru, dude," J.L. said, his words stilling the group. "Probably figured out who she was when Raven saw Damali, in state, and—"

"Another reason why Marlene didn't want Damali out in the street battling so close to the time. What I can't figure out is why this compound isn't under siege as we speak? Rivera already got close and confirmed any hunch the vamps might have had."

"While we've got good security, J.L.—thanks to you, now we're sitting ducks. Before we were safe, because not even the phone company had an address, everything routed to the bogus location, and then switched here. We had the P.O. box; we drove in a different way each time. We've never sustained a breach. But they came right through our door. My question is, what, aside from UV light and our lockdown at the moment, is keeping them from trying to get in again?"

"Don't lose faith," Big Mike warned, his focus on Shabazz. "Beyond all technology stuff, that's our secret weapon. Faith. That's the first and last ring of defense—prayers."

"It's the alpha and the omega, buddy," Rider agreed, picking at the edge of the table as he spoke.

"You know, now that I think about it, it wouldn't have been to Raven's advantage to unseat her own reign," Shabazz said, trying to calm himself and restore confidence to the team. "The planetary alignment told the vamps, just like us, that a Neteru is on the earth, and that her time is near—but the planets never say where. Not to mention, we have every holy order in vigilant watch prepared for battle, knowing the time is near. Something went down. If Damali is so valuable, Raven wouldn't have tried to off her. Nuit wouldn't tolerate that. And, Rivera showed up in here and didn't attempt an abduction. Hmmm . . ."

"Problem is that at present, a lot of energy from the side of light is getting squandered while we duke it out topside with general-purpose chaos, instead of doing what the vamps just did—coming together and doing this thing united." J.L. raked his fingers through his hair and looked out the window.

"I know, J.L. We're losing good warriors daily who have been manipulated and compromised by the politics." The reality made Big Mike search out a stool and sit down heavily. "Doesn't make sense."

"True dat," Shabazz said in a far-off tone. "The head vamp has been searching for her in the chaos which covers his tracks, and the trail to find our hidden Neteru had to have led him to the one guardian, gone bad, that could have gotten close enough to her . . . that guardian would be in her head, she in his head . . . the chemicals connect at the soul level. I don't think that thing between them has ever been broken, plus, he's a born tracker, courageous fighter, master strategist."

"Don't tell me," Rider sighed. "Carlos was definitely her destined-pair guardian? For real?" Rider shook his head. "Now I'm done. Just stick a fork in me."

Shabazz's voice became very, very quiet and he put his head down on the table as he finished his thought. "Until we all just sat here and talked it out, I just didn't want to deal with it. That's the link. Raven just got in the way for the second time. But there's a sure-fire vulnerability that our Neteru has, beyond all these other transitional issues, and they found it."

The team glanced around and only Jose was brave enough to say what they all had known for a long time.

"Carlos."

Shabazz nodded. "He took the fallout, and the poor bastard didn't even know it. Just like in our camp, they turned vamps all around him to keep an eye on him—so close to Damali's time. The vamps wouldn't even trust human helpers to stay with him and on the Neteru's trail. It was too important. That's why they've come for our folks, too. They knew he was the one—because Carlos spotted her years ago, and had the instinct to protect her . . . even he didn't comprehend why she was so important to him. If she'd gone with Rivera and entered the drug life, she would have been so susceptible to the forces of darkness, and they thought they had her—then we got her away from him, and therefore away from them . . . but the link, oh, fellow guardian brothers . . . damn it all . . . the link between them was never severed." Shabazz swallowed hard with his eyes closed, and he breathed through his nose with his head still down.

"Carlos still has the Neteru scent from when Damali first mildly cycled seven years ago—he didn't even know it. He never touched her, because she said no." Shabazz sat up, glanced at the door, and flexed his fists. "I would have felt it if he did. But he had the scent—tracker, par excellent. Makes sense. He came from good people, was surrounded by prayers, women of faith, made a good warrior from the streets, but he walked from the light into the dark for power, money, material gain, and got marked. The dark simply picked up on her scent from him— 'cause *she's in Rivera's head*, man, like a life raft—and she instinctively knows she is, and won't let him drown— they're linked in spirit, even though she wouldn't go along with his program then, and I pray she won't now. But they've been in a spiritual tug-of-war to pull each other to their respective sides, paths, *for years*. What else can I say?"

"Deep," Rider murmured. "You can feel shit like that, brother?"

Shabazz dismissed him with a hard glance and spoke

to the rest of the team, straightening himself up and giving Rider his back.

"Free choice, their paths were being separated by choice, then. She went light, he went dark . . . and with every negative transaction, Rivera came closer to the lower-realm provinces. She was still a kid, and didn't have the trinity number on her—twenty-one—so her trail wasn't as strong. That original scent held by someone sliding deeper into the negative side of the choice gray zone brought them to him," Shabazz whispered, "and Rivera is the only one that can deliver her to them. She trusts him. We saw that tonight. He could get her to relent . . . they need his head to get inside of her head. You dig? Now drop it. This upsets me too much, and I can't talk about it anymore, like Mar can't."

"We gotta talk about this, Shabazz," Big Mike said patiently. "The fellas need to know the deal." He looked at the team. "Why do you think Marlene is always on us to guard our words? Words are formed by thoughts; when spoken, they vibrate and cause tone, tone sends vibrations to the realms. I'm an audio guy, I know. Words are a manifestation of thoughts—you must think it, before you can do it or speak it, hence Damali's gift. The spoken word. Thought is energy. Energy, like electricity, travels, astral travels, is airborne—and J.L., you ain't got enough security to lock that down."

"That's why Rivera being in her head is so dangerous. He's a thought." Shabazz pushed himself up from the table and yet spoke quietly toward it, looking at no one. "The Prince of Darkness is prince of the airwaves, and all his legions down below can mess with thought. That's why one's mind is the beginning or end of all things, must be guarded—can't let any and everything assail the psyche. Everything is corrupted at the thought level first. That's what the dark side enters first to break a spirit—it's the mind, then that directs the body, and the spirit is history. Get it. Dig it. Never forget it. They are coming for our Neteru's head to get to her body and spirit. Okay?"

"Oh, shit . . . if they've picked up some of my thoughts over the past few months—might as well hook up a black box to my skull and call it adult cable." Rider wiped his palms over his face. "I liked it when I was drunk, and foolish, and an irresponsibly free man. This is for the birds. *This* is living on the edge—not what I was doing before."

Jose chuckled. "You can always go back and do it alone, fighting lower-realm demons solo, dude. Remember Arizona?"

"Jose—"

Mike stood, walked to the door, and listened hard, which stilled the argument brewing between Jose and Rider. "Wrap it up, fellas."

"But wait, Mike," Dan protested, his eyes still wide since the time he'd been stalked by Raven. "Carlos guarded me! You guys said he was supposed to be guardian material, but made a choice. If he was bad, then—"

"Damali's link, before he turned vampire, was to what good was still left inside him. All of us have a light side and a dark side, that's the yin and yang principle, the ancient ones knew. So, even though she stepped away from Rivera and his drug life, a part of her always wondered, *what if* the light can prevail. That's not just the way of a Neteru—that's the way of a woman. Period. That's what gives women strength to raise children, the divine aspect of forgiveness."

When no one spoke, Shabazz gave Dan a piercing

look. It was not one of contempt, but one that was sent to convey the seriousness of what he was telling Dan.

"'Cause I did time," Shabazz murmured. "I watched a lot of sisters keep coming to the glass for brothers who were put away for a long sentence, or for terrible things . . . and I could feel them all hoping for the same outcome—'What if he changed?' It was the saddest thing in the world to witness . . . even sadder was, if those men dug deep, they actually could have changed. Dark claimed them first, though. That's the margin of error— you just never know what free human will is gonna do. Even the angels don't know. Made me philosophical."

"Can't we just keep her here until this situation passes?"

"No! Then it's not a choice, it's just circumstance, logistics—her soul has to decide. She has to let the choice wash over her, feel the intensity of a dark pull and *know* that she is in full control of her impulses, or she'll forever second-guess herself. That moment of hesitation in battle, or when faced with a vampire seduction or second-guessing when in a demon zone, could cost Damali her life. I'm done with this subject!"

"Wrap it up, gentlemen. Mar is on the move and about to come into the hall."

Shabazz held up his hand to Rider, Jose, J.L., and Dan who still had more questions as Big Mike motioned for them to quickly drop the subject, backing up Shabazz's earlier request.

CHAPTER EIGHT

BLOOD FROM the faucet couldn't run fast enough, and when the tank had drained, he'd ripped the plumbing out and sent it crashing against the wall. The rack of bottled elixir of life was soon also gone, and he stood before the marble butcher-block island in the middle of the lair, holding himself up on outstretched arms, heaving in air from the exertion of the sudden gorge. The worst of it all was that he was still hungry. There wasn't enough adrenaline in the tap or in the bottles, wasn't enough fight-or-flight hormone left in the concentration. It had aged, wasn't fresh, wasn't potent. The substitute was okay for an old don who didn't still have the hunt in him, but not for a twenty-three-year-old master! His nails dug into the marble. Tonight, after what he'd just been through, he had to eat. Now.

The noise behind him didn't make Carlos start, just growl. Bring it on. He needed a good fight . . . a bloodletting. He wasn't afraid of anything at the moment, especially not Nuit.

Carlos turned slowly; if Nuit touched him he'd die.

"Whew . . ." Nuit said quietly, his expression awed as he rounded the butcher block, and Carlos squared off on him.

But Nuit's tone wasn't threatening; it was oddly reverent . . . if the word could even apply. Carlos watched him, his snarl becoming a deeper growl coming from inside his chest.

"If I didn't know better," Nuit said, thoroughly appraising Carlos, "I would swear you were a master. There is not even a flicker of deference or fear in your eyes. The Neteru drug has that effect?"

"If you touch me, reach out to wipe a drop of sweat off my brow, you'll draw back a nub. I promise you."

Fully transformed, a low rumble came up from Carlos's insides to back up the threat. Nuit smiled, and simply inhaled.

"My friend, I don't need to. The air is so filled with her scent, I'm getting a contact high just standing in your kitchen." Nuit shook his head as the sensation riddled him. "We sent a tracker—to watch your back—and they followed you to her sanctuary."

Carlos pushed away from the center island. His gaze narrowed. He was prepared to attack, but needed to know Damali's condition. That was the thin thread of reason that held him like a frail choker chain.

"Talk to me!" A section of the island fell away, made instant rubble under Carlos's fist.

"Relax. We followed you because we thought you were in imminent danger, and you're valuable—you're family."

Carlos kept his gaze steady while Nuit circled, watching him become intoxicated and aroused by the air around him. The hair stood up on Carlos's arms, and he could not retract his incisors now if his life depended on it. Even sharing her scent with another male was intolerable at this point.

"We have had men stationed beyond the light border at her compound to protect her from incursion by the Vampire Council since last night," Nuit explained. "We are on the same side, you and I. Remember that. And our trackers saw you arrive, call her right through the barriers— just breach the compound and slice through significant prayer lines."

Nuit opened his arms in total disbelief. "It was the most awesome piece of undercover work, and demonstration of pure lust—power—I have ever experienced. We all stood out there, watching you—awed."

Carlos relaxed his stance a bit, the imminent danger to Damali making him garner reason. Logic thrust past the battling emotions he could barely contain.

"You seduced her to tell a team of guardians to literally turn off the lights? We were all out there just dumbfounded, looking at each other. We watched you through the gates once you'd breached their prayer lines. You stood before *guardians*, Rivera! Walked past holy water. Goddamned brilliant execution! Then gave them some ruse that flamed up in their hands, and took her—right in front of them, scored their wall, slammed their generators, and walked out." Nuit shook his head. "I'm still trembling from just watching you work."

Nuit put shaking hands behind his back. "There's not enough territory to mark for something like this. My remaining dons stood with me; I called them. They had to see it for themselves. I brought them away from a feeding fest just to witness the incomprehensible. A brand-new second? Then you rent the air with her scent and howled till it ran through us all. She had you under the moon, on your knees with your arms outstretched begging her for mercy, setting off coyotes in the hills. It was unbelievable. And she came to you, snapped a cord to them, and said *yes*. We heard her broadcast it. We all just looked at each other—stunned. The connection was so hot, Rivera, she sent you back an evolutionary step into practically a level-five werewolf transformation!"

Nuit paced like a caged animal as he spoke. Total, gripping fury mixed with vampiric humiliation tore at Carlos till he had to send his line of vision to a point on the wall. But then he had to pull his glance to anything but a wall. This violation might as well have been a wooden stake, and that, with the frustration of his request being heard and blocked was almost more than he could bear. If she only knew. Only a very thin thread of his objective remained . . . *play the game*. This time for her. So, he said nothing, and took the abuse, thinking of how many different ways one could kill the same entity.

"Carlos, we were in a state of pure awe," Nuit ranted on, too excited to be anything but oblivious to Carlos's reaction. "You looked back at her compound and *through UV*—called her again—even after they knew what you were, *and she came to you?* Her guardians had to hold her to keep her from your call . . . Neteru—a vampire huntress? Unheard of! Absolutely unheard of . . . I told them, we were watching a new generation of vampire being evolved, and I had made it—invented it, and it was born within my line. Maybe the demon alliance is creating a new mutation within us, a stronger hybrid when there's a serious vengeance issue at hand? Who knows?"

Nuit threw his head back and laughed, totally high,

and then looked at Carlos. "I am so proud. What do you want? Name it . . . except her."

"I want the Jamaican's territory. Tonight. I want access to the third-level demon tunnels so I can travel at high speeds. I like New Orleans."

"I don't know . . ." Nuit hesitated.

Carlos wiped his brow and walked over to Nuit, and slapped his face with a lightning strike of force. "Think about it." Then he stalked back to a neutral position. "I want access, and power, and the package I'm delivering is worth it. I told you. Don't fuck with me, I'm in—and she's got no natural defense against me."

The blow made Nuit hold on to the edge of the sink for balance as the drug of Damali's scent washed his system and convulsed him. It took him a moment to recover, and he pulled himself up slowly. He gazed at Carlos with open admiration. "It's *pure* Neteru. She's never been with anyone . . . at her human age? Undiluted. There's undiluted first-love passion in it . . . not illusion. Even transformed, she had no fear of you—and the woman wanted you back as much as you wanted her? Do you know how powerful that is? How *rare*?"

Stunned, Nuit touched his cheek where Carlos's hand had landed. "The Jamaican and I have had a long-standing relationship as far back as the sugar plantation export days in the islands, but business is business. That was then, this is now. His territory comes under new leadership tonight."

Carlos nodded, trying to collect himself. "What's the plan at the concert? How do I bring her in? My cover is blown with her people. My personal defenses are down— I'm compromised. I don't know if my system can handle another invasion . . . I'm too near the border . . . real close to the edge of taking a stake to try to get to her. Almost got torched tonight." There was so much truth in what he said that Carlos could feel his hands shake.

Nuit noticed it, too. The credibility of the emotion couldn't be denied, and it sent a shudder through Nuit as it passed through Carlos's system and connected them for a moment. Nuit exhaled sharply and hissed.

"Damn, the drug is so pure—we'll have to help you detox before you try to go in tomorrow night. You've got one-hundred-percent, totally open Neteru in your nose. Carlos, listen to me. You have to clean your palate; you must eat and get something to bring you down—you're too high right now. You're not in full control, and that's never good. You'll OD, and I'll have to kill you. You're shaking like a junkie."

Carlos closed his eyes. "I know," he admitted, not able to deny it. "It was the kiss, and the telepathy spar. Don't ask me to go back in without a plan. One more hit like that, and you will definitely have to kill me. The Vampire Council already sent a sniffer for me—put one of their marked human helpers on the force . . . had to do him tonight."

"We saw it in the newspapers. Heard about it in the alleys—but couldn't get to the innocent cop, because he'd said a prayer out there in the darkness. The light got in our way, so we had to let him go. But we do know they're setting you up to have your assets taken. No matter. We'll give you everything in the Jamaican and Dominican's zones. Your human territory was small anyway, by comparison. We have plenty of people in the media to reverse the story to give it a better spin to your advantage."

"What's the plan?" Carlos steadied himself, trying to keep his focus, his bearings. He had to know.

"I have compromised human stars. The Stars D'Nuit—

the stars of the night. They get a few drops from my veins each night . . . the human digestive system is so fragile and their food is so easy to taint. It keeps them connected, but not fully turned . . . they have to cast an image, but they also have to do my work."

Carlos nodded, listening intently as he watched Nuit lower his guard.

"Each one will keep the crowds mesmerized at the five concert stadiums in Russia, China, Australia, South America, and terminating in North America—L.A. If you noticed," Nuit added with a smile, "it forms a giant pentagram, with Africa, the Middle East, Europe, and much of the Caribbean in the middle. The lines mark our borders. Everything in the center of it is the sixth jewel—the territory."

"I thought you wanted her to perform in my club, not the stadium." The change of venue without him knowing about it first made Carlos wary, and it was going to be a stretch to convince Damali of anything now. Surely by this point, like him, she was coming down, and coming to her senses—which meant she'd be on full alert against him.

"No," Nuit replied after a moment. "Your club is too small, and I want her surrounded in a venue where hundreds of my forces can contain her. I want to be sure that we have no problems. You'll have to get her to agree to broadcast live from the larger venue."

Carlos nodded; she had just talked about wanting to do that. Interesting.

"I think I can do that. I'll tell her to think of the possibilities—how many more people she can reach . . . and I'll tell her I'm taking her to meet the man who can give her access to the world—on stage and on film. From there, you gotta work it."

Nuit chuckled. "If you can get her to me, and manipulate the dark side of her desires to the surface, maybe using the lure of fame, or her ego . . . then trust me, Carlos, I will, as you say, 'work it to the bone.'"

It took everything in Carlos not to react. He just offered a nod.

"Souls of the audiences will be open, receiving, willing, and hypnotized with our vibration from the under realm, and per your promise, and excellent seduction, we'll bring Damali out last. The crown jewel that will crown all of our territory. When she comes onto the stage, she will have the audience on their feet, and at the end of her act, we are going to open up a cavern right there onstage and pull her in. The audience will think it's the best theater they have ever witnessed. Magic. Poof, she's gone. Our time, she'll be gone an hour; topside, it will seem like only a few minutes. Be right by her side when the silence comes. All I need is an hour, Carlos. You understand?"

Carlos became very, very still. He studied Nuit. "In the tunnels," he murmured. "What am I supposed to do, then? I don't have demon passage yet."

"Be her escort, we'll handle getting you amnesty. I made you, so once the Amanthras pick up your hybrid scent, it will be done. The tunnels are getting dangerous, though, even for the demons on our side to guard. They, too, have factions you should be aware of. Their old councils don't want to embrace the change—but, like us, they have rogues we've been able to develop alliances with. However, the Vampire Council has sent up a hit squad, too. Their messengers are half demon, half vampire, loyal hybrids made to allow the council members to feed from the topside without risk of a nightly surfacing . . . and these messengers know the tunnels well. We lost a few good seconds tonight in foreign territories—that's why I ordered your full protection from all my topside forces."

"But, once I'm in the tunnels . . ."

"Non-sanctioned vampires move slower because of their full vampire density—unlike hybrids that have the lighter demon portion of their structure, an attribute of the higher realms above the sixth. But remember, if any master or several seconds get into a demon zone, we are formidable. Don't worry. We have every one of the demon traits of evolution from levels one down: invisibility of the ghosts, kinetic energy of poltergeists, possession capacity, shape-shifting, we have the wolf hunt in us like our once-removed brethren, werewolves—but by the time one has evolved to level six, we have more power—which is why we grace the top of the food chain. Jealousy is rampant amongst the levels; all aspire to be where we are."

"If I'm hearing you right, we're denser and move slower in the tunnels, and can be surrounded easily by faster-moving entities underground." Carlos studied Nuit hard. "Why didn't you show me around down there before, so I wouldn't have a problem?"

Nuit smiled. "We had a trust issue then." His smile broadened to offer a hint of fang. "I gave you a glimpse of my topside assets, but would never show any new turn the route to my lair . . . however, I think we've resolved those issues between us."

Carlos nodded. "I don't like moving slower than anything else down there, especially carrying precious cargo."

"Alas. That, I have no power over. It's supernatural law. What I can give you is the slight speed advantage through my amnesty pact with the demons on level three."

Again, Carlos nodded. "A human female might slow me down, because of her density, which will put her at further risk. Her body heat alone will draw demons and vampires from both sides like sharks. The blood scent will create a feeding frenzy."

Nuit walked in a circle. "That has been a concern for me, too. You'll have to carry her in your arms for delivery speed and safety. If she goes willingly, she won't struggle and further slow you down. Bring her quickly to New Orleans. I'll have a bridal chamber waiting."

The two stared at each other for a long time. It came down to this: once Damali left the stage, it was on. He and Nuit would battle in his own lair.

Nuit studied him through narrowed eyes. "You're so distracted right now that I cannot get a telepathy lock on you, although I don't need that power to know the thought of carrying her gives you pause. Your energy and attention will be scattered as you travel at high velocity . . . carrying cargo that you can't feed on for nearly forty-five seconds, and carrying a woman that you want so badly you'll be ready to risk your own neck. It gives me pause, too. But while you're traveling I can't meet you, even halfway. The tunnels don't work like that. We'd pass each other or collide in the vampire band we've been allowed to travel within. If I snatch her onstage, she will fight me, slow me down, and the demons we have no alliance with will only register a slow-moving object—and attack us both. Even some of our allies might mistake the heat tracer the Neteru gives off in their zones. She must travel without a struggle. I'm going to have to bank on your knowledge of what I'll do to you if anything goes wrong. We do understand each other, *n'cest pas?"*

"Once I deposit her, then what?" Carlos held Nuit's line of vision in a deadlock. "If I'm jonesin' that bad, I'll need something to bring me down fast."

"I'll have a brand-new second generation laid at your feet, three if you want. New Orleans's best cuts, I promise. Or, just three innocents that are still warm? You'll be weakened, disoriented, and shaking—and will need to immediately feed. Don't forget yourself and try to fight me for her. That won't be a good idea, because I assure you, I will have just fed to be ready for her . . . and will not be suffering from any such weaknesses."

The threat was an honest one. Carlos smiled. Cool. He'd been warned. Information was power. But he also knew Nuit would be alone. Even he wouldn't risk having a couple of seconds or thirds in his lair with a Neteru dropped off at his door—her scent was potent enough to make his own guards try to take him down.

Obviously accepting Carlos's smile as agreement, Nuit relaxed again. "Good. We understand each other. After you come down at bit, you can go topside, and enjoy New Orleans nightlife, pick out a lair. Listen to some jazz and relax. Or, go to London, Romania; take a transatlantic transport to see some of our most glorious historic sights. Amuse yourself."

Carlos shrugged. "Tell me more about this *Raise the Dead* ceremony at midnight."

Nuit smiled. "Brilliant, isn't it? With that many humans focusing on a dark prayer at the same time, all around the world, it will open every lair portal that has been sealed since my line has been in existence . . . When the Vampire Council incarcerated me, I was unable to protect my provinces then, and every time the humans have killed one of us in-coffin, it has sealed an important lair. But, with those old gates opened again, we will come up through safe passages—with our demon allies, feed at will, and turn two hundred and fifty thousand innocents at once. While the concert feeding takes place to resurrect and strengthen those once lost on my line, I will take my bride—and bring her back out onstage when I'm done with her—to face the new world."

"Two hundred and fifty thousand of us will wipe out the food resources within months, maybe a year."

"But our daywalker gestation doesn't take a year. One bite, vampire-to-vampire, even from an infant, and the virus spreads. It's exponential. My inner circle will receive it first, and we'll spread it quickly to the deserving members of the Minion colonies. Like I told you before, I have six hundred and sixty-six in mine . . . the other masters in other regions . . . alas. Like everything else, he who has the gold makes the rules. Power is supreme."

"The existing council?" Carlos began pacing again.

"They become second-class citizens. Total wipeout. They will not be given access to topside, the new virus, or other food sources. Those we don't kill will eventually starve—then the demons can have total access to their sixth realm. We won't need levels one through six, we'll all be topside. That was the truce, and the demons loved the concept."

"Sounds like a plan," Carlos said in an even tone. Made sense for Nuit not to have clued him in until he'd proven inner-circle-level loyalty. This was a crazy-major expansion. A total coup. He hated to admit that it was brilliant. But there was a flaw to Nuit's plan and his mind raced to seize the advantage.

In their lust for power, the rogue demons hadn't considered the environmental effect. With no more humans topside, and daywalkers too strong to possess . . . where would demons multiply, populate, and eat? They had been very short-sighted. Stupid, for short-term gain. Their old councils were correct. What good were the levels, if there was no one to haunt, to make scream, to devour?

Carlos remained quiet, watching Nuit watch him. He wondered what ruse Nuit had used? Wondered if Nuit never told the Amanthra rogues how deadly a daywalker infant bite would be, or how short a vampire gestation of this kind would be?

That made sense, since there was no archive of history about this in the demon realms—only a council throne member would have such knowledge. They'd probably assumed they had more time or had been promised to be made ultimately into vampires—something Nuit would surely renege on. Carlos almost laughed. He'd have to figure out a way to make contact for a discussion—so he could move slowly without attack. A messenger might be the answer, and a messenger had brought him the maps.

"Nuit, I'm tired," Carlos finally said to break the deadlock. "I'm not thinking clearly and I need to feed, so, if you'll excuse me . . ."

"I brought dinner." Nuit laughed. "After what you just went through, the loyalty you just demonstrated—you think I wouldn't honor you? I do have manners, and a hell of a lot of respect for you now. I am a Southern gentleman of high breeding, after all. There are just some things that are done a certain way, with protocol. Period."

To Carlos's horror, upon Nuit's signal he watched a young girl come down the steps of the lair escorted by his best friend, Juan, his brother, Alejandro, his cousin, Julio, and his homeboy, Miguel. Sadness impaled him as he watched his family. They were in too deep, just like him. He'd never wanted it this way, and he knew there was only one way to release them from the bondage . . . the Vampire Council had sanctioned the hit. They'd just never know the real reason why.

"Yo, *hombre!*" Julio shouted across the expanse.

"Yo!" His other two friends yelled in unison.

"Stranger, *que pasa!* Man, why didn't you tell us? This is da bomb! You livin' large. We been eating and partying all night!" Alejandro said laughing, going to Carlos for the first embrace, the young girl in tow.

When Alejandro hugged Carlos, he caught a whiff of Damali and his eyes slid closed in ecstasy. Nuit laughed. His brother held him back at arm's length and gazed at him with amazement.

"Oh, shit!" Alejandro whispered in awe. He held out his fist and gave Carlos a pound. "Daaaayum! See, I told you Carlos was always the one. He got da *product of life*! You descended, bro, moving *serious* weight, now. Doing good for yourself, as always. Damn."

Carlos kept his gaze steady on the young girl. She was high. Couldn't have been more than fourteen. She was in a den—a freakin' lair with a hungry pack, and had no idea and no way out.

"Look. She's too young. My brother can tell you, I never did them that young. Send her back to her mother. Now."

Nuit simply chuckled. "That's because you've never tried a young one before. Tastes like veal—still tender, succulent, no gristle or tough skin. Smell her, Rivera. The fattened calf, for everything you've brought to the family. I know it will never compare to the offering you just had to walk away from, but, on me. Please. *Por favor,*" Nuit crooned seductively, "unless you want an infant?" He smiled. "Perhaps next time?"

"Send her back to her mother, man," Carlos said as his brother smiled, fully fanged.

"Who do you think gave her to Nuit for us?" Alejandro chuckled.

"Her mother pushed her into my limousine, said make her a star . . . didn't care as long as she got paid." Nuit shrugged. "You know how many parents come to me of their own free will and just hand over fresh kill for a few dollars?"

"I'll do her," Alejandro said anxiously, retracting his fangs before the girl saw them. "Carlos was always a picky eater," he added, joking and glimpsing the girl from a side-glance.

The young girl giggled and swayed, totally blitzed. "All a'y'all is fine. Damn. The money don't hurt neither. You can take turns. I can hang. My momma don't care, as long as I break her off a li'l something something when I get made into a star—so, shit, why should I care? Don't nobody care about me, but me."

Carlos looked into the child's eyes and saw Damali. Heard the same words—*Don't nobody care about me, but me.* And he remembered shaking his head then, and telling her that wasn't true. He did. He swore he'd protect her . . . wouldn't let harm come her way . . . remembered how she'd turned her chin up to him, trying to be brave and not cry, when she'd realized she was homeless, on the run, with nowhere to go—street wolves and danger had been all around her, and his baby had thought she could hang . . . he didn't violate her, she was just an innocent scared kid, and he'd put her under his gun, and protection, till Marlene and the guardians stole her away.

"Do you pray?" Carlos asked the child, hoping she did, so maybe when she died tonight her soul could rest in peace.

"You playin', right?" The child laughed. "Pulleeease. I ain't no church girl."

Carlos closed his eyes.

"She ain't tainted, *hombre*. Won't leave no aftertaste." Alejandro glanced at Nuit. "My brother is used to da butter. Don't consume anything but the best. Never did, dats why he's *da man*."

"I know." Nuit sighed. "Once you acquire a taste for the best—"

"Send her home—or somewhere else, but—"

"See, he's a punk," the child said boldly, motioning to Carlos and sauntering over to Nuit, who just smiled.

"No, *cheri*. You just aren't woman enough for him. Pity." Nuit shook his head. "Delightful, isn't she? Has attitude. May even put up a small struggle. She will be afraid, I promise you . . . That helps, *oui?* The adrenaline kick off of this one might help you come down, Rivera. Consider it."

"My name ain't no Sherri, and your boy is too a punk," she taunted, rolling her eyes at Carlos, outraged that he didn't want her.

"He's got Neteru in his nose, bitch," Alejandro corrected. "He don't want you after that."

The girl laughed and leaned on Nuit, stroking his chest. "I'll try Neteru. How you do it—what's it like? Ecstasy?"

"Oh, to be sure, but better," Nuit murmured low in

his throat. "You've never experienced anything like it. Trust me."

"Send her home, y'all," Carlos said, his tone low. "Not this one. Not here."

"Yeah, he didn't even want Juanita when we was all living da life," Juan said in a wistful tone. "Told my crazy sister to do my boy right—but you know, Nita was raised in the Church . . . prob'ly couldn't hang wit what my boy was throwing down. But, like, I was trying to keep it all in the family and shit, so our money would all be linked in the squad."

"You've got a wise group of associates," Nuit murmured, stroking the girl's nylon wig, his gaze roving over her scantily clad body. "We used to do that in the old days—arrange the marriages, keep the power lines uninterrupted. Your daughter marries my son, we all stay wealthy, you know how it was done."

Juan chuckled. "Yeah, but my sister was always in Carlos's face about leaving all that behind, so she got dumped. Prob'ly why he's squeamish about this one, too. I was gonna go home and turn Nita myself for him, and my mom, maybe hook my little brother up in the business, but they had this bullshit prayer line around them."

"Yeah, mine, too," Alejandro sighed. "Forget them. That was then, this is now."

Relief for the living dueled with the remorse that ate away at Carlos as he heard his life being reviewed, but not understood. They just didn't know. Nita had been pushed away for her own protection, so she could maybe have a normal life; even while he was alive he'd made that decision.

"This one ain't worth it," Carlos said, keeping his tone even, casual. He neared the girl, sniffed her, and turned up his nose and shook his head while his insides churned from the tension.

"I'm worth it. I can show you." The girl laughed. The vampires around her did, too.

Carlos just stared at the young girl for a moment, then walked away. Juanita had said the same thing, always jealous of Damali. She'd also taunted him to take her just to prove a point, a misguided offering of her body to make her appear more grown, more woman, and more willing than Damali . . . until he'd succumbed to the temptation after Damali left—but it hadn't changed a thing. That was before he knew better; you couldn't replace what you really wanted. Carlos glanced at the girl. *Baby, sometimes you ought to let sleeping dogs lie . . . sometimes when the big, bad wolf says he'll pass, you oughta let him. You might wanna be in the mix, but some company you don't wanna keep.* This child simply didn't understand. Neither had Juanita. Carlos sighed.

In those days, it wasn't a fatal bite; it was a fatal life he was trying to save an innocent from. At his side, Nita could have gone down one day in a war, and like Damali's, her heart was too soft to come to an end like that. He'd stepped away from both for the same reasons . . . albeit Damali was the one that he had never been able to forget. The other women after her had all been living vampires, like Raven, only with a heartbeat. This young girl was about to fall in the latter category, if she didn't die.

But he didn't have time to think about all that right now. The child had to get out of there. Carlos couldn't take his eyes off the girl who was getting ready to be dinner for a devil. Maybe if he could get them to hand her over, he could tell them he wanted her for all himself, and could take her to safe—

"We gonna eat, or what?" Alejandro smiled. "I'm hungry as a motherfucker, and Carlos is just playing with his food . . . walking around, sniffing it, trying to decide, and just looking at it hard."

"Can't wait for the concert, though, man," Miguel said, laughing and pounding his fists all around. "We'll be off the hook—we're doing the tunnels wit'chu to watch your back—like old times, while you make that important delivery—might have to drop a few bodies . . . then, we gonna eat, drink, and be merry. Cool? You got our high-speed passes, right, Nuit?"

"Yes," Nuit said with a level gaze on Carlos. "Your inner circle will escort you to my door, then immediately take you back with them. We'll reconvene onstage shortly thereafter. I'll have food for all of you left at my front door. Like I told your brethren, eat it in New Orleans, or wherever, just help Carlos feed and get the drug out of his system so we can all stay brethren without incident."

"I feel you. Cool," Alejandro replied in a cheerful tone. "We got his back—won't let him do nothing stupid while high, then everything stays smooth."

His posse nodded. His homeboys gave Alejandro a fist pound and nodded in Carlos's direction.

"Exactly," Nuit murmured. "No unfortunate incidents."

Carlos's gaze shot between his homeboys, his brother, Nuit, and the girl. He was definitely in Hell. Everything dark that he'd ever done was now topside, twisted, but similar in so many ways to the predator life he'd lived. Nuit was skillful, his brother and his friends were thirds and an easy takedown, but hard for a weakened second to combat alone . . . and Nuit was banking on that moment of hesitation that he knew would be there—dead or alive, it was always hard to do family, so he'd sent them to escort him to New Orleans. Just to be on the safe side. Wise move. A variable he hadn't considered while under the influence. His bad.

In the split second of contemplation while he thought about his family, Carlos watched without being able to get in between the child and Nuit's body fast enough.

Nuit's hands had gone to the sides of her babylike face, and she'd closed her eyes and leaned up to offer her mouth with a smile. It happened so quickly that time seemed to stop and restart in slow motion. Carlos simultaneously reached for the girl, opened his mouth, and yelled, "No!" unable to get her before Nuit's massive jaw had unhinged while the child's lids were down. In a flash, Nuit's mouth had covered her nose, her lips, and had blown out a powerful breath. Her lungs expanded, Carlos came to a skidding halt as her ribs cracked, blood ran out her ears, then emptied the sockets that had once contained her pretty, doe eyes. Her back had exploded, sending quivering meat and organs flying, and then Nuit calmly dropped her at his feet.

"What's the problem?" Nuit asked with annoyance. "I gave you first shot, you declined."

"Yo, Carlos," Juan said with concern, "you can't expect a man to pull up from a kill like that, right in the middle, past the point of no return." His gaze nervously shot between Carlos and Nuit.

"Was your timing, *hombre*," Miguel said, shaking his head, then shrugging. "We can bring you something else after we eat. Let it go. Nuit gave you first shot—you slow, you blow."

"Well, shit, don't just stand there," Alejandro argued while laughing. "Have a rib." His brother closed his eyes and moaned when he put bits of flesh into his mouth. "The meat is just falling off the bones, Carlos. Try it— damn, this is tender."

The fact that saliva was building in his mouth as he watched them eat upset Carlos so badly he had to get away from the scent.

"I'm going to take a walk," Carlos muttered. A child was dead in his house. She would never go home. In the blink of an eye, she'd been murdered. There was no home for her to go to, anyway, but the concept just fucked with him. He had to get air.

"Rivera, I am sorry," Nuit said, putting a hand on Carlos's shoulder as he passed him. He then looked at the confused group. "A hunt interrupted twice in one night, give him some space—he's ready to kill."

"Can we crash here, Carlos?" his brother called behind him. "This place is all that."

"Only if you stay here and let me go to the Jamaican's—alone!"

"I'll go take out the Jamaican right now while you hunt," Nuit offered. "Let them remain here, and feed. You go hunt, and gather yourself. By the time you get back, the Jamaican will be ash. Fair exchange is no robbery. Some ethics must be adhered to, or there'd be no honor left in the land." Nuit sighed and nonchalantly wiped the gore off his suit.

"Peace. It's all good." Alejandro shrugged and glanced at his feeding friends who also just shrugged.

"Whatever," Carlos snarled and bound up the steps.

Nuit licked his fingers. "He's coming down—Neteru's wearing off, and he's going to be nasty and hard to live with for a while, until he eats and regains his composure."

Alejandro nodded. "Whatchu gonna do? You know my brother has always been stubborn. You offered him a Valium," he said, glancing at the remains of the girl on the floor. "But he didn't want one."

Nuit shook his head and sighed. "My stubborn son . . . what will I do with Carlos?"

The group murmured agreement, snarled, and continued to eat.

"Sanctuary! In the name of God, we claim sanctuary, Neteru! The Covenant needs your protection! Open the doors!"

"We got hot body readings—two," J.L. yelled across the room. "On camera and incoming!"

The guardians all stared at the screen as a sword-bearing knight of Templar in a blue Catholic priest's robe huddled against the compound door with a Moslem cleric. Both were yelling, brandishing weapons, and looking behind them as though something invisible, but horrible, was chasing them.

Marlene gasped. "Open up fast, and let them in!"

Rider swore hard as he paced between the monitors and weapons table. Shabazz, Big Mike, and Dan got to their feet as well.

"It's like a revolving door tonight," Shabazz muttered. "But they're human, let 'em in out of the dark."

Big Mike picked up a cannon. "Get Damali, Mar. This is deep."

Within moments, the huge metal doors unlocked as J.L. worked the control panel, and the terrified men rushed through it. UV lights flooded the hall and their boots splashed through the receding puddles that had been caused by the sprinkler system.

The team waited for them at the end of the hall, both sides still waving weapons.

"Hold up!" Shabazz yelled as they neared the entrance to the equipment room. "Damali's been through enough tonight. She doesn't need any additional drama, and ain't throwing down in no battles that aren't hers. You need to know that up front, so state your business."

"We need to get word to the Neteru. An important message from On High."

"Stand down," Marlene ordered, "and let them in."

No words were exchanged as the motley team quickly advanced into the weapons room. They were dirty, ragged, looked like they'd been in a serious battle. Both of them were breathing hard. The guardian team glanced at each other in confusion. Damali ran down the hall, hearing the commotion, and came to a halt, her eyes widening in surprise. She stepped forward and looked at the one dressed in royal blue who wore a cross.

Immediately the man before her dropped to one knee and turned his sword to point down, the hilt facing the ceiling. The other man followed suit, their heads bowed in deference. She stood there, shocked, not knowing what to make of it.

"I am a knight of Templar, and Asula is of the Moorish order. There are twelve of us total, and we all form the Covenant. We pledge our allegiance from all sectors. Neteru, it is an honor that we never thought we'd achieve. Bless you."

"A Templar knight?" Marlene whispered, then blew out a long breath. "Oh, y'all, this is big. Trust me. These guys usually don't do house calls—only visions."

Dumbstruck, Damali glanced around at her team. Shabazz shrugged, Marlene stood wide-eyed, even Rider looked perplexed. Everyone in her group simply stared.

"Uh, gentlemen," Damali began slowly. "Ummm . . . well, first, stand up."

Damali stood back as the men before her slowly stood, looking at each other for approval to do so.

"I don't quite understand," she said slowly.

"The fallen have begun amassing forces tonight," the man in blue said. "Your compound was surrounded, just outside of the line of light." He used his sword to point toward the windows as he continued to explain.

"We kept hidden in the foliage around the dwelling inside the ring of light. Then, mysteriously, the lights went out for a few seconds."

The guardian team cast a glance at Damali, who cleared her throat.

"Yeah, well, we had an issue . . . uh, go ahead. I'll explain later."

"Yes, we knew of this issue, and that is why we were here. But many creatures immediately drew to the darkness. Thankfully, they were wary of the perimeter, and it kept them at bay. We waited," the man in blue said, still trying to catch his breath. "Then we realized there had been a breach of the fortress when the lights went out again, and the dark entity that had been inside your compound sanctuary fled. But we couldn't tell which entity it was." He looked at Damali hard. "Neteru, were you harmed?"

"No," Rider said casually, "just had her mind blown for a minute there, but our girl regrouped."

"Shut up, Rider," Marlene snapped.

"Praise Allah," the Moor said, relaxing his hold on his machete.

"Good. Praise the Almighty," the blue knight added, letting his breath out hard. Relief visibly washed through the two warriors. "Then it went deep into the woods across the road—we didn't give chase because there were too many of them. But we could hear his howl for miles. We weren't sure if it was wounded, or if it was gathering more forces. So we prepared to battle within the perimeter of your lights." The knight looked at Damali squarely. "If we are to die, so be it. We do so with honor. It is a privilege!"

"The bastard wasn't wounded, per se," Rider quipped. "But she did get him in the heart. Homeboy was in agony when he left here, that's—"

"Rider! Watch your mouth in front of clergy, for starters. And we can do without the comic relief," Damali snapped. "Let the man continue." She folded her arms and tried to steady her breathing. She could only pray that these guys didn't have a seer in their group. She was still struggling to bring her thoughts under control.

"He attacked you . . . You got him in the heart?" the knight asked, looking at his brethren, confused. "But it didn't die?" He cast another glance around at the other armed cleric. "If you drove a stake, or the Isis, and it was able to still move, then we're dealing with something now, that . . . I understand now why the warrior angels told us to stay by your side. To answer your call. They said you wailed in abject defeat, and that we had a Neteru down . . . slowly losing hope, faith . . . maybe even love. They left us, didn't even disperse the demon line—just said, 'Have faith.' The dark line retreated as soon as the one maimed stopped howling. We waited until we thought it was safe to approach your door. Oh, Neteru, but we were obviously too late."

The Covenant members hung their heads, their weapons held in relaxed grips as they stared at the floor.

"The angels heard me cry?" Damali then covered her mouth and closed her eyes. This could not be happening.

"Always, Neteru. Your tears are diamonds. Your heart holds light. Your words are a beacon. Your thoughts have power. They heard it all. They sent us, but we're too late."

"Can we just stop beating around the bush with these guys?" Rider asked as he walked around in an agitated circle. "Everybody always says, 'Rider, shut up.' But I think this is one time that a straight without a chaser approach is called for. Geeze Louise."

Marlene nodded. "For once, I agree with Rider."

Rider opened his mouth and then shut it, and raked his fingers through his hair. "Gee, Mar . . . now I don't know what to say."

"Damali let it in here, because she trusted it—it wasn't her fault," Big Mike said in his deep, soft voice.

"He had us all going for a moment, and even duped us with phony maps of Hell. Can you believe it?" Shabazz said, the anger clear in his tone. "We all dropped our guard, so Damali isn't at fault . . . silver-tongued bast— I mean, devil."

"That she trusted him, like that, had our poor sister in tears," Jose said, shaking his head. "She deserved better."

"Wait!" the knight said. Both Covenant soldiers

seemed to revive as they passed excited glances between each other. "You say he brought you maps?"

"Yeah, but they burned," Damali said quietly, her gaze going to the window as she turned toward it. Having the light shine upon her most private weakness made her feel too open, too vulnerable, and it was still so tender a wound. "It was only an illusion."

"You said that the Neteru had injured it, had struck it in the heart?"

"Yeah," Rider said on a long breath. "The guy had a thing for her—*before* he was turned—and crossed the threshold on *her* invitation." He gave Damali a sideways glance. "Then he gave us the maps, explained all this bizarre stuff about Hell . . . am I allowed to say that word in front of you guys?"

The knight nodded with impatience. "Just speak, man! All of our sensory capacities are overloaded after our encounters with the beasts."

Rider looked at the group with a sheepish expression while Damali walked farther away, her arms wrapped around herself.

"Okay. So, we were all reading the phony maps, and he kept looking at her like he'd eat her alive—and we *now know* that *he will*—so we were on guard because something was fishy. Then Damali went to him, hugged him, and, I don't know how to describe it." Rider raked his fingers though his hair again while walking and shaking his head. "She kissed the sonofa . . . she kissed him," Rider sighed, checking himself, "and he snapped."

Damali's team nodded as Rider opened his arms, using his hands to talk.

"It was like, wild. He grabbed her, laid one on her like

I have never seen a man kiss a woman in my life, the maps burst into flames, our alarm system went into a frenzy, she was crushed against the wall—trying to scratch him to get him off of her—then he took a chunk out of the wall with his claws!" Rider pointed to the wall where five grooves remained as evidence. Satisfied when all heads turned and then looked at him again, he pressed on.

"The girl was in shock, I tell you. She couldn't breathe and the SOB hit the lights so he could get out, passed our sprinklers, which initially wouldn't respond. J.L. was going nuts at the panel, trying to get our shields back up. It happened so fast, not one of us could get a shot off. Then Marlene took her—because he howled and poor Damali had this dazed look on her face like she might go to him. With me and Shabazz and Mike holding her, I thought we were going to have to put her down. But thank God, she came to her senses." Rider was breathing hard and his voice became quieter as he took a breath to deliver the last part of what he'd witnessed. "Then, we heard her sobbing . . . I never want to hear her cry like that again. I'll kill whatever tries to take our baby sister there."

All of the members of Damali's team nodded their silent agreement with Rider.

"That's our baby," Big Mike said in a low, but forceful tone. "The only reason we know she got him was that his shirt had a big hole in it over his chest—when she got that in, who knows? There was so much chaos."

To everyone's surprise however, the knight and the Moor were smiling. They each blew out sighs of relief and began slapping each other on the back. Damali looked around at them, turning slowly, just as confused as her team by their sudden jubilation.

"Forgive me, fellas," Rider carefully asked, taking his

time, "but we just got our butts kicked, got breached, and had a Neteru almost go down. This does not seem to be Miller time, if you ask me."

"She got him." The knight laughed joyously. "Right in the heart."

"Did you hear what Rider said?" Shabazz boomed. "He walked through a holy water barrier—held our sprinklers back. He had a hole in his shirt, but not in his chest! Maps of the demon realms burned under our lights, and our systems went down, twice!"

The foreign squad kept chuckling, and Damali's team stood tense, waiting for them to explain.

"That was our marked man. Had to be Rivera." The knight glanced at his comrade for confirmation. "There were two master vampires out there, hence our alarm. But the one we're protecting got into the compound, and exited safely."

"Carlos Rivera?" Damali walked closer to them.

"Get outta here," Marlene whispered. "The Covenant is protecting vamps these days?" Marlene weaved a bit and leaned against the weapons table for support. "Now I've heard everything."

"Yes. He's a possible double agent. Delivered the maps as we requested—and didn't deliver a death bite . . . when . . . uh . . . how can I say this delicately, Neteru? . . . uh . . . it was very difficult for him not to." The knight swallowed away a smile and looked down at the ashes on the floor. "Those were the maps?"

"Yeah," Damali said quietly, watching the knight and his partner hard.

"Then we reconstruct from memory."

"Not before you tell me about Carlos," she said in a distant, quiet tone.

Again the entire group went still.

"We are not at liberty to fully disclose—"

"What happened to him?" she yelled, rushing forward. "You do not get maps, we do not continue to talk, unless I get some answers. I have walked out on blind faith, time and time again . . . and yes, I have hit a personal wall where I need just a little hope, just a small sign, something to help me deal. Now talk."

Marlene let her breath out hard when the knight glanced at her for support. "I've already called on the warrior angels with constant prayers. They aren't getting in the middle of it because of the choice factor."

"That's what they told us as well," the Moor said with a sigh.

"Okay. But about Rivera . . . ?" Damali said, not letting the knight off the hook.

"He was marked by the darkness," the knight replied in a slow, steady voice. "They manipulated him to full rage and pain, in the way they'd killed his family—but his lifestyle was setting him up to be turned anyway."

Damali nodded. "I always told him that, but he wouldn't listen to me." Her voice was sad, no longer charged with impatience. She studied her hands.

"A master vampire, Fallon Nuit, bit him—but he immediately turned. That doesn't happen. It usually takes three days. But not only did he immediately turn, but turned master, which also violates supernatural laws."

"You mean a master vampire just waltzed in here and kissed our girl?" Rider slapped his head and walked away. "Marlene said he was, but me and the fellas were like, nah. If he was a master, this conversation now would be moot."

"But he didn't bite her?" Marlene glanced at the nervous team. "Or us?"

The knight shook his head. "At first, when he fell and came back so strong, we thought it was because the darkness in Rivera's heart was so powerful. But then we came to know that the Vampire Council had breached supernatural law, and made him. They have a division in philosophy, are at war amongst themselves—which means they aren't unified, and that presents an opportunity for light to seep in where it is dark."

"So, okay—the council made him? And—"

"Damali," Rider interrupted, "I'm still stuck on the fact that they have a council . . . like senators, and shit?"

"Rider, shut up," Shabazz urged. "Your language. Let the man speak."

"Because the law was violated, that gave us three days to match against their three stolen nights. The warrior angels aggressively went in at the moment of Carlos's death and retrieved his soul—which is in Purgatory as we speak. The Vampire Council cannot find it in the realms of Hell, and they are quite distressed. Carlos Rivera's soul is extremely valuable to both sides. He is a hardened sinner, worth the soul weight of one hundred good souls. For them, he is the only access to you . . . and he will fill a territory for the Vampire Council with one of their own to replace Nuit."

"What happens if he makes the wrong choice?" Damali asked in a strained whisper, almost afraid to know.

"The man is walking a very thin line," the knight replied, drawing a line with his sword on the floor. "He can go deeper into the dark cavern of the nether realm, and take the offer made to him by the Vampire Council. He can take up with the rogue vampires, whom Nuit calls the Minion, and assist Nuit's plan to turn two hundred and fifty thousand at once at the concert. They will soon be daywalkers. Or, Carlos Rivera can side with us . . . but we cannot guarantee him life or ascension without a period of atonement." He looked up at Damali. "But you have been heavily tipping the scales in our favor. The kiss, without a bite, was like a drug."

"What . . ." Damali came closer to the knight and put her hand on his shoulder. "I don't understand . . . and daywalkers?"

"There is much at stake for Carlos Rivera right now. The dark realm's offers are much more seductive. We have little to bargain with. But you got him in the heart with all three weapons at our disposal. Your guardian seer-mother will explain all that there is to know about this . . . and will reveal the dark realm's plan as her visions increase." The knight stepped back from Damali and lowered his gaze.

"Tell me some of it, at least." Damali's gaze went from face to face in the room. Impatience seized her. "All this waiting, and stuff about being ready. I can't stand it another moment!"

"Faith, that the man could change," he said in a tense, emphatic tone. "You believed that he was better—could do better, and it pierced his conscience." The knight leaned in, his hand motioning to Damali as he counted off the points one by one using his fingers.

"Hope, that the man could see his own potential one day, and that he would embrace the right path. And, like you, he hoped that one day there would be a way for him to claim you, and you him. Very powerful shield against darkness." The knight let his breath out slowly, his gaze level and unwavering. "Then you drew the sword of truth on the man, coated it with love, and sent it right through his heart."

He stepped back and used his sword as a pointer. "You are girded in spiritual armor, young Neteru. The belt of truth, the breastplate of righteousness, the helmet of salvation, the shield of faith, your feet are shod in the gospel of peace—which you preach from the stage—and in your hand you have the sword of the spirit, the truth, which is the word of God. You were not unarmed when he approached you, and you vanquished the darkness within him—if only for a moment, or you would not still be standing. So, take heart, and do not ever lose the faith!"

Damali slowly looked down at her own body where the knight had pointed. Her team remained stunned, gaping. The knight and the Moor had gone to one knee again. Her eyes met the knight's. So much responsibility and she was still so young.

"Our young are the future," the knight murmured. "The task is daunting, but the young always lead the way, once the old become too blind to see. Joan of Arc was but a girl—"

"That is *not* a good example, dude," Rider said quickly. "Not if you're trying to get a pep rally going for our trip to Hell. The beginning of Joan's saga was great, but the ending sucked. Feel me?"

"What do you want me to do?" Damali glanced at the weapons table. A level of energy, power, confidence . . . something she couldn't define had reignited within her.

"It's your choice, and we cannot guarantee the outcome, or Rivera's choice—but lead us, and we pledge to follow you . . . yes, even to Hell and back, Neteru. All twelve of us will accompany you and your team on the mission. Every major faith will be there, united. The cause is great, the mission perilous; we have been instructed to go where you lead. One very entrenched sinner turning back is worth his weight in holy men."

Damali nodded. "Carlos could hand me over to any side, if he decided he wanted the power . . . and that has always been his weakness. It blinded him, and I am well aware of that."

Everyone nodded, and Marlene went to stand at Shabazz's side.

"I'm not afraid of him—or myself—anymore. And nobody is ever going to get me to go where I just went, again. I refuse to give up and be slain by some emotional drama." Damali looked at the group. "My choice has always been the same and it has been the light. I love Carlos, but I will dust him in a heartbeat for my family, or for the cause. It's bigger than him."

She pushed the existing weapons back from the table. "I am standing. So, we will go inside the belly of the beast, or die trying."

"I think she's cured," Marlene said quietly.

"You'd better hope so," Shabazz said, rubbing his jaw.

Damali glanced at them and then looked at the knight and his partner. "You gentlemen ever do a concert?"

"Oh, boy," Rider said with a whistle, his glance darting between his team and the Covenant representatives. When the knight and the Moor shook their heads, Rider found a metal stool and flopped down on it.

"We're taking in the whole squad," she announced. "I want knights in the corridors on flank, but they need to be on stage, too, to get in." She stopped, waited for them to nod, before pressing on.

"I want some new artillery, J.L.—new light systems; Dan, Big Mike, Shabazz, work on a new stage intro—I'm going to give them diva to make them think my ego just went over the top so they'll go along. Then I'm going to flip the script and do unauthorized songs—Rider, tune up your axe, and make that baby hum; the rest of you all work it out—heavy percussion, strong bass lines, take 'em up with chimes, cowbells, I want that joint rocking off the planet. I want some def' defying music out there when I do my thing for the crowds. We've got a little bit of time and a whole lotta work—and new people to add into the mix."

She walked around the table, her index finger tapping her lips. "Dan, get Nuit's people on the horn in the morning. Tell him I want to do the stadium, not Carlos's dinky little club—that'll suck them in. Tell them I want to talk contracts with Nuit, alone. But I insist on my own crew to set my stage . . . as a diva, I have that right. Then we lay for 'em, and breach their tunnels to seal them up. Nuit is mine. Can't wait to meet him. Dan let him know that I am practically trembling for the opportunity . . . and be sure you say it *just* like that, baby."

Again, the group remained mute, and gave their silent agreement. Their expressions seemed to contain a mixture of astonishment, revived commitment, and a little bit of practical apprehension—which was wise. But as she spoke and rallied the team, and they developed their plan, her spirit quietly revived from the blow it had sustained. No guarantees were needed. She had hope.

"Gentlemen," she finally said with a smile. "We are going to rock da house and bring down the light!"

PART TWO

Thus the highest realization of warfare is to attack the enemy's plans; next to attack their alliances; next attack their army; and the lowest is to attack their fortified cities.

—Sun Tzu, *The Art of War*

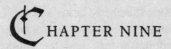

CHAPTER NINE

"SHE CALLED, Carlos. I don't know what you said to her, but her people called."

Nuit closed his eyes and inhaled slowly. The ear-splitting decibels of the music coming from the stage provided no cover for the sigh of anticipation that he'd released. Carlos monitored his cool. He had not called Damali, or made contact with her people since the previous night and they had never spoken about the concert. That she would call Nuit on her own meant there could be a serious variable that was raising the odds on the long shot.

Nuit swallowed with difficulty as though trying to keep his calm. "Her business manager, Weinstein, said that after the concert, she wanted to meet with me privately to talk about her career . . . and to bring contracts. My human assistants sent word via Amanthra demon alliances that are impervious to daylight. They woke me up in the lair to tell me . . . I couldn't even go back to sleep after receiving such news. They told me he'd said, quote, 'She was trembling for the opportunity.' Then they said she wanted her own crew, her own stage lights, her own diva entourage." Nuit snatched Carlos's arm. "I told them to give her whatever she wants! She's coming willingly, with ego, and power-lust, and the ruthless desire for fame."

"Your fangs are showing in public, dude. Uncool for a master. Even if we've brought out a colorful crowd to-night." Carlos appraised Nuit with a sideways glance, who only nodded in agreement.

"You're right. I have to collect myself."

"Maybe you should go underground and wait for her in the lair. If you get a whiff topside, you might really embarrass yourself on stage." Carlos chuckled. It was partly the truth.

"Her whole crew . . . anybody she shook hands with, hugged . . . they're trailing it all over the place!"

"I know," Carlos said as calmly as possible. "It's going to affect you more, because as a master, you have a lower tolerance for it—the others don't have the nose. So, you can either stay up here, and watch her do twenty minutes . . . under the hot lights, while she works out, sweats, and puts more of her scent in the air, or you can be cool, and chill, and go sub. She's on in less than fifteen minutes. Make a decision."

"I don't think I can take it," Nuit murmured, beginning to pace.

"Wise choice. Been there. See you in New Orleans."

To find out where she'd been stashed was a no-brainer. The other vamps had positioned themselves closely to her quarters and a ring of guardians eyed the vamp forces in a tense standoff. The problem would be getting to her dressing room. This variable had to be dealt with. No element of the plan could go haywire at the last minute. Whatever she was cooking up could put everybody in harm's way. When he spotted Shabazz and Big Mike on the door, he approached more slowly.

"Gotta talk to her before she goes on," Carlos said in a calm voice.

"I don't think so," Big Mike said low in his throat.

Shabazz shook his head.

"Call Marlene for an appraisal—but on the DL. If you haven't noticed, the rafters are loaded and have eyes," he said, motioning with a nod above. "The walls have ears, too. But she can't be bitten until after the show—girlfriend has to cast an image. We got three minutes to talk, or we can stand out here and bullshit and put her in harm's way."

"Three minutes," Big Mike said as Shabazz stepped aside begrudgingly.

"Cool," Carlos muttered as they followed him into the room.

Damali was at the far end of it. Marlene was opening with a prayer, anointing the group, but immediately stopped mid-sentence. Twelve knights and the rest of Damali's crew drew weapons. And then it hit him—*she was wearing all silver.* He could taste the acrid metal even from this distance. It registered a warning so visceral to him that the hair bristled on the back of his neck. But it also had a stabilizing effect.

Carlos held up his hands. "Three minutes. Say a prayer of concealment against dark forces. I have information. Need to talk to her. Everybody can stay. But the info is power."

"Let him speak," Damali said quickly. "Do it, Mar. We don't have much time."

He watched as the team rimmed the room, held hands with him inside their circle so the words would seal in what he had to say, but he was forced to cover his ears as the sound of Marlene's murmurs almost made his ears bleed. Once the pain stopped, he dropped his hands away and wiped the sweat from his brow.

"Are we sealed?" He glanced around at the faces that nodded, and tried to shake off the effect Damali was also having on him. "As soon as you close, the floor is going to drop out from under you—you'll be in a tunnel."

"What!" Rider snapped. "That is not the plan—"

"Rider, let the man speak," Damali warned in a low voice. "The prayer has him affected, and we need to know what we're dealing with."

"It's not just the prayer," Carlos said on a deep inhale, letting it out fast. "Your scent is an aphrodisiac . . . you can use it to your advantage."

She stared at his back as he turned away. Her group of guardians parted as he went to the door and leaned against it on an outstretched arm. All of them watched him as his back heaved from deep breaths, almost expanding his tailored suit till the seams ripped, and then collapsed, repeating the hypnotic motion as his breaths became more labored with each exhale.

"Masters have a low tolerance for it. Male vampires can smell it for miles. This concert site is packed with them. Sends the lower generations into a feeding frenzy. Females, however, will fight you—will attack at the drop of a hat. You've got Nuit's human helpers out there with orders to take down any male vamp with a stake if they rush you. So, topside, you should be cool. But the tunnels are filling.

I've been designated as your escort to Nuit's door—he doesn't know I'm a master . . . or about my alliances."

"He tells the truth," the Templar said quietly, placing a hand on her shoulder. "The demon is suffering, but might have to be exterminated if . . ."

"You can't trust me," Carlos admitted. "I can't even trust myself, at this point."

He turned and looked at her, his gaze riveted to her horror-stricken face. Her team drew closer to her. Dan leveled a crossbow at him. Carlos closed his eyes, willing his fangs to retract. They were slow to respond.

"Oh, shit . . ." Rider said in a quiet voice. "You got an antidote for that, man? Something to keep you on our side while we're in Hell with you?"

Carlos carefully appraised Damali, the pain in her eyes haunting him, but he couldn't look away from her. "There's only one, but it won't sit well with the group."

For a moment silence stood between them.

"All right. Talk fast, man. Lest we have to smoke you in here."

Nodding, Carlos began to pace, trying to shake off the effect of Damali. Shabazz had a point. "Yeah, Shabazz. You might have to—because I have to catch her when she drops—or the demons will get her, or the Vampire Council, or any other possible rogue vamps that want her. If she travels at a high speed with me—it will be directly to Nuit's door. But by then, I'll be in a very compromised state, and a weakened one. I'll be no match for him alone . . . and I don't even know if I can hold her—she's wearing silver."

The group cast stricken glances between them.

"Templar, can you do anything?" Carlos murmured. "If I drop her, the suit will only hold back a few vamps, but as you know, Hell is infested. She won't be able to find her way back to the portal. Eventually, if the Amanthras get to her and pull her in deep enough, the suit won't do shit for her."

Warily, the knight approached Carlos, glancing between him and the group. "On May tenth, Venus, love, and Mars, war, were in exact conjunction in a very rare celestial alignment during the Neteru-signaling period. It hasn't, and will not occur again for decades. We didn't know what it meant, in the midst of the other signs. Love would collide with war, we initially thought. But perhaps it meant aligning love within the same war. We can attempt a prayer, but only for her, that will also cover you . . . which might also help you keep focused. But we won't know if it works till she drops, or you touch her."

"I'll take the risk." Carlos turned, his gaze going past the Templar and the team of warriors surrounding Damali. Silver notwithstanding, her pull was incomprehensible. She looked at him and rocked his mind to semidazed awareness. Yeah, he'd take the risk.

"How fast to Nuit's door?" Damali asked, walking in a circle.

"*Be still* . . . you stir the air," Carlos hissed.

Everybody looked at him and she stopped pacing.

Carlos let out his breath slowly, and closed his eyes, unable to simultaneously process the sight and the scent of her. "Forty-five seconds. If you go by foot through the tunnels—it's still astral speed, just not as fast. Time is different down there than up here—seems like hours and it's only minutes. So be prepared for the time distortion. Any human in the tunnel, or non-sanctioned vamp, will be moving at topside time approximately ten minutes behind you . . . but anything human or otherwise without what amounts to an Amanthra passport will be attacked."

He stopped and briefly gazed at her again, having to close his eyes once more just to be able to speak. The sight of her in a body-fitting wetsuit, her locks down on her shoulders, her eyes boring a hole into him . . .

"Can we get you some water, or something?" Rider asked, shaking his head. "Damn. Hurry up and say what you gotta say. You're giving me the heebie-jeebies!"

"Damali," Carlos murmured. "If you come with me, you and I can take Nuit—"

"No," Shabazz said immediately.

"Definitely not." Marlene walked away and leaned against the far wall.

"What they said," Rider agreed.

"You must be crazy," Big Mike rumbled, shaking his head slowly, and then pounding J.L.'s and Dan's fists. "Must be missin' yo' mind."

"Hold up, everybody," Damali interjected. "If the silver doesn't maim him, the man can get me to Nuit with Madame Isis in hand in forty-five seconds, right? And he's not going to bite me, because he wants Nuit dead as bad as I do—Nuit did his family . . . so he's not going to bite me."

Again, the group's attention went to Carlos, who now opened his eyes.

"Can't promise that, baby. Never could."

Rider folded his arms over his chest. "At least the brother is honest. Look at him, Little Red Riding Hood. That is, for real, for real, the big bad wolf!"

Carlos just nodded, too ashamed to be able to do anything else.

"Then why is he here?" Damali started toward Carlos but he held up his hand and turned away.

"Don't."

The room went still again, and the blue-clad Templar stepped in between them. "His time to make a decision is running out and even he doesn't know what that decision will be. If he goes with the Vampire Council, he can have infinite power at the ground level. If he goes with Nuit, he will be a high-level advisor with a vast topside territory and daywalker power. If he goes with us, five mob factions, the FBI, and other police forces will hunt for him, or until they find his body . . . and that's only assuming he gets a chance to live. He might have to die if he becomes human again because the bite was so horrendous. And, once this double-cross is uncovered—both sides of the vampire empire and all its factions will hunt him till the end of time."

"Shit. And here I thought homeboy was holding aces." Rider shook his head and looked at Damali. "Don't even think about hugging him under these circumstances—not even to keep hope alive, as Reverend Jackson would say."

"Man, you got yourself in a totally fucked-up position," Shabazz said. " 'Scuze me, all present. But, there's no other way to describe it."

"The tunnels," Damali said quickly. "If our men go in, led by Marlene, what advantages can we leverage?"

Her voice was like a knife, carving at his libido, slicing it away from his reason.

"In the slow areas," Carlos said, releasing a deep breath. "I have forces—the Vampire Council's messenger demons who do not want Nuit's goal to be accomplished. They will sense anything in there moving slow, and will help you get to his door to kill him. That was our deal."

"Demons?" The Templar and the members of the Covenant pulled back and huddled in an agitated conference, arguing the merits of Carlos's newest strategy, and the way it might be misunderstood within their own hierarchy.

"Listen. We don't have time!" Carlos began pacing. He'd been in the room longer than three minutes. The show preceding hers was wrapping up. There would be a brief break, and then she'd have to go on stage. Someone would knock soon to tell her it was time.

"The demons I worked a deal with agreed," Carlos said. "However, there are rogues amongst them that will attack slow-moving objects—any vampire not traveling at the higher speed, or humans. The way the tunnels work is, if something is moving slower than the tunnel's speed, it belongs on a different level, not theirs. They don't ask questions, they attack. And humans aren't even supposed to be anywhere down there. Your bodies are slowed to topside time, not astral time, and you draw them. Not to mention, the scent of your blood is a tracer."

"This is a bad—"

Carlos stopped Rider's comment and pressed on. "Nuit's forces are expecting six of us to go down there with Damali in tow—me, my brother Alejandro, as well as Julio, Juan, and Miguel. The five other vampires made by Nuit's line, and me, are the only ones that have high-speed amnesty—not even Damali can be cleared. Which means as soon as the floor drops, while in the center of a zone, I'll have to do them . . . may their souls rest in peace. From there, we can go fast, or slow, but we won't have much time. The longer it takes me to get to Nuit's door, the more suspicious and on guard he'll be, and the higher the risk of attack from other subterranean forces."

"Oh, Carlos," Damali murmured. "Nobody should have to do their own family . . ."

Carlos looked away from her.

"Once I . . . take care of them, you can pick four men to replace them, but they have to enter the tunnel immediately after you and me or they will be viewed as intruders. If they miss that window of opportunity, they'll have to risk the slower corridors with the rest of the group." Carlos studied the serious faces that stared back at him. "If you don't get to Nuit's door in time, Damali will be between me and Nuit. The only thing you'll have to your advantage, and the only possible way to get her out, is if he and I square off—which is inevitable."

"I told you, they did his fam—"

"No, D!" Carlos yelled. He looked at her hard, and finally told her the truth. "It's not because of my family. Two male masters, one female Neteru . . . If I kill him down there, you'll have to kill me. Got it? So will your team, when they get there. Make your strike swift, make sure you get me on the first blow. If not . . ." He put his hand on the door and didn't look at her as he spoke. "If not, I start an empire. Choose well, and be decisive."

The assembled group didn't say a word. The expressions on everyone's faces said it all. Damali walked over and picked up her blade, and checked the sharpness of its edge.

"Say a prayer, Templar," she said in a low murmur. The knock and curtain-call yell didn't even make her look up. So much adrenaline had hit her system it was making her ears ring. The tone of Carlos's voice, the look in his eyes . . . the unconcealed desire. Yes. She might have to kill him.

"C'mon, people. We've got a show to do."

She could feel them watching her as she stood on a small platform under the stage, waiting for it to raise her to stage level. It was like being in a shark cage underwater, each beast swimming by, circling, waiting for the opportunity to strike. Seconds seemed like minutes. Damali gripped Madame Isis tighter, checked the battery belt on her silver suit, as well as the Isis dagger on her hip, and picked up the medieval, silver, double-bladed battle-ax the knight had offered. They were gonna get it on when she dropped, and she'd have everything she needed when she did.

Special-effects thunder and lightning strikes could be heard above, as the crowd's clapping roar swelled when Big Mike turned up the volume of the FX section of his soundboards. Marlene's voice rang out with the introduction, and she began an African chant that the crowd followed.

Stage boards creaked overhead to the beat of Marlene's repetitive, "Oooohhh, nanana." The team was jumping up and down overhead, giving Watutsi homage and anthem from the motherland. Deep bomb blasts that sounded like M-80s soon followed, and Damali knew it was show time.

She held up Madame Isis as she rose. A dark blue and a purple haze awaited her entrance when she got to the top, then more bomb blasts, and the stage went white with light and gold smoke. More thunder sounded as Rider's guitar started to wail. Jose, as sick as he had been, was throwing down conga hard, J.L.'s keyboard was serving it hot, but Shabazz was walking the bass and had it thumpin'. Marlene was working out on cowbells as the crowd went nuts. Damali laughed. So, they liked the twelve warriors with weapons onstage, huh? Cool.

Electricity ran through her. There was nothing as exhilarating as a performance when the crowd was like this. And even though there was everything in the world riding on the situation, the music had her swaying. All those innocents out there, waving UV unknowingly. She was gonna blow the doors off!

Rising slowly, she heard Big Mike's booming voice lead off and blend in with Shabazz's and Rider's, as they each took turns to yell into their mics.

"She leaves 'em smoking, on fire!"

"Baby got da ansa, for any desire!"

"Hot—burnin' with emotion!"

"Betta wat'chure back, 'cause she ain't jokin'!"

The floor opened and a wave of audience screams assaulted her as more stage bombs went off, white and gold smoke surrounded her, and the lights changed. The music tempo picked up, and Damali stepped forward holding a medieval ax out from her boot ninety degrees on the left and Madame Isis raised on her right. She gave out a war cry, and the crowd erupted again. Dropping the ax for a nearby knight to catch, she strutted to the front of the stage to the music, pulled her dagger from her hip belt, lowered her sword toward the crowd, breathed in, and let the words ring out.

"I leave 'em smokin', dead or alive. Dis ain't no job like a nine to five. Ain't scared of the dark, 'cause I bring my own light. Make a choice, fast, and make it right. Been to Hell and back, might go there again—but you betta watch yours and take a friend. My sword's name is Isis, and Momma draws heat. Watch her work, when we drop da funky beat!"

Carlos was riveted to Damali's image, as she owned the stage. He couldn't move from his position beside his squad in the wings as she began her routine. It was pure, fluid adrenaline, charged atmosphere. Her body was like liquid silver fire, and the crowd was off the hook. The UV lights kept him in the shadows, it burned off some of the scent, but it didn't keep him from seeing her work. She took full possession of fifty thousand screaming fans, however many crew and vamps in the wings—and him. There was no description for it. The music throbbed inside him as Shabazz and Rider took the rhythm frenzy to the next level, and Damali swung a sword and dagger in between stanzas.

"Yo, man, how's your head?" Alejandro whispered. "You need to step outside for a minute and get some air, so you can do this delivery in a few? You don't look so good, *hombre,* but I got'chure back."

"I'm all right," Carlos growled, his gaze glued to the stage.

"Listen, man, you gotta stop watching her or you ain't gonna be no good by the time the floor drops. Plus, the silver suit wasn't expected. How you gonna hold her and not go up in flames, *hombre*?"

"I'm already there, bro. You have no idea. The suit doesn't even compare."

"I think he's over the top, man," Miguel said nervously, looking at Carlos and then at the others.

Carlos pulled his gaze away, and turned his back on Damali's performance. "I'm all right. I'm good. She won't be in the tunnel that long." He watched his brother's expression from a side-glance. Despair fought side-by-side with the effect Damali was having on him, all of it clouding his judgment. "But I just needed to watch her for a little bit, before it's time."

"Damn, man, I can dig it," Alejandro agreed, his gaze fixed on the stage. "I remember when she was just a kid, free-styling in the old neighborhood—begging to get a shot at a mic. Look at her now . . ."

Unable to withstand the pull, Carlos found his line of vision drawn back to where he had forbidden it to go. It was now possible to see a thin sheen of perspiration on her brow, and she'd licked her lips, opened her arms, and leaned back with a weapon in each hand. Incredible.

"If I die with honor, then they say it's all good. But I'm about livin', not jus' survivin' in the hood. So keep your light, and block the shade—tell 'em don't hate a player that the light above made! *'Cause* . . . I leave 'em smoking wit da truth, everything I'm telling you got da juice. Been standin' on the high road, but can go low, might hafta drop a body, so act like you know. Ain't no game, ain't truth or dare. What Grandmomma told you is your only prayer—"

"Man . . . go get some air, brother, for real for real. Your hands are shaking," Alejandro warned. "You are way too high right now, and—"

"Shut up!" Carlos shouted as the music took another turn, and Damali paced toward the back of the stage, allowing the drums a solo.

His boys looked at him hard. Alejandro shook his head when Juan, Julio, and Miguel came up behind Carlos and stood with him. His breath was coming out in short bursts now, and his shoulders were gaining in thickness. Carlos wiped his nose with the back of his hand as a shudder ran through him again. He swallowed hard and could feel his gums beginning to bulk. He closed his eyes, leaned his head back, and sucked in a huge gulp of air.

"He'll take a limb," his brother warned. "Go get him something to eat."

"I don't need to feed on garbage!" Carlos growled.

His boys hesitated, and Alejandro signaled for them to wait and ride it out. They stood by him with a wary distance between them. When Damali went into the last stanza, Carlos held on to the wall for support. Against his better judgment, he opened his eyes and again watched her work.

"*Yeah* . . . I leave 'em smokin'—so watch your back. Night is the time when creatures attack. Bring the word; stand in the light. We got one shot to get it right! Ain't a game or a battle, it's a fight for it all. Make the wrong choice, and you'll take a fall. Runnin' down the high road, dodging from the low, pressure starts to build, but that's when I blow . . ."

The lights blew, sparklers went off, the keyboards screamed with the guitar, and Damali lit up in full UV— the crowd went wild, and he had to turn away. The light temporarily blinded him, dazed him like a sucker punch. His boys covered their eyes with forearms and snarled. But the pain worked like a slap of reality. The UV so close to her skin, burned off the residue of potent scent for a moment, and it helped to break his trance.

"Downstairs, now!" Carlos circled his team, and pointed to the lower level.

"Yo, man, but—"

"She's only got a few minutes to be lit up, judging from the battery sizes on her belt. She's got two more songs, and we roll." He was breathing hard as he walked away from the stage, his squad in hot pursuit. "You wanna

be the one to explain to Nuit why we weren't in position
to catch her when she falls? If the wrong demons claim
her, or another vampire does, he'll have everybody's
head—do it now!"

Without further argument, his posse followed him. He
couldn't speak as he got farther and farther away from
Damali. The pain that riddled him felt like an eerie with-
drawal, but if he didn't get away from her now, he
wouldn't be able to later. A female vampire holding a
clipboard scowled as he walked by.

"This was not on her docket, nor was real *silver*! That
bitch flipped the script," she said low in her throat.

Carlos came to a halt. "Tell it to Nuit. He said to make
her happy, and give her whatever she wanted."

"She's got this place feeling like an oven, and temporarily sealing lairs near wherever this sound travels or
is broadcast with all this light bullshit! She's got the
crowd with UV wands in their hands, and—"

"Say anything to make her anything less than happy,
and Nuit will rip your heart out," Carlos said evenly. "He
wouldn't care if every portal sealed worldwide, as long as
I bring her to him. You understand? No interventions topside, or after this is over, I will personally hunt you down.
We clear?"

The female vamp smiled. "Promise?" she purred.

"Forget her, man," Alejandro said, pulling his arm.
"Let's do this thing."

Carlos nodded, then brushed past the female and made
their way to the lower level. He could hear Damali above
finishing her first act, and the scent of her was so strong in
the tight confines near the lift that he had to keep walking
in circles—motion, anything to wear it off, wear it down.

"Man, in just a few, everything will be cool. Just hang in there."

He closed his eyes as he heard Damali prepare to go into a baleful poem-song above his head. He could tell by the music that she was sending him a message as much as she was working the audience. It made him stand still as he braced himself to listen to the words, and the guitar and keyboard accompanied her in sad harmony. Marlene's violin felt like it was cutting him, sawing through his ribs to get to his heart. The flute, the chimes, soft bells, making him go back to the place where he'd found her; Shabazz's bass connecting it all like a pulse. *Don't do this . . .*

"Remember, baby, how it used to be," she began singing low and sweet to the audience. "Before it all got crazy—when we just were kids . . . and *so* free.

"Now, I know we've gotta move on—and that's life. Still I can't help going back to our past—just once or twice . . . Just remember, baby, how it used to be—before it all got crazy, when we were just kids . . . and so free—please, baby . . . don't forget."

Damali's voice had risen with the violin, stroking his memory, turning a blade in the center of his chest, and had ended on a whisper . . . *please, baby . . . don't forget.*

Carlos looked up at the black underbelly of the stage. The area had cooled; the lights had gone low to a blue haze. He could see a ball casting a prism of stars around the glimpses of stage periphery, and he shut his eyes to see her and join with the emotion in her. She stood in the middle of a blue universe of stars, wearing her silver, her sword held low as though in defeat, her dagger clenched in her fist, her head back, her eyes closed, tears glistening at the corners of them, as she sang her heart out. Yes, he remembered. How could he forget? She stood in the middle of his world, and was his universe.

"Don't listen to her, man," Juan murmured. "That was a long time ago, *hombre*. It's all different now. Power, money, women—she didn't understand the life. Never did."

"Don't let it mess with your head, bro," Julio said with worry. "You got everything in front of you—leave the past behind and may it rest in peace."

"Yeah, man," Alejandro said with growing concern. "Only thing you need to remember is you got a delivery to make."

"Word," Miguel murmured.

Carlos didn't respond to his best friend, cousin, or brother, nor did he shake off Miguel's hand on his shoulder. He had to do what he had to do. But her words were like an echo, a whisper that wouldn't leave him . . . because all he could do was remember. Everything.

"Alejandro," Carlos whispered, as he walked toward his brother and Miguel's hand dropped from his shoulder. He needed to stand close before Alejandro to help him understand. "Listen to the words," he said, locking his brother's gaze within his.

"You all right, man?" Alejandro backed up a bit when Carlos placed his hand in the center of his chest.

"I'm fine. Close your eyes. Remember when we were kids—playing ball in the street, running for ice cream, hanging out?"

With caution, Alejandro closed his eyes, and gave in to the sway of the memory that Carlos projected. "Yeah . . . man, those were some good times. We'll have good times again."

"Yes, you will, my brother. But remember how I tried so hard not to bring you into the life—how I'd chase you away?"

Behind him, Miguel and Juan laughed with Julio. Alejandro opened his eyes.

"Little brat was always following us, getting in the way of a deal." Julio shook his head. "We had to finally let you in, before you got yourself—or one of us—shot."

Alejandro just laughed, and covered Carlos's hand over his chest. "But I wanted to be just like him." Tears filled Alejandro's eyes suddenly and he looked away. "Would do anything for my brother, even this."

"When's the last time you saw Mom?" Carlos's question was a murmur.

His brother shrugged and the laughter among his friends died down. Silence enveloped them.

"I want you to remember her face when she was happy—before any of us died . . . before Dad lost his sense of what was right and wrong . . . before he hit her. I want you to close your eyes and stand with me and remember her laughter, the peace in her eyes, the sound of her voice when she'd call us for dinner, and remember how much I tried to push you away from my life—because I loved you so much, then, and knew what I was, then . . . what that life meant. And I'm doing it again," Carlos said, sucking in a deep breath, "because I love you."

He'd reached into his breast pocket so fast with his free hand, without removing the other from Alejandro's chest, that his brother only had his eyes half open before the stake replaced his palm.

"Rest in peace, Alejandro." Carlos stepped back from the burning ash, and breathed in deeply to steady himself.

The wailing song above held him as he stared at what was left of his brother.

"Oh, shit! Carlos, man—you did him? What the fuck! You're too high—you just did you own brother! Are you crazy, man!"

"It was about my brother's soul. I'll never have one, but I always wanted him to have better than me. The song made me remember how much."

Carlos didn't move as his boys circled him, their fangs now showing, ready to attack. He watched them through narrowed eyes.

"He went soft," Juan spat. "I don't fucking believe it! And he's supposed to bring the huntress to Nuit? You don't even deserve the honor. You disgrace our family—our line!"

Miguel lunged at him first, and lost his heart to Carlos's fist. Out of friendship, he made the snatch instantaneous. A master's reach slammed into breastbone, ripped away anchor tissue, and left a gaping hole in Miguel's chest. With Miguel's heart still beating in his hand, Carlos drove the point of the stake through the bloody organ and flung it away, watching it burn as his friend was immediately incinerated. The only comfort he took was that his friend had stopped feeling before he even began to burn.

Julio tried to escape, but that couldn't happen. Carlos grabbed the back of Julio's suit, pulled his cousin to him, lodged the stake where it needed to land, then stepped away from the inferno. But perhaps the hardest pair of eyes to meet were Juan's. Unlike Alejandro, cornered, Juan saw it coming. The pleading expression almost made Carlos hesitate. The question "why" hovered on his best friend's lips as Carlos held him by his throat and killed him at close range.

It had to all end here, quietly, under the stage—which it summarily did. Carlos stood over each pile of ash that had been his friends, his family, closed his eyes, and saw again how he'd driven a stake into their hearts—using the same one that had allowed Alejandro to rest in peace. They had not been on a tour of Hell, of that he was sure. They would never know where their souls could have been trapped . . . not even a dog deserved to be held hostage there.

Tears threatened his eyes as he realized he couldn't even pray over their remains. Such a transgression would scorch his tongue. All he could do was look down at what was left. Four members of what was once his family . . . what had been and was no more. Young, vital humanity, with promise, turned inhuman, all in the blink of an eye.

Carlos listened to the end of the song as he wiped ash from his hands and the stake, putting it back in his breast pocket as he slowly stood. "Rest well, my friends, my cousin, my brother. Remember what it was like when we were just kids, and we were still free." That was the closest thing to a prayer that he could utter.

She had begun her last number. The lights were back to burning brightly overhead. He could feel the heat, but somehow it didn't have the same effect. Damali had heavy reverb going, the stage was thumping, and he could hear the crowd on their feet stamping to her throbbing beat. Three minutes, and she would fall into his arms, and it didn't even faze him. He just had to finish this. End the madness.

But reality spread through him like a fast-moving cancer; it would never end. Killing Nuit would just stop one line out of many. Just like her prayers and songs of light were only one torch competing for brightness with so much darkness all around it. She could hold up the lantern with her words till it looked like only a small match in the distance. Maybe her prayers closed a few portals tonight, but others would always open.

Sure as he was standing under the stage, evil would reconstitute itself elsewhere, in another form. Even with Nuit eliminated, the Vampire Council would send hunters to track him down, just like the world of light would. Topside, bottom side, Heaven or Hell, what did it truly matter? Her guardians were right, he was in a fucked-up position. However, the different sides closing in on him needed to recognize one thing—a man, or a vampire, with nothing to lose, was a dangerous variable.

She was yelling, "Bring it, people! Bring the light! Pass the flame!"

Carlo shook his head as sound started to evaporate around him. The clock was ticking. Only four of her guardians could go with them. He looked up, sensing her footsteps, her position, as the crowd roared around her. Another smoke bomb went off, and he felt the air whip at his trousers, scattering the ashes at his feet.

Then she dropped.

It happened so fast that she couldn't breathe. Air felt like it had been vacuum-sucked out of her lungs. She gripped the Isis sword and baby Isis dagger, and held on to the smoldering body that had caught her. When she looked up, her team was sprawled on a cavern floor, trying to scramble to their feet. Carlos had instantly let go of his hold on her and backed away, snarling.

"Choose four, fast, and let's move," Carlos commanded. Intense agony riddled his body. The damn suit. He looked over the scorch marks on his hands and his clothing, which still emitted a light white haze of smoke. But there wasn't time to deal with the pain.

Damali and the Templar immediately assessed his condition, and she issued a quick order. "Rider, Shabazz, Big Mike, Marlene—"

Before she could finish speaking, demons entered the black space as J.L., Jose, and Dan quickly lit concert lights in the small area. Misshapen, grotesque forms lashed at them in the confining area. They needed to fan out, so the weapons would have swing range. Carlos had blocked one side of the cavern, giving her team room and a chance to run down the dark corridor.

"Protect the Neteru at all costs!" the Templar yelled over his shoulder.

"Bring her in this tunnel behind us!" Rider hollered.

"No, hot demon and vamp territory!" Carlos roared. "She takes high-speed transport. It's the only way."

Damali's blade swung as the hair on her neck bristled. Something was happening to her; she was more aware of things down here than she'd ever been. The environment was pumping her up; the urge to fight was stronger than when she'd tracked Raven. She was inside her body, but also not, as she beheaded a foul creature, spun around, kicked its burning head away from her foot, and let out a throaty battle yell. It was fucking on! Her guardians were in her way, as were the Covenant warriors. They were trying to circle her to protect her, but they were interfering with her kill.

"Fan out!" she ordered, slashing at something she couldn't even see until her blade connected with it. The thing materialized and dropped, turning to a mass of putrid, bubbling tar.

Her eyes didn't even have to strain in the dark. Each creature she brought down, the sharper her senses became. It was exhilarating, a rush, and created a hunger to push forward. She was out of the team's circle, had left the ground with a hurling kick to stun a beast before she put her foot on its chest, then planted her sword in the center of its ugly flat skull.

Back-to-back in tandem, Shabazz and Big Mike took out three slithering entities. Their grotesque claws grappled at the wounds that tore into their greenish nude human bodies, which ended in a black serpent coil for legs. Their eyes glowed yellow, and their massive viper fangs dripped acidic-smelling ooze as they screeched a death shriek.

Awful wails from dying demons battered their senses. Mike had unsnapped the sides of his wide-legged leather pants in one deft motion, and pulled out two double-barrel snub-nose cannons, blowing away two of the demons. Shabazz ducked as creature gore splattered from Mike's assault, and while stooping, he released a black magnum into each hand from his sleeves to explode the third predator that was about to rush them.

Marlene used her stick to stake one screeching creature through its temple and then its gizzard, which left green gook and entrails at her feet. Dan got the one behind her with a holy-water grenade-slingshot hit dead-aim into the eye of the thing he battled, making half of its head ignite and then explode. J.L. and Jose were working out on instrument-converted mini-crossbows. Their weapons adapted to fire like automatics and released multiple rounds of silver-tipped wooden arrows, creating a plume of sulfuric smoke around the team as they took out screeching targets.

They gave Rider cover in their center by flanking him while he locked four sections of a machine gun together and released a hail of hallowed earth within the pit. "Back the fuck up!" Rider hollered, his arms shaking as he sprayed into the black network of endless tunnels.

Members of the Covenant swung battle-axes and machetes, sending geysers of green blood and gore from spindly, gruesome necks that began smoking. Damali beheaded another creature with the Isis, as she glanced at the Covenant team to be sure she didn't lose any of her men. The Templar sliced the chest of a pale, withered beast that squealed a high-pitched call as it slumped. The Ninjas had a vampire between them: one going for the beast's head with a kick, the other using discs to incinerate it from behind. Blocked from the high-speed zone by four demons spinning wildly, the team fought to open a hole toward safety along the other routes to enter the slower tunnel— while Carlos went after the creatures that blocked his passage to the high-speed zone.

Damali glanced at Carlos, and his form took her aback. *He was huge.* The fangs he now bore were six inches long and at least three-quarters of an inch wide. His eyes glowed red. The muscles in his forearms and shoulders and thighs had burst seams in his tattered suit. His silk shirt was hanging open, the size of his chest looked like two cinder blocks had been affixed to it, and his stomach rippled with eight, well-defined muscular bricks. Heaving from exertion, sweat rolled down his temples and the center of his chest. His adrenaline was palpable, the scent of it nearly intoxicating. He'd abandoned using a stake as a weapon; now he used his bare hands.

The low rumble that came from his throat sent a shiver through her. For a second their eyes met. The force of his projected thought momentarily stunned her like she'd been punched. For the first time in her life she witnessed a master vampire in full battle mode. It was both horrifying and awesome.

"Damali!" Marlene yelled, breaking her trance.

Stabbing at a new wave of creatures with the Isis blade, Damali opened access closer to the portal Carlos was fighting to clear. "I won't leave my team down here!" she yelled toward him.

When she spun around, however, the Templars and her guardian team were blocked in the slow cavern by multiple beasts that gave chase. She could hear her squad running and yelling, each telling her to go fast with Carlos and they'd meet her on the other side.

"Trust me," he said, grabbing her arm even though his hand began to sizzle. "If you resist, we'll fall back into a slow cavern—just the two of us. They at least have a fighting chance," he told her.

Beasts seemed to be pouring into the pit from all sides, and oddly she couldn't see now that J.L.'s lights were being carried farther away. Before J.L. had even fired up the torches, she could see in the dark, hear everything coming before it rushed them, feel the creatures' presence— sense it, taste it—but in an instant her internal battery was low. It was like her own power had dipped the moment she'd been slammed with Carlos's thoughts.

She squinted, regaining her night vision, yet she had to work at it, concentrate. Holes she hadn't even noticed came alive. Rock was transforming into entities, gravel under her feet clutched at her as hands came up from the ground. Things overhead grasped at her head, pulled her hair. Invisible threadlike tentacles and fingers snatched at her arms and legs while she slashed at everything with her dagger in one hand and Madame Isis in the other.

As soon as she stopped pulling away from him, Carlos swept her up while she held her sword and dagger close to her chest. The suit burn made the surfaces she touched slowly ignite, but he tightened his hold.

Hurtling so fast, there was no way to breathe. He could feel the pressure push oxygen out of his lungs, make his eardrums nearly burst, sight was impossible, everything was a blur, and all he could do was continue to cradle Damali in his grasp and keep her close as she practically fused to his skin.

She thought she was dying. Her chest felt like a thousand pounds of forced weight was upon it. She couldn't suck in because her diaphragm couldn't lift. Her ears felt like they were bleeding, and the high-pitched whine was like that of a turbine engine inside of them. The foul, smoldering air and the whiz of motion burned her eyes, which she could only shut tightly now. She began a prayer, and she heard Carlos howl with pain as they slowed and his hold loosened on her.

No! Not in my arms! It wasn't Carlos's voice, but his mind that told her.

Somehow she knew that her survival was predicated on them getting to the other side. She could immediately feel things scratching at her when they'd slowed down, and her mind fixed on the objective, which instantly kicked them back up into high gear. Find Nuit.

Almost as suddenly as they had begun to hurl forward, the swirling energy behind them snapped shut, making Carlos lurch forward and stumble to a stop before a massive, black marble door. He was heaving in air, and fully transformed. He dropped her down fast, then backed up and drew quicker pants. Knowing the suit had hurt him, weakening his fight condition, she stepped away from him as he gasped for a breath in the putrid pit around them. She could see in the dark again. All her senses were keened once more. She was in full-blown huntress, having also transformed herself. The hurling action had sent an adrenaline shot through her, and tapped into her survival core. She was ready.

On the ground behind her were a heap of six dead women. The sight of them lying limp, their necks snapped, their eyes wide open, had turned her knuckles white on the grip of her blade. Every lapsed sensory gift was so heightened that she was almost shaking where she stood. The smells, the distant sounds of lost souls screaming, the still air, the taste of dark realm sulfur, and her lack of need for light entered her system from her spinal column—spreading out to the tips of her fingers, toes, and the top of her head in one internal electric current. She used the blade to motion toward the gore.

"What the hell is this, Carlos?"

"Dinner, I presume," he muttered. "Nuit is a man of his word. Two for me, one for each of my boys." Carlos spat and walked around her. "I'm not hungry, though."

The burn, the high-speed travel, and the battle combined, had initially been enough to slightly bring him down to divert his attention. Now Damali just stared at him, could even see him in the dark; it was reversing the effect, like an anesthetic wearing off. The heightened Neteru scent of her mixed with another fragrance that he couldn't place. It created something close to delirium within the tight, unventilated confines. Blood was also in the air from Nuit's substitute offering. But Damali's adrenaline was pumping, the silver suit's effectiveness rapidly diminishing, as the scent of her numbed the pain. He had the feeling he could just tear the silver from her body with little difficulty. He shook his head. They had to breach Nuit's lair now or he wouldn't be responsible for his actions.

"You've got about two seconds to make a choice. We go in there and fight him right now, or I won't be myself. *Que pasa?*"

Damali leveled her blade at the man who had changed in size and density right before her eyes. His shoulders had gained another three inches in bulk. Threatening strength circled her, occasionally tilting its head. His incisors had taken on saber-toothed proportions, and his transition was worse than what she'd witnessed before. His eyes occasionally flashed deep gold, like a cat's within the darkness. As he circled and stalked her, a low panther-like rumble came from his chest and went through her body and settled in her marrow. He breathed in deeply and the glowing orbs disappeared in the blackness. But she could hear him circling, ready to strike, and she turned with him, Madame Isis always leading their dance. Then, he vanished.

"Fear mixed with a sudden burst of adrenaline . . . you better kill me on the first blow—you're taking too long," he said, his tone urgent and strained. "I tried to tell you, baby. I didn't want you to see me like this, ever."

His voice echoed off the walls and suddenly she went still, using all her senses to locate him, because his footsteps had also suddenly disappeared. Then he was behind her, and had her by her shoulders. His hands didn't burn now, and it sent a shot of pure terror through her. The instinctive reflex seemed to make him shudder and only tighten his hold. She tensed, bracing for his bite. Instead, he'd groaned against her hair.

She was not trying to go out like this. Struggle was impossible under his vise-like grip. His entire body pressed against her like stone. He nuzzled her shoulder, up her neck, smelling her hair, the growl moving up from his chest to his throat. Again, she became very, very still—remembering that there was another one—two males that would battle to the death over her.

"I didn't want it to be like this . . . especially your first time," he murmured harshly against the exposed skin of her cheek, sending a hot shaft of pure desire through her body. "But I'm way too far from redemption at this juncture, baby. . . . Since last night, I ain't been no good."

She could feel his fang-packed jaw, the power of the muscles in it grazing her cheek as his body trembled against her spine. Instead of only feeling a sense of horror, she was also feeling a strange draw of desire. What was wrong with her? She leaned her head back to allow Carlos's ardent nuzzle. She couldn't help it. He issued another primal sound from deep within his throat as her body relaxed against his. The ache to make love to him almost made her cry out. An incisor slid past her earlobe. As it did, her survival instinct kicked in. She screamed the last name she ever thought she would.

"Nuit!"

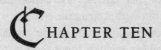

CHAPTER TEN

"BODY COUNT? Ammo? Who's wounded? Status, now!" Shabazz hollered as the besieged guardian teams huddled and re-marshaled forces.

"We lost four men," the Templar yelled, heaving in breaths. "We're down to eight, and we've got a man bitten and dying slow."

"Ammo is almost out," Rider shouted. "From this point on, it could be hand-to-hand and we're only halfway there—judging by the reconstructed maps!"

The teams surrounded the Hindu monk that had been among the knight's team. The large Moor had him in his arms and the Moor was breathing hard from the exertion of the run and the battles, like the rest of them. With his eyes, the Templar asked the question, and the Moor shook his head no in silent reply.

"Vampire. If it was a demon strike, we could bring him up and exorcise him. But . . ."

The monk hissed as the Moor gently put him on the ground.

"With honor, my friend," the Moor said, his normal voice coming out with a struggle.

Blood ran from the corner of the monk's mouth, and when he turned his head, a huge section of his shoulder was gone. The Moor stood back, and the guardians watched in horror while the blue-clad knight raised a silver battle-ax over his head.

"Go with God, and rest in peace—and in honor."

The blade came down, and all gathered turned their faces as the dying man's head rolled past them on the dank cavern floor.

"It is the only way to assure that any of us will rest in peace," the knight said in a strong voice as he looked behind them. "We knew this going in, and have dedicated our whole lives to this. We have no way to tell which line the beasts come from. Do not let any man or woman with us suffer. Do this, if we are compromised."

"We need to get to Damali. Mar, can you see anything down here?"

Marlene shook her head in answer to Big Mike's question. "We're in too deep."

"We need to move," Rider said quietly. "Jose doesn't look good."

"If he falls, I'll carry him . . . he ain't heavy—he's my brother." Big Mike slung his arm around Jose's shoulder as Jose struggled for air.

"I'm slowing you all down . . ."

"Shut up, Jose," Dan yelled. "We don't leave anybody down here to perish. We go back for our own, and bury them ourselves. Come on, I got his other side, Mike."

"While we were topside, did you give Damali that extra battery, J.L.?" Shabazz lit a concert torch as the one he was holding began to die.

"Yeah. If she can get to it fast enough, she might have a prayer."

"Let's hustle, folks. I hear movement again behind us," Rider urged. "The monk's blood and our body heat is drawing 'em out again."

Marlene touched the knight's shoulder. "I'm sorry . . . but I have to say this. If they stop and feed, it gives us time. When we go topside, you tell them that your brother guardian gave his life so we may live."

The knight just nodded and swallowed hard as the group began to jog deeper into the pit.

The force of Carlos's push had landed her against a pile of gore with a soft thud, but she hadn't lost her blades. She instantly shrank away from the dead women who had cushioned her fall. The doors had flung open, and something worse, much worse than Carlos, was standing between the marble slabs now hanging from broken hinges, and it issued a threatening growl. Red, gleaming eyes peered at her through slits, as Carlos's golden ones glistened with challenge. Oh, shit . . .

The thing standing in the doorway was a head taller than Carlos, and it not only had fangs but claws to match. They squared off and circled one another. While the two vampires focused on each other, she scrambled low, undetected for a moment, into the larger space behind them. The room she had sneaked into was lit with wall torches, and had more space for her to maneuver within. The massive black granite slab in the middle of the floor was something that she could use to shield herself with, and she knew she could leverage her position to fight around it when the time came.

"My delivery is five minutes late!"

"We were attacked in the tunnels—four of my men went down."

She watched as the first creature withdrew with caution, and could only assume that it was Nuit. He let out a guttural roar, which drew the same sound from Carlos. But they had stopped circling.

"Unfortunate, but I left your dinner at the door as promised—now leave me my bride."

A bride . . . and Carlos asked for bodies to be left? She saw him glance at her, and the implicit threat in his eyes chilled her. Two masters in such close proximity were screwing up her telepathy. But she caught part of Carlos's response. *Play the game.* Right.

"Don't sweat me about the minor time lapse! She called you," Carlos rumbled. "That should tell you something, despite my condition. You know the high-speed access portal has taken its toll—and as the courier, I was required to do battle, and then had to suffer holding her! Can you blame me?"

Damali was behind Nuit and could see his muscle-distorted shoulders begin to relax. She knew Carlos's style well enough to sense something was going on, and she locked in on his gaze. But she was too far from the menacing thing in front of her to wield the Isis, or effectively use the dagger. They would have to do this as a team, and Carlos was backing up Nuit in his lair.

"No, I guess this was to be expected," Nuit finally growled, stalking from the entrance to turn his attention on Damali. "You've done well," he said as she continued to back up, her glance going between Nuit and Carlos as she moved with Nuit, her sword cocked and ready to swing. "The package is wrapped in silver," he snarled. "Unwrap it."

"Are you insane?" Carlos said, shaking his head. "I held it, nearly caught fire. If I unwrap her, she's mine."

"You were to bring her to me without her barriers!"

"I lost my brother, my cousin, and two of my best friends to make this delivery—and fought in the tunnels . . . and didn't violate the package. We need to have a discussion about the territories, and my new, expanded cut. Then, maybe I'll unwrap her for you."

Damali glanced at Nuit as he tilted his head to one side, his gaze going between her and Carlos. Anxiety swept through her, as did hope. All she could do was pray that Carlos hadn't totally gone over to the other side, and that he wouldn't have turned her over for mere territory—and what did that mean, anyway? Territory? For what? She was afraid to fathom the definition as she thought of the dead women on the ground outside. But the thought of a prayer brought Nuit's attention back to her.

"Not down here," Nuit said in an even tone through his teeth.

Carlos cast a warning glance at her.

"You're frightening her," Carlos said carefully.

"Good—it just intensifies the lure."

"You want her to submit willingly, or the seed might not take. Be smart."

Outright indignation accosted her, and she stepped toward the beast. "Seed? You must be on drugs." She would ice this sucker.

"I am, sweetheart. Totally blitzed by you. But you *are* mine."

Damali glared at Nuit. Oh yeah, she would cut his

heart out. "Who I choose is my decision, asshole! And I haven't made up my mind! But it's safe to say, if you're one of my choices—*not*."

Nuit stepped back from her for a moment, and then laughed. He inhaled, and closed his eyes briefly and began circling her. "Carlos . . . you were right. She's fabulous. Absolutely intoxicating. The defiant rage in her is like a power hit."

From the corner of her eye she noticed Carlos had slipped into the chamber behind Nuit. She knew she needed to hold Nuit's attention to give the other stalking vampire the advantage—then they could cancel each other out. But, again, as soon as the thought crossed her mind Carlos stopped, looked at her, stunned, and Nuit had spun around to see Carlos well inside his lair.

"We'll discuss your territory later. I told you, for this delivery the bride price would be high and well worth it!"

Carlos nodded and backed away. Mortified, she leveled her blade to defend herself from both of them. But she needed to even the score with Nuit first.

"Nuit! You killed my father and my mother! Took out several of my guardians, made Raven. We have a debt to settle!"

Unharnessed fury coiled within her and she could feel it nearly curdle her blood. But the effect of her increasing anger seemed to only strengthen the thing in front of her, as well as Carlos. Suddenly Nuit reached out, and as she swung her blade, Isis ringing, he drew back his hand and licked the ooze coming from the slash.

"Carlos, close the doors on your way out. You can have all of South America, Africa, whatever . . . she's amazing."

"I will cut your fucking balls off," Damali said evenly, flexing her wrist that held the dagger.

A shudder ran through Nuit, and his eyes glowed a deeper shade of crimson. "Close the doors, *now*, Rivera—she's blowing my mind."

She heard a low growl coming from beyond Nuit's shoulder, and she knew he would turn to address it. The moment he did, she swung the long sword, and rolled over the slab to keep it between her and Nuit. He threw his head back and roared at the slash that had slit his suit and drew black blood. But it gave Carlos time to spring from his crouched position by the doors.

In an instant the two entities were in the midst of a death struggle. Carlos had opened a huge second gash in Nuit's back, and when they fell, Carlos had scored Nuit's face with a swipe on the way down. But the returned swipe from Nuit had gashed Carlos the length of his abdomen, beginning at the center of his chest. Immediately the two beasts parted, circled, and then lunged at each other again, taking out a corner of the granite slab and a section of rock wall when they hurled against it.

They were moving too fast for her to get between them to get a decisive strike in to cripple Nuit. She couldn't understand it; the Isis wasn't drawing smoke. It was cutting like a regular blade. It seemed like both of them were now impervious to the normal Isis-delivered wounds that rendered vampires impotent—but the more she fought, the more she tried to claim her part of the battle, it seemed to heighten their blood lust to destroy each other.

Rock and marble fixtures along with torches went crashing, as teeth locked upon sections of bone that wouldn't give way. She could also feel herself getting stronger, and was soon able to keep pace with them and get out of the way, as she jockeyed for position to get in lightning-quick strikes, slashing Nuit's back, which made him round on her. She threw her dagger, and he caught it before it opened his chest.

"Stay out of it so you don't get hurt! You are too important!" Nuit yelled at her, casting away the dagger, and pushing her so hard that her body slammed against a jagged wall.

The silver suit ripped. Blood oozed from Damali's elbow and shoulder where it had connected against stone, and Carlos's eyes went from gold to red as he hurled a punch.

"Motherfucker, I will kill you!" Carlos roared. "Don't you *ever* touch her!" He'd grabbed Nuit by what remained of his suit at the chest, raised him overhead, and slammed him to the floor.

Nuit scrambled quickly, nursing the blow that he seemed to now feel, finding a neutral corner as his eyes went from red to gold. "You're a master? What the fuck . . . When did that happen?"

"Shit happens, and I made a deal—several, in fact," Carlos breathed out, sucking in huge breaths. "You made her bleed. You did my squad, so I had to watch my back." He inhaled again deeply and cast off Nuit's ring. *"She's mine."*

"The Vampire Council?" Nuit's eyes began to normalize, only flickered gold intermittently.

"Yeah," Carlos snarled. "And I'm coming for you to pull a bone out of your ass."

He was on Nuit so fast that when they fell, Damali almost lost her sword. Nuit's leg was exposed, and she raised the long blade above her head and came down vertically, pinning Nuit's leg. The trapped beast let out a howl and Carlos looked over his shoulder.

"Back off," Carlos roared. "My kill. Check the doors—company."

She pulled her blade out of Nuit's leg, who was scrambling to get away from Carlos. Damali rushed to cover the open entrance as fluttering sounds came from just beyond it. But Nuit's attempt to evade another blow from Carlos was in vain. Carlos had grabbed the back of his suit and flung him across the room. Nuit's body slammed the rock, and when he looked up, dazed, Carlos bitch-slapped him with the back of his hand.

"Remember Alejandro!" Carlos bellowed, taking out the bottom section of Nuit's jaw with one powerful swipe. "You're neutered, *bitch*. Fair exchange is no robbery."

Gurgling in agony, Nuit covered his face with both arms as Carlos's foot found the center of Nuit's chest. Like a cobra's strike, Carlos tore away one of Nuit's arms, bones snapping, as the forearm bent backward unnaturally. Damali stood transfixed. In a blur of fury Carlos's hand immediately went to Nuit's throat, the other inside Nuit's mouth, and came away with tissue and incisors. Carlos stepped back, spat on the ground, and showed Nuit what remained of his vampire powers, then his fist slowly closed over the dripping teeth and meat.

A piteous scream came up from Nuit's gaping face. The flutter at the broken doors stopped and a cloud of bats dispersed and shape-shifted into six guards. But when they landed, and saw Nuit with Carlos growling over him, they hesitated.

"You were made from whose line?" one of the entities beyond the door shouted.

"I was made by Nuit," Carlos stood, breathing hard, as

Nuit slithered into a corner to take cover, then he dropped Nuit's teeth and threw the bottom half of Nuit's jaw to them for inspection.

They sniffed the air, and sniffed Carlos from a distance, and then nodded.

"That's fucked-up, man. You're a second, and did him like that—with Neteru running through him?" One of the assembled hit squad snarled a smile in Damali's direction and licked his lips.

"Don't even think about it," she whispered, her blade leveled in their direction.

"Wait till the boys hear this shit," another of the creatures beyond the door said with a chuckle. "Humph."

"We report to you, now, or what? You taking his New Orleans lair? This bitch, Nuit, ain't good for nothin' now, dude. Damn."

"I haven't decided yet," Carlos said slowly, and very cautiously. "Need to let my bride finish Nuit off." He nodded at Damali. "Only reason I saved you some is 'cause you asked me to. You wanted his heart—cut it out."

"Damn, dat's cold," one of the vamps at the doors said, shaking his head and laughing. "Aw, man . . . this territory hit is going down in history, boss. Look at this shit; let a Neteru do him in his own lair as her first birthday present. Brother, what's your name? Just so I can say I was here."

"Rivera." Carlos nodded again, staring at Damali. "You wanted vengeance? Then do him."

She looked at the creatures at the doors, looked at Carlos, and glanced at the bleeding, cowering creature at Carlos's feet, which couldn't even beg for mercy. Black blood gurgled up where a plea might have been issued, and she took her time coming near the living carnage.

"She'll get a stomach for it," one called out from the cavern. "Give her time, man. She's fine, though . . . can see why you had to do him for her." It shrugged and pounded fists with the others. "If I was your rank, woulda done the same thing, man. It's all good."

"The longer you take, Damali, the longer this sonof-abitch suffers. If you're gonna be a huntress, then hunt, Neteru. Or, if you want him to suffer, that's cool, too. Your choice, baby."

"You already put him down," she whispered, staring down at Nuit. "I've only done them while in the heat of battle—never like this."

"Then I want you to think about it this way—there are several women on the ground out there who I have to be-head to be sure they don't wake up one night. I had to stand there and tell my brother I loved him and rip his heart out while I put a stake in it. I had to drive a stake through my boys' hearts, and it drove one through mine—trust me. And this motherfucker will reconstitute in a few days and come looking for you. Make a choice, Damali, like you said for the audience—make it fast."

She stood over Nuit and said a mental prayer. Carlos backed away. Then the prayer found her lips, and Carlos covered his ears while Nuit began to screech and smolder. The creatures in the hall hissed their discontent. And she asked that Nuit's soul be saved, sending him into the light till he caught flame. She waited, watching the slow fire, before she plunged Isis with her full weight behind it.

Weakened, the other vampires covered their mouths and shook their heads while dry heaving. Carlos leaned against the wall as Damali turned to all of them and nar-rowed her gaze on them.

"Damn . . . sister . . . that was cold. You didn't have to

go there. Coulda let him have a little pride on the way out. A prayer? Deep."

"Fucked up, is what it was, for real for real. Burnt off the contact, too—damn, she blew my high behind that."

"Aw, man, brother—you got a cold woman on your hands. You got dat!"

"I still can't wait to tell the brothas how this hit went down, though. We be out, boss."

"You want this take-out cuisine left at your door, or do you need it for later, you know . . . after you and the lady hook up? Just asking, don't wanna to see good food go to waste. We can leave you one, as an appetizer?"

"Take 'em," Carlos murmured. "Just don't let them wake up and walk."

She stared at him as the beasts left the cavern entrance and half shut the broken doors. Smoldering ash remained, emitting sulfur in a slow, steady stream. Carlos sat down heavily on the end of the slab and studied his hands, cleaning them with his mind.

"I better take you to go find your team, and get you back onstage," he whispered.

"Yeah," she said quietly. "It's all done down here."

He shook his head, and glanced up at her. "Baby, it's never done down here."

"So, what are you going to do?"

He chuckled. "I don't know. Just started a legend . . . had to save face—couldn't have 'em say I was no punk." Carlos stood. "The sulfur is dying down, the prayer is wearing off, the silver's effect ain't jack right now, but the way you look in the suit is killing me. You're working it like you worked the audience . . . and working me along with it. You're stronger. I've just seen you do some incredibly sexy shit, and you smell—" Carlos swallowed hard and paused. "Woman . . . listen, it's almost past midnight. I burned a lot of energy, I'm extremely hungry, and I need to get you to your people. Hopefully your team is intact."

He watched her hesitate and he closed his eyes against the slow pull she was having on him again. "I heard your song . . . I remember. Trust me. I kept everything you wrote from those days, like you used to read to me on the beach. But—a lotta shit has gone down, to put it mildly. And you see how they deliver take-out down here. A vampire and a vegetarian is a stretch. So, let's go, while I've got a little noble left in me."

She nodded, and stooped to pick up her dagger. "I hope you choose well. Would have liked to see you around again."

"Damali, noble is wearing thin. Get your blade, baby. Keep it, and me, in front of you."

"We have to take the slow tunnels. My team went in there—maybe we can meet them halfway."

He stopped and turned around and stared at her for a long time, branding her image into his mind.

"If they took the slow tunnels, I doubt they made it, D. The Vampire Council is looking for you, and the registry just ran blood—a master went down, and a whole line is up for grabs. You're in a war zone. All seconds and thirds are dusted upon my command. Only weaker strains remain, and they get folded up under my turf. It's done like that, so I can pick my own lieutenants without issues, but I don't have any at present. You understand—the tunnels are crawling, the demon empires just went to war on those rogue demons that sided with Nuit, and I probably have some real old, powerful dudes on my ass looking for you to be with me."

He winked at her, appraising her and letting out a deep breath as he stood. "That's the only reason you're getting out of this room right now. I ain't that noble, survival has somethin' to do with it."

"Watch your back," she said, trying to resist the pull to him. He'd normalized and she held that image of him in her mind.

Carlos rubbed his jaw and turned away, glanced at the door, then glanced at her, and tore himself from the seductive thought—it left a warm spot where his mind had touched her.

"I can't, no, correction, I won't leave my team."

Deadlocked in a standoff, she began walking.

"I'll go in alone."

"No, you won't."

"Then watch my back," she commanded. "You might run shit down here, but you *never* ran me."

He smiled as he followed her. He wasn't sure why he was allowing himself to be led into a sure kill, but the rear view of her in ripped, dirty silver from this vantage point was threatening his reason.

"Look," he called behind her. "You need to get back to the main cavern in the next five or less. They're doing the *Raise the Dead* act above, but it's been neutralized. The portals are closed from your prayer-songs, and the head of the line is toast. However, when your team steps back into the center of that cavern, based on the ceremony timing, it's going to suck everything in it up onto the stage again. You *don't* want to miss that elevator ride."

She peered at him and he backed away into the shadows.

"Raise your sword, baby. Send a signal; give the people hope. Show five continents that tonight, the light was what got raised from the dead. It came straight up from Hell, and was gorgeous."

"Come with us!"

"No. If I come up with you, I'm a marked man. The televisions can't pick me up—but the Vampire Council can send a hit to do me right there onstage, if they think there's been a double-cross. You understand? I have one goal, to reunite you with your team in that center cavern, then I'm gone."

"But—"

"No buts about it. I need to handle my business. You are already handling yours."

"You could have bitten me at any time—why didn't you?"

She saw two glowing orbs in the shadows disappear and then reappear with the sound of a deep inhale.

"You have five minutes of juice left in the new battery on your suit. You could have toasted me and Nuit at any time, and gotten rid of both of us. Why didn't you?"

For a moment, she said nothing.

"Yeah, I feel you, baby," he murmured, his voice smooth, controlled, sensual in the dark.

"I need to find my team."

"Yeah, you sure do."

"You need to take the lead down here," she murmured. "I don't know the way, and I should probably stay downwind from you so we can make it topside."

"Glad you finally understand where I'm coming from," he said on a ragged breath, rounding her in the dark and taking the lead. "Wise choice."

<hr />

A low flicker of light made Carlos and Damali start running faster. Moving bodies ran toward them, dragging wounded, and the numbers had considerably thinned. Carlos's line of vision narrowed, and he could sense her trying to see farther than was possible. Even with her unique ability, the night was his, and he had the advantage.

"Listen, D, brace yourself. There are only twelve standing, and not all twelve are completely standing. You started with a squad of nineteen. The reason we made it this far without incident is probably because they took the weight as decoys."

"Oh, no!"

"Yeah—but it wasn't your fault. That's their job . . . they're guardians. They have to be willing to lay down their lives for a Neteru."

Running beside Carlos, she let the remorse sink into her bones. No person should have to make that choice, no matter how honorable. Guilt dug into her side as the run sent a stab of pain through it. The battling, the stage, the run, were all taking their toll. The twinge felt like it was gouging her appendix, and she slowed her gait, and had to catch her breath as another shooting pain ripped through her abdomen.

Bent over, she heaved in air, and in slow motion, she watched Carlos stop, turn away from her, and growl.

"Get to your team! Now!"

She could barely breathe, much less run, and she pushed herself up and looked at the dim light that was coming closer. "I don't know what it is. I think I may have been hit . . . when I fell, some internal injury that just—"

"Get to your team," Carlos said in an agonized voice,

but much softer. "Please, before they kill me. Run toward the light—I got'chure back."

Half running, half dragging herself, she brushed past him. Isis was making a line in the rock at her feet as Damali stumbled forward pulling it behind her, one arm in front of her waist clutching the dagger.

"Neteru!" the Templar called out. "Are you hurt?"

"No," Damali wheezed, making it to the border of light, her gaze counting faces, heads. "Roll call," she whispered, tears now streaming down her cheeks.

"Rider, Mar, Shabazz, J.L., Dan, Jose," Big Mike boomed, his breaths labored. "And me." He then fell quiet, breathing hard, as the blue knight stepped forward winded and exhausted.

Damali looked around as her assembled guardians each nodded upon Big Mike's roll call. All of them were leaning against portions of the jagged tunnel walls, trying to catch their breaths.

"They took the weight, li'l sis," Mike said while grappling for air. "Died with honor—said it was their job as front line. We're second line, and they held back things I cannot even describe. They helped us put down the guardian squad from our unit that had been nicked topside . . . so we didn't have to."

"Templar," Damali huffed, "we cannot begin to thank you and your men. There are not enough words."

"That you are still with us unscathed, Neteru, is all that we had hoped for," the knight said on slow, heavy exhales.

"We have to move, we only have a few moments to rest," Marlene whispered, drawing ragged inhales from the run. "D, you don't look good."

"I'm not." Damali winced. "But I'm not nicked. It's

my side. I cut Nuit's heart out, after Carlos neutered him. But I think I hit a wall." Damali stopped mid-sentence, tried to catch her breath, and continued more slowly. "Might have some internal injuries. You're right, though. We've gotta move, the Vampire Council is looking for Carlos, and will flood the tunnels soon. We have to get back to the open cavern in the center and wait for a lift in a few minutes or less. I'll be all right."

"Where's Carlos?" Rider said, an odd level of concern in his voice.

"He left me, about twenty-five feet back and told me to run toward the light. He had my back the whole time—save one minor incident." She chuckled sadly. "But he's gone."

"He's not gone," the Templar warned, glancing around. "He's a master, and he's showing a lot of discipline, Neteru. Unparalleled restraint at the moment. If you can withstand the pain, we have to get you out of here before his restraint falters."

Damali doubled over again as another stab in her side ripped through her abdomen.

"Tell her, Mar," Shabazz murmured. "Once and for all."

Marlene looked at Damali and glanced at the darkness behind them.

"It's almost midnight—you were born at twelve-oh-one . . . and, baby, you're in the middle of Hell, and you just started ovulating—the first adult Neteru menses. It's a rough one on the human system, that's why it hurts so much—you aren't injured. You've gotta move, now, without us."

Damali's gaze locked with Marlene's.

"Baby, you can take a body blow, or a bite, and you can

see in the dark . . . Read minds, and you are making him crazy. So, baby, *run*. We got your back; let Isis have your front. We're dragging wounded and will slow you down. You'll draw sharks in this cavern in the next minute or two. *Run!*"

"Run with me, Marlene—everybody. Or we all go down fighting together. We all go up into the light, together. That's the only way I'm going down that tunnel—as a team."

A low growl behind them made the group stop and turn fast.

"I tried to reason with her, too, Marlene. I tried to stay upwind from her," a low rumble whispered. "Tried to explain what she was doing to me, but . . . she's so damned stubborn."

When J.L. moved a light near the voice, it was summarily flung away.

"Oh, shit . . . uh, look, Carlos, man—"

"Shut up, Rider! Go with her, if *that* will make her move. I'll watch your backs; you will *immediately* get your bloody, mangled team out of here. You're drawing more of us, and more of them to her—the longer you all stand and have a summit meeting in the fucking cavern about this!"

A section of the cavern wall gave way, and falling gravel and dirt made the team cover their heads.

"I can keep them from your back, but I can't guard your front," the voice said more calmly.

Heavy breathing echoed in the cavern, as the group remained still.

"Come with us, Rivera," the Templar said quietly. "You had faith that she could trust you, hope that you would vanquish Nuit . . . and love, or the Neteru could not be here with us, not without one of you being dead. Rivera, your choice is—"

"Move her, now, priest! Or I take her deeper into the lair zones. You'll find that choices are very limited in my world. Decisions are also swiftly made."

"Carlos," Damali's voice rang out, still refusing to leave without him or her team, "you'll be a sitting duck here for the Vampire Council. There's safety in numbers! We fought good together."

Two golden orbs in the dark disappeared and came back red.

"That cannot be a good sign, D," Rider said fast. "Let's not argue with the man. He's made his decision. He has serious issues. So let's get the fuck out of here."

"Wise choice," the voice rumbled. "All of you need to roll. Quickly. You're between a rock and a hard place—me at your back, and whatever at your front. You all smell like blood, and I haven't eaten all night . . . and she smells . . ." The voice paused. "*Fabulous*. Get my woman out of here. I'm not myself."

"We get the picture," Big Mike murmured, as the group began to move out. "Let's give boss some space. He's compromised—and it's real cool of him to give notice."

"What did you say?" Damali murmured as she walked toward the darkness, and Big Mike put a hand on her shoulder.

"Her *voice* is running all through me . . . Baby, go 'head. For real. You don't understand this craving . . . *yet*." The red glow disappeared from the darkness.

Marlene and Shabazz glanced at each other.

"Uh, people," Dan whispered, "I think that's our cue."

"Y'all deal wit your shit later," Shabazz said, his tone firm. "We be out."

"Big time," Rider yelled as the group backed up. "See, that's youth. People our age only gotta be told once."

"Leave him, D," Marlene said, as a growl came nearer.

"He's one of us—we don't leave our own! I saw him fight back there. He fought like a guardian. He didn't harm me. He was once a guardian, too, and it may not be too late! Carlos, listen to the Templar and come with us—"

"I'm not one of you, *beautiful vision . . .*" Carlos's voice echoed through the cavern in a low, seductive murmur, bouncing off the walls, now making it difficult to locate his position in the darkness. The intensity of it made the sounds beyond them go quiet for a moment, the way birds and crickets go still when a loping predator passes. "Damali, raise your sword, baby, before you have to plant it in my chest."

His voice was rendered at such a low, sensual octave of warning that the walls vibrated from the sound of it even after he'd stopped speaking. Wisdom instantly assaulted her, and she turned away from the darkness to quickly usher her team through the cavern toward safety—but her mind was left in an invisible corner as they ran, and she glanced back repeatedly hoping what was in it would follow. He was one of them; they didn't leave their own. Running as a small huddle, they turned after a hundred yards when they heard a fight ensue behind them. Loud snarls and snaps and screeches echoed behind them. Damali turned to head back.

"Leave him, huntress!"

Reality jolted her and they continued to run, now in a flat-out dash down the treacherous area before them. Hideous sounds were advancing, a loud cry rang through the cavern—it was male, it was low like a mortal wound . . . it was Carlos.

"No!" Damali turned again, but Big Mike held her, shoving her ahead of him.

"Push forward toward the light. You can't help him now—whatever's got him, got him!"

She ran as hard and as fast as she could, helping to drag the knight's wounded teammates, helping Jose, her side killing her, the sound of a fierce vampire battle behind her stabbing her heart. It was a vertical thrust with no mercy in it, goring her as she listened to Carlos's roars of agony behind her. "Die with honor . . . but live with pride," she whispered as she raced. "Live!"

They stood gathered in the small, confining space where they'd first been dropped—the allied teams gasping for air, sucking in the sulfur, the putrid after-stench of vampire extinction. Guardians surrounded her in Templar formation; her team a center ring, then the Templars, and she at the core. Damali glanced at a revived Jose, who could now live, also knowing his loss, like hers, would never be erased. She briefly closed her eyes, the burn of the environment becoming grit behind her lids, waiting for the lift, and listening as the pathways behind them went still. That's when her hand found her mouth, and she looked back just one last time. What if . . . *Please, God, even down here.*

Things of the night slithered into the space around them, vampires, demons, all manner of creatures unnamed. And as her weary team drew together, surrounded, back to back, the last of their weapons readied to go down as one—she quieted her team with a silent prayer, and lit herself as a torch.

Ultraviolet light filled the space from her suit and fried everything in its wake that wasn't human. Billowing black clouds mixed with yellow and deep crimson,

screams so horrific that the guardians covered their ears
and a small avalanche started. Damali raised her sword
upon a whisper . . . "For Carlos. Rest in peace."

It was not clear whether the subterranean disturbance,
the timing, or the light jettisoned them upward, ejecting
them back to the place where they'd first been swallowed.
But her team stood firm, surrounding her—then fanned
out one-by-one on an electric blue–lit stage with black
smoke behind them, the Vampire huntress in the circle's
center, all slowly stepping forward for the cheering
crowd, her sword raised in salute to those who got left
behind.

Media swamped them, the crowd rushed the barri-
cades, and the team looked on as commentators thrust
microphones in their faces . . . there were no words. Who
cared that they'd brought the house down? It wasn't
magic; it was a miracle, and there was no way to explain
something as complicated as that.

Damali closed her eyes, leaned her head back, swallowed hard, and raised Isis higher for the applauding,
cheering crowd . . . the refrain of a very sad song echoed
in her mind. She tried to send it by thought to someone
she once knew.

Remember before it all got crazy? *Please, baby, don't
ever forget.*

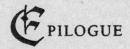PILOGUE

DETECTIVE BERKFIELD sat at his desk, looking at the package that had come to him with no name and no address. The note inside of it said simply, *The Jamaican Territory—as promised.*

For a month, nothing, and now this came in the mail? He looked up as his new partner leaned in his doorway.

"Hey, Dick, I know you're brown-nosing for the next big promotion, but it's getting late. You wanna get something to eat?"

"Naw," he said slowly, holding the package in his hands. "I think I'm gonna hang here for a while longer."

"Why, man? You have to eat. You're gonna mess up your biorhythms, working all night all the time, and then crashing at dawn."

"Yeah, I know . . . but I got a funny feeling I'm going to get a phone call soon." Berkfield's gaze slid out of the window toward the blue moon. "Don't ask me why, I can't even tell you—just a feeling, is all. Next time. Be careful going home though . . . say a little prayer; works for me. Catch ya later."

THE LEGENDS CONTINUE WITH

THE HUNTED

A VAMPIRE

HUNTRESS

LEGEND

AVAILABLE FROM
ST. MARTIN'S GRIFFIN TRADE PAPERBACKS

Take a sneak peek

HE HAD to get out of there. The look of shock, relief, disappointment, and rage on Damali's face was working every cell in his body. She hadn't said a word, just circled him, staring, her blade held low, moving counterclockwise to him like she'd lunge at any moment. Her team was not his greatest danger. The Covenant team was not his greatest danger. She was. He needed to roll.

"J.L., hit the exteriors, all right?"

J.L. nodded, but Damali held up her hand. Everyone stood still, waiting. The room crackled with quiet. The hum of air-conditioner compressors created a sumppump sound in the distance. A stereo was on somewhere in the compound. The humans had enough adrenaline oozing from their bodies to give him a contact high. He could see their eyes blink in slow motion as they stared at his and Damali's circling forms. The pores on their faces enlarged within his peripheral vision. He could detect the moment a bead of sweat exited their skin. His tongue glided over his lips and he tasted salt. The tension in their muscles increased, springs wound so tightly that at any moment they would pop. It fused with his reflexes. He felt the air, sensing for a weapon release. He smelled their blood, twelve nervous humans with hearts beating a rhythm out of their chests.

"I have to go," Carlos murmured, his gaze steady on Damali.

She shook her head slowly no. It was a millimeter of movement. Her locks swayed ever so much. The adornments in her hair and her earrings chimed. Lion's teeth, a tiny silver charm . . . Ankh fertility symbols created natural music at a nearly imperceptible timbre. Her pupils had eclipsed her irises. Shea butter, almond oil—the scent of her was an intoxicating blend with something else she emitted . . . something different from Neteru. He'd smelled it on her before, but couldn't place it. Her face and arms glistened. The muscles beneath her smooth skin were a network of taut, steel-like cable. He could hear the blood pumping through her veins as she stalked him. She was gorgeous, poetry in motion. The crocheted white dress had holes that showed skin. As she moved, the dress moved with her body, barely concealing it. The fluorescent lights glinted off of Isis and sent shards of illumination against patches of warm, damp flesh.

He allowed his gaze to roll over her in a slow undressing. "I have to go," he repeated more firmly, his voice dropping an octave. He had meant it as a statement, but even to his own ears, it had come out as a plea.

"You talk to me," she whispered through her teeth and stopped circling.

"Oh, shit . . ." Rider backed up a few paces and leveled his shotgun.

"Shut up, Rider," Marlene snapped.

Damali's eyes had never left Carlos's. All she did was hold up her hand and her team went still once more.

"We should leave," the eldest cleric said quietly. "Before somebody gets hurt."

Carlos shook his head *no.*

"Oh, what the fuck." Rider threw Big Mike a crossbow, and he caught it, nodding. Rider glanced at the clerics. "I thought you had an understanding with dude?"

"We do, and it's time to leave," Father Patrick insisted. "If it's not too late."

The Covenant team backed up, cautiously rounded Damali and Carlos, standing the line on the side of the guardians with weapons raised. J.L. had armed himself with a battle-ax; even Dan and Jose now had silver-tipped stakes in their hands. Shabazz had pulled Sleeping Beauty out of her holster.

Marlene folded her arms and leaned against the weapons table. "Steady, gentlemen. Nobody get an itchy trigger finger. Stay cool. Have faith."

"Have faith? Mar—"

"Shabazz, we know how this has to go down."

Damali blocked out the other voices, her goal singular, focused. There was no shred of trust in her as she looked at the master vampire that had made her taste fear. She had to remember what he was, not allow the illusion to get to her. This liar had fooled trusting clerics. Carlos was dead. This was something else. And this entity possessing a familiar body, had shape-shifted to trick her team, had rolled up on her in a battle station–ready compound, and dissected her while she was blind. The worst part of it all was he'd been right. If it had been Fallon Nuit, she would have been dead . . . or worse. What did this thing want?

"Speak to me!"

"It's me, Damali—Carlos . . . use your third eye!"

"You're a liar! Carlos is dead!"

She circled, she moved with him. She was indeed more dangerous to him than sunlight at present.

"I can't get a mind-lock," Carlos told Marlene and the seer cleric, his line of vision shifting quickly to gain their assistance. "She's in a mental black box."

"Don't screw with my team! They don't have the telepathic capacity—I don't care what illusions you throw at them—"

"No, Damali," Marlene argued. "Listen—"

"No! They sent this one as a trap; it's a decoy. I heard Carlos die—I saw it! Vamps are masters of deception." She narrowed her gaze on the entity before her. "How dare you assume his shape . . . I'll gut you," she seethed, her grip tightening on Isis.

"Then plant Isis," Carlos said. "Plant it right in the brand." In one deft motion he tore away the black T-shirt to expose his scar. Hot tears of frustration stood in his eyes. "How did I get that, then, huh, Damali? Ask the damned men who pulled me out of a cave in the desert! Ask them how they found me! It saved my life and I suffered for three nights in the fucking desert."

Carlos slapped the center of his chest as Damali's hand slowly covered her mouth. "I got this carrying you, baby," he said, his voice fractured. "You're the only one that can do me in this room."

He closed his eyes, outstretched his arms, and leaned his head back. Her legs moved beneath her, hurling her toward the thing claiming to be Carlos, sword raised. She heard Marlene scream, "No!"